Lye in
Wait

FORTHCOMING BY CRICKET MCRAE IN 2008

Heaven Preserve Us

A Home Crafting Mystery

Lye in Wait

Cricket McRae

MIDNIGHT INK
WOODBURY, MINNESOTA

First Edition
First Printing, 2007

Book design and format by Donna Burch
Cover design and photo by Lisa Novak
Editing by Connie Hill

Midnight Ink, an imprint of Llewellyn Publications

Library of Congress Cataloging-in-Publication Data
McRae, Cricket.
  Lye in wait : a home crafting mystery / Cricket McRae. — 1st ed.
    p.   cm.
  ISBN-13: 978-0-7387-1116-4
  1. Women artisans—Fiction. 2. Soap trade—Fiction. I. Title.
PS3613.C58755L94   2007
813'.6—dc22   2007018060

Midnight Ink
Llewellyn Publications
2143 Wooddale Drive, Dept. 978-0-7387-1116-4
Woodbury, MN 55125-2989, U.S.A.
www.midnightinkbooks.com

Printed in the United States of America

ACKNOWLEDGMENTS

Writing a novel is never done in a vacuum, and so many people helped me in this endeavor. Thanks to Jacky Sach, my terrific agent, and to Barbara Moore, Connie Hill, Brian Farrey, and all the other hardworking folks at Midnight Ink. I feel indebted to my writing buddies Bob Trott and Mark Figlozzi for their constant support, inspiration and willingness to listen to my whining. Others who cheered me on by reading drafts, providing feedback and pushing me forward include Edward and Rochelle Cattrell, Tom Martin, Jody Ivy, Stacey Kollman, Mindy Ireland, Kevin Brookfield, Marjorie Reynolds, Jeff and Denise Weaver, Rod and Nita Lindsey, Margot Ayer, Stasa Fritz, and Aimee Jolie. Thank you, too, Jane Isenberg and Larry Karp for reading my manuscript and saying such nice things about it. Apologies to anyone I've forgotten to mention; everyone who was willing to take a look at this novel has my gratitude.

The local members of the Puget Sound Chapter of Sisters in Crime have been staunchly enthusiastic on my behalf. Police Chief Chuck Macklin answered my questions about Cadyville's police force and its procedures, and Officer Charlie Frati answered my questions and let me ride along in his patrol car. Frank Borshears told me all about the chemical properties of sodium hydroxide and how it mixes with other substances. I take full responsibility for any information I changed for fictional purposes or that I simply got wrong.

ONE

THAT THURSDAY MORNING HAD been going so well until I found the local handyman dead on my workroom floor. Walter lay on his back, twisted to one side. His right hand was pressed to his throat. The left clenched the chambray work shirt in front of his heart. Streaks of moisture along the cuffs and in uneven splotches down the front darkened the blue of the shirt's fabric. I recognized the signature yellow suspenders first, then the gray hair pulled back into a ponytail.

Staring down at the ruin of his face, I covered my mouth with one hand. His eyes were squeezed shut and his lips drawn back in a horrific grimace. The interior of his open mouth was inflamed and raw. His teeth, now a disturbing shade of dark gray, jutted from what remained of his gums, and angry blisters welled on his chin and jaw.

My gaze shifted to the open doorway, to where the sun had finally pried its way through the clots of gray sludge above. The Japanese maple in our backyard blazed incandescent orange against the evergreens along the neighbor's cedar fence. A chickadee called through October air so crisp it would have crunched if you bit into it…

Then I remembered to breathe. A long, shuddering inhalation, and the oxygen hit my brain. Practicality surfaced through my horror, and I spun and ran up the interior stairs to the main part of the house. Through the kitchen and the foyer to Meghan's massage room, where I burst in without thinking. Thank God her client was still dressed. Meghan's eyes widened.

"Call 911," I said.

She dropped an armful of white towels onto the massage table. "What happened?"

"Walter's dead in the basement. Call 911."

She nodded and went through to her office for the phone. As she called out to the client that she'd have to reschedule, I turned and ran back downstairs. I'd never been more grateful for Meghan's no-nonsense approach to things than I was at that moment.

Back in my workroom, I leaned against a counter and looked around at anything except the body on the floor. The spacious thirty-five-by-forty-foot room had been plumbed and heated when Meghan and her husband—now ex-husband—bought the house. I'd hired Walter to install plasterboard, two rows of track lighting, a few appliances, and several work surfaces. He'd made it into the perfect place to produce the soap and other items I market under the name Winding Road Bath Products.

A glass lay on its side at the edge of the braided rag rug in front of the sink, an oblong splatter of liquid extending out onto the bare concrete. The room smelled of the rosemary and peppermint essential oils I'd used to make a foot scrub the previous afternoon, but another odor rode the air, far more subtle and so familiar it didn't seem out of place until I realized what it was: sodium hydroxide. Lye. I used it to make soap, but I hadn't mixed any batches of cold-process soap for over a week.

With a growing sense of dismay, I tiptoed to the glass and the spill on the floor and crouched beside them. Then, like an idiot, I stuck my finger in the liquid. The slick consistency was instantly familiar, and I hurried to the sink to rinse it off even as my skin began burning. I had to step over Walter to reach the faucet. My hands were shaking. No wonder his mouth looked like that. Leaning over the sink, I gulped air and tried to quell my rising stomach contents.

"The paramedics are on the way," Meghan said from the doorway. "Poor Walter…hey, are you okay?"

I turned from the sink and tried to nod. Meghan started toward me, then faltered as her gaze dropped to the form on the floor.

"Oh God, Sophie Mae. What the…" She looked up at me. "What happened to his face?"

"He…" I swallowed. "I think he drank lye."

"Holy shit." Her voice was low, almost a whisper.

We heard a thump and the doorbell rang upstairs. Brodie, Meghan's old corgi, let out a series of sharp barks from the top of the stairs, and my housemate went up to answer the door.

Two uniformed EMTs, a woman and a man, clumped down the narrow wooden stairs and hurried to the prone figure. Meghan followed behind them, stopping on the bottom step to watch from the doorway. Kneeling beside him, the paramedics blocked my view of Walter's head and torso. I heard them mutter to one another in low voices, and moments later they stood up, shaking their heads. The man took a walkie-talkie phone from his belt and stepped out into the backyard. Through the window I saw two firemen talking in the alley.

The woman told me in a gentle voice they couldn't do anything to help Walter—not much of a news flash, but her kindness brought a sudden lump to my throat.

The other paramedic returned. "They're on their way."

"Who?" I asked.

"Police."

"Oh." And for the next five minutes we stood in awkward silence, waiting for whatever would come next.

TWO

THE DOORBELL RANG AGAIN and Meghan went upstairs. She returned with a uniformed officer in tow. He looked about fourteen years old, though he must have been at least in his twenties. Nice looking, with hair the color of sand and wide blue eyes that grew wider when one of the EMTs said it looked like Walter had died from something he ingested.

No kidding.

I imagined how the lye would have felt going down: nothing, then the fierce burn, the realization of having made a terrible, utterly irrevocable mistake.

I started to tell the officer about the lye, but he waved me off and pulled his phone from his heavy belt, murmuring into it as he walked through the open door to the backyard, just as the paramedic had.

The EMTs went back upstairs, and I heard Brodie's muffled barking; Meghan had shut him in the laundry room, away from all the comings and goings. She still wore her work clothes—loose yoga pants paired with a soft pastel T-shirt. We sat down on the third step, where the wall and the corner of a counter blocked the body except for Walter's work boots pointing toward the ceiling. "Turning up your toes" had been my grandmother's euphemism for dying, and when it popped into my head I had to fight down the sick giggle that threatened to erupt. Instead my stomach rumbled, and the urge toward inappropriate laughter turned to consternation. Even under these circumstances, my body still insisted I'd skipped breakfast and owed it an early lunch.

The sandy-haired cop came back in but hovered near the back door, looking as though he'd rather be almost anywhere else. I couldn't really blame him.

The EMTs must have let in the next arrivals. We heard them coming down from above and moved off the narrow stairs so they could enter the room. First came a tall, thin, balding man who looked like an undertaker, but wore the same dark blue uniform as Sandy Hair. He introduced himself as Sergeant Zahn. Behind him came another man, wearing jeans and a maroon, collared shirt under a sweater the color of fall chestnuts. Sawdust clung to the elbow of the sweater. His dark hair had begun to gray at the temples, and his brown eyes moved around the room, lingering for a moment as something snagged his interest, then flicking to the next detail.

Looking relieved, the young officer hurried over to them. The three men talked for a minute, then Sandy Hair went upstairs. I'd been able to identify the paramedics, the firemen, and the police by their uniforms. Who was the guy wearing jeans?

"Ladies," Sergeant Zahn said, "I'm very sorry for your loss." It sounded like patter right out of a TV crime drama, and I could tell he was really thinking about something else. "We need for you to move upstairs while we process this room. Detective Ambrose here will need to ask you some questions."

Ah. Detective Ambrose.

Sergeant Zahn went outside and took out yet another cell phone. Meghan moved back to the bottom of the stairway, but I shifted closer to the spatter of lye on the floor, guarding it from the feet of the emergency personnel. Detective Ambrose looked around the room again, his gaze methodical, his attention pausing for several seconds on Walter, on the glass lying on the floor, and then on my face.

He raised his eyebrows, and I thought he was going to chastise me for not hopping to obey the sergeant's orders.

But instead he said, "You found him?"

"Yes."

"And you are?"

"Sophie Mae Reynolds.

"You live here?"

I nodded.

Ambrose waved toward Walter. "What about him?"

"What…Did he live here? No. Across the alley, in that little cottage." I pointed. "Walter is—was—our local handyman, fix-it guy, whatever you want to call it. He was going to build a new raised bed for our vegetable garden this morning."

He walked over and gazed down at the body. "Poor bastard," he said. His brow furrowed and he bent to take a closer look at Walter's face. "If you could go ahead and wait upstairs, Ms. Reynolds, I'll be there in a moment. I'd like to take you over to the station in order to get a proper statement."

"I just wanted to tell you to be careful where you step," I said. "This spill's caustic."

Ambrose straightened. "What is it?"

"It's sodium hydroxide," I said.

"Sodium hydroxide."

"Lye."

"Lye? Why would…" he trailed off, looking back down at Walter.

"I don't know. I mean, I think it's there on the floor because he drank it and then dropped the glass, but I don't know why he'd do that. Drink it, I mean. I can see why he'd drop the glass, of course." I closed my mouth to stop my babbling.

"How do you know it's lye?"

"By the smell. And I stuck my finger in it."

He raised one eyebrow.

"I know, I know. Stupid," I said. "But I was a little rattled. Anyway, it's slick, definitely alkaline. And has that flat, almost sweetish smell. It's quite distinctive."

Ambrose leaned over the stain. "All I smell is something minty."

"Peppermint." I leaned forward, too. Sniffed. The peppermint scent *was* coming from the pool on the floor. "But I can smell the lye, too."

He straightened. "Not many people'd be able to peg lye by the texture and smell."

I let that hang.

"Any idea where the stuff came from?" he asked.

"I don't know. Can't be mine."

"You don't keep any on hand to clear sink clogs?" His tone was mild, but he never blinked and his eyes never left my face.

"Um, not for that, no," I said, flustered. Behind me I heard Meghan make a noise in her throat.

The skin seemed to tighten across Ambrose's features. "Meaning…?"

"Well, I use lye, yes. But," I said, pointing to the liquid on the floor, "that's not mine. Or at least I didn't mix it up." I stopped and took a deep breath. "Look, I keep lye here. Plenty of it, but I haven't needed any for a week or so. I don't see how the lye Walter drank could have come from my supply."

"Your supply."

"Yes."

He sighed. "Ms. Reynolds, perhaps you would indulge me with an explanation of just why you have 'plenty of lye' on the premises."

"Oh. I guess I haven't been very clear, have I? I use sodium hydroxide to make cold-process soap, which is a large part of my handmade toiletry business. You mix the granules with water to activate the lye, then combine it with oils at certain temperatures. The resulting chemical reaction produces soap." I just managed to stop myself before I began spewing information about saponification and superfatting.

A displeased expression settled on Detective Ambrose's face. "Show me where you keep it."

"Sure." I went to a lower cupboard beside the refrigerator, knelt in front of it, and reached for the combination lock.

"Wait." He squatted next to me. Up close, his sweater smelled of fresh-cut wood. Pulling on a pair of rubber gloves, he asked, "What's the combination?"

Staring at his hands, my mind went blank.

"Ms. Reynolds?"

I blinked and my brain came back online. I gave him the numbers and carefully he spun the dial forward, back, forward again, slid the lock off the hasp, and opened the door. Inside sat two five-gallon buckets of sodium hydroxide granules with snap-on lids and skull-and-crossbones labels. Several empty gallon jugs sat on a shelf above, each of which had a rough skull and crossbones drawn on with permanent marker and the word POISON in bold red ink.

Detective Ambrose stood. "So what are the plastic jugs for?"

"When I'm going to be making a lot of soap—and when I make soap, I make a lot at a time—it's expedient to mix up all the lye I'll need at once. It doesn't react with plastic, so these work well for storing it. I always keep the solid sodium hydroxide in here—and the liquid lye once it's mixed. I'm careful about keeping the lock on."

He crossed his arms over his chest.

Meghan spoke from where she waited by the stairs. "She's very careful with the chemicals, Detective. I have a ten-year-old daughter, and Sophie Mae would never do anything to endanger her."

I flashed her a grateful glance.

"And you are?" Detective Ambrose turned to face her.

"Meghan Bly. I own this house." Her voice trembled at little at the end.

"I see." He turned back to me.

"So how would…Walter, right?…How would Walter get access to your lye? Did he know the combination?"

I frowned. "No. I never told him. Never needed to."

Ambrose looked skeptical. "And that's all of it there in the cupboard? You don't have it anywhere else, maybe in liquid form?"

I shook my head.

"You know, Ms. Reynolds, anyone can make a mistake."

"That is *not* my lye."

He stood watching me and, as I felt the flush creep up my face, I cursed the Scandinavian complexion that showed my every emotion.

"So despite the fact you have literally buckets full of lye here in this room, and a man lies dead on the floor apparently from drinking lye, you don't think there's a connection?"

"I don't—"

"A man, who, I might add, doesn't even live here? Who could have accessed the lye without your knowledge?"

"I never told him the combination. Not even the girl who works for me can get into that cupboard if I don't open the lock for her." I paused, realizing what Ambrose had just said.

Since stumbling upon Walter, my thoughts had been focused in a tight beam, concerned only with tamping down my visceral reaction so I could concentrate on the practical details of how to deal with a dead body in my workroom. Now it occurred to me to wonder why he'd taken a swig of lye in the first place.

"Wait a minute. He…he did it on purpose?" I rubbed my hand over my face. "Oh, God. He…of course…he committed—" But I couldn't say it, struggling to swallow away the dread that settled into my chest just from thinking the word.

Ambrose's gaze held mine in an almost physical grip. A few beats while no one spoke, and finally he looked away. But before he did, something gentle—sympathy? kindness?—passed through his eyes. I tried not to be obvious as I let out my breath.

He put the combination lock in a plastic bag. "I'll be happy to drive you to the station for that statement."

Meghan said, "We'll drive right over, after we freshen up and get our nerves under control. Say, in half an hour?"

Ambrose didn't look happy but agreed. In Meghan's former life she'd been a lawyer—technically she could still practice—so I guessed we were within our rights. And the ugly truth was that Walter's death, besides being horrifying and sad, could present legal issues since he'd died in her house.

I wondered if I could somehow prove he hadn't used my lye to kill himself.

Zahn came back in, and Ambrose turned toward him. Meghan started up the stairs, but I just stood there, looking at our handyman still lying on the cold concrete, and hated myself and pretty much everyone else for having to think about liability at a time like this. I'd liked Walter Hanover a lot. He'd been a fixture in the neighborhood for years and had been a great help to Meghan, her daughter, and me. He lived across the alley in the former guesthouse for the larger house facing the street behind ours. A gentle soul, he worked hard and always had a cheerful word for everyone. Whatever despair had driven him to deliberately choose such a horrible death must have been grim indeed.

My eyes felt hot. I blinked, hard.

Freshen up, Meghan had said. Not a bad idea, come to think of it. A splash of cold water on my face and a splash of Scotch down my gullet. Or perhaps better to wait on the latter until after I'd given my statement. I trudged upstairs to find a cold-water spigot and talk to my housemate before heading over to the Cadyville Police Station.

Below, I heard Zahn say, "For God's sake, Ambrose. I don't care if it is your day off—go home and change. Makes the department look bad."

As I walked through the door to the kitchen, Brodie's vigorous displeasure at being shut away from the excitement drowned the detective's response.

THREE

Meghan and I were roommates at the University of Washington. Then she went on to law school, and I married Mike Reynolds and went to work in the administration office of the Lake Washington School District. The job was comfortable—boring, but comfortable—and I never got around to looking for another one. Then, six years into our marriage, lymphoma struck Mike a killing blow. The doctors caught it late, and only three months later I was a widow. Like finding a new job, we'd never gotten around to having children.

Meghan married Richard and had Erin. After she passed the bar, she and her husband bought the house in Cadyville, about twenty-five miles north of Seattle, and she opened a practice specializing in contract law. Three years later, her husband turned out to be a real jerk, with both a secret gambling habit, which had drained their savings, and a not-very-discreet girlfriend.

She divorced him, closed her law practice, and apprenticed as a massage therapist. Less than a year later, my husband died.

The offer to come live with Erin and Meghan came at a miserable, lonely time in my life, so I quit my job, moved to Cadyville, and went to work at the local bookstore. I started selling my soaps and personal care products as a lark, but last year I took the plunge and quit my day job. Now Winding Road is my full-time business, and I love it.

As promised, Meghan drove us to the police station. After a gray-haired officer took our fingerprints—just routine they told us, but it gave me the creeps—Ambrose talked to each of us separately. In addition to asking me the same questions he'd asked before about the lye, he also wanted to know about anyone who might have access to my workroom, when I'd last mixed lye for soap, and whether there had been any left over. I told him I often left the outside door unlocked and always did when Walter was doing work back there, and that I'd last mixed lye eight days before and had used it all to make that batch of soap. I told him the glass on the floor didn't belong to us, that Walter must have brought it with him.

Ambrose had also asked about Walter's family and friends. Appalled at how little I knew about these aspects of his life, I found myself unable to provide any useful information at all. It still disturbed me that evening, as Meghan and I cooked dinner and discussed the police interviews.

"So you stayed with exactly what you did and saw and kept all your opinions to yourself," Meghan said. She smeared a dollop of pungent garlic butter on a piece of Italian bread and reached for another slice.

"It's not my *opinion* that I didn't leave a bunch of lye sitting around for Walter to kill himself with." I whacked a carrot in two with my knife. "If that detective would have just listened to me."

"Sophie Mae, tell me you didn't piss Ambrose off."

I shrugged.

Sighing, she arranged the bread on a cookie sheet and placed it under the hot broiler. Turning back to me, she said, "What happened to Walter wasn't your fault."

"I never said it was."

She held my gaze for a moment, then shook her head and stooped to check on the garlic bread. "It was a pretty weird way to commit suicide."

"Oh, I don't know. The choices people make? They seem perfectly normal to them." But I wasn't thinking of Walter when I said it.

She started to nod, then grimaced and ran a hand over her eyes. "Oh God. I'm such a jerk. I completely forgot about your brother."

I waved off her chagrin and forced a smile. Bobby Lee had killed himself so many years ago that now I could sometimes go for a week at a time without thinking of him, but all that afternoon, memories had crept around the edges of my awareness. I changed the subject.

"So tell me, would I be in trouble if I'd left the lye out?" I kept my tone light.

She narrowed her eyes at me. I could tell she wanted to say something else about my brother.

"Well, would I?"

She sighed, giving in. "You can get lye in the cleaning aisle at the grocery store. They'd have to prove criminal negligence. No prosecutor would touch it."

"But they brought in the forensics people and took our fingerprints," I said.

"They do that anytime someone dies an unnatural death."

"Why doesn't that make me feel better?" I tossed the carrot scrapings in the covered crock we used to collect vegetable matter for the compost bin. "Did they ask you about Walter's family?"

"Yeah."

"Could you tell them anything?"

She shook her head. "Not really."

The water was boiling, the steam clouding the window over the sink. She dropped a handful of spaghetti in the pot, stirring it with a long wooden fork to separate the strands. "This whole thing scares the bejesus out of me."

"Me, too." I finished slicing green onions and sprinkled them on top of the salad. "I'm glad you believe I'm careful when I work with the lye."

"Of course I do. Do you think I'd let you make soap in the house if I didn't have every confidence it was safe for Erin? And I've seen your soap-making getup: rubber apron and gloves, goggles. I'm surprised you don't use a gas mask."

"I open the windows," I said.

"Even better." She stopped stirring, though her hand remained curled around the wooden handle. "Sophie Mae?"

I looked up.

"Is there any way it could have been an accident?"

I put the salad on the table. "I just can't see how. You have to mix the sodium hydroxide granules with water. That's not something you do by mistake."

"And you're certain you didn't have any already mixed?"

I groaned. "God, not you, too."

"Stop being so dramatic. Can't you buy liquid drain cleaner?"

"Sure. It's usually colored. Blue, I think. The liquid on the floor was clear, but there may be some brands that pour clear. Still, you don't buy liquid drain cleaner and drink it by accident, either."

"Hmm. Guess not." She took the toasted garlic bread out of the oven and put it on the butcher-block kitchen table where we ate most of our meals.

I couldn't get the image of Walter's grimacing, blistered face out of my mind. "I've heard of people drinking lye...but why do it here?"

"Instead of at home like any other self-respecting suicide?"

"Well, yeah, something like that. Did it have something to do with us?"

She blew out her breath, a sound of frustration. "No way to know now, is there?"

"Maybe he left a note," I said.

She went to the doorway and called up the stairs, "Erin! Dinner!"

Hearing footsteps on the wooden stairs from the second floor, we dropped the subject. I went to the stove and tested the pasta. Al dente. I dumped it into a colander, drained it, then drizzled a little olive oil over it and slid it back into the pot. Meghan tossed it with home-canned red sauce while I got the salad dressing out of the refrigerator and Erin washed her hands at the sink.

I turned and saw mother and daughter from behind, one a smaller version of the other. Dark curls reached almost to their shoulders, blue jeans and T-shirts hugged their short, slender frames, and when they turned together I saw only slight variations in their almost elfin features. Meghan doesn't wear makeup, blessed with a face that needs no improvement. Her blue eyes can get this intense look that makes me think she would have been a good courtroom lawyer if she had chosen that path. Erin's eyes were grayer and sometimes struck me as old for such a little girl.

Settled at the table, we loaded up our plates with food. We were having spaghetti because it was Erin's favorite meal, and she felt pretty low about Walter. I didn't feel particularly hungry, and I doubted that Meghan did either, but for Erin's sake we made the effort.

Erin swallowed a bite of spaghetti. "Mom?"

"Yeah?"

"How old are you?"

"I'm thirty-four."

Erin played with a piece of lettuce in her salad bowl. "How old are Grandma and Grandpa?" Meghan's parents had moved to Taos, New Mexico four years before.

Meghan put her piece of garlic bread down on her plate. "Grandma is sixty-three and Grandpa is sixty-six." She waited for the next question.

"Sometimes people live to be a hundred, don't they? But usually not that long. Is there any way to tell how long someone's going to live?"

"Not really. Some families have genetic tendencies toward certain diseases, and how someone takes care of themselves—not

19

smoking, eating right, that kind of thing—can affect how long they live."

"Yeah, I know about that stuff. But the family stuff—do we have any of that in our family?"

"Well, I can tell you my grandmother lived to be ninety-seven, which is pretty close to a hundred. And my grandfather lived to be ninety-four. Is this about Walter?"

"Well, of course it is, Mom." Erin sounded a little exasperated at the question. Then a wry expression crossed her ten-year-old face. The look flickered away, and she said, "At least it sorta is."

I said, "Walter had an accident, Bug. His age didn't have anything to do with it." I didn't know how much Meghan had told her daughter about the details of the "accident." The police had still been down in the basement, sampling or measuring or doing whatever it is they do, when Erin came home from school. She'd wanted to go watch them, but Meghan nixed that idea.

Erin nodded. "Yeah. But him dying just made me think about other people dying, is all." She leaned over her plate and stuffed a huge dripping bite of spaghetti in her mouth.

"Do you want to talk about it?" Meghan asked.

Erin shook her dark curls. But a moment later she swallowed and said, "Walter said he used to drink a lot."

Meghan shot me a glance, and at that moment I was really glad I wasn't the mom, didn't have to handle all the tough questions. Though Erin still managed to hit me with the occasional unexpected zinger from out of left field.

"Walter was a recovering alcoholic. Some bad things can come from drinking, but you have to understand that it's a disease. It didn't make him a bad man," Meghan said.

20

There, I thought. I never would have handled that so well. She seemed to find just the right words.

But Erin looked stricken. "I never thought he was a bad man." Her fork clattered to the table, and she pushed her chair back. Tears welled up in her eyes. "I loved Walter. He was funny and nice and he showed me how to plant things and build things and he let me help him sometimes and he liked to talk about baseball, and…and…" She turned and fled up the stairs to her room, crying in earnest now.

Meghan shot me a helpless look, then picked up a whining Brodie from the foot of the stairs and carried him up to help console her daughter. I sat alone at the wooden table for a few minutes, poking my fork at strands of pasta. Then I got up and started scraping the mounds of food from the plates.

Sometimes the right words just don't exist.

FOUR

AFTER CLEANING UP THE dishes I went downstairs. Three whole-sale orders of soap remained to package, box up, and send, and I needed to make up for some of the time I'd lost that day. But once in the basement, I knew I couldn't work down there that night. I was so tired my bones felt mushy, and the stark pools of fluorescence from the track lighting hurt my eyes.

The authorities had been very tidy; there was no indication Walter had ever been in my workroom. The glass was gone, but the spilled sodium hydroxide mixture had eaten into the rag rug and soaked into the concrete floor, creating an ugly stain. I got out the apple cider vinegar I used for much of my cleaning, poured some straight onto the stain and left it. It probably wouldn't remove the mark, but the acid would neutralize the alkaline in the lye. As I capped the bottle, I caught a whiff, and the spicy-sour smell lodged in my throat.

I tossed the rug in the garbage.

A smear of black powder came away on my hand when I closed the hasp on the cupboard. I'd have to get another lock. Besides sodium hydroxide, the cupboard contained potassium hydroxide, which is another kind of lye used for liquid soaps. I had only a small amount, as I didn't have any liquid soaps in my current product repertoire. Considering it now, I realized many of the substances I used could be dangerous. Peppermint could burn skin if applied full strength, as could clove or cinnamon oils. In fact, I didn't know of any essential oils that could be used full strength with any guaranteed safety. Only wintergreen oil is actually regulated by the FDA. But none of them could do the kind of damage the lye had done, and frankly, all were far milder than some of the chemicals you would find in a typical cleaning closet. Still, I'd pick up a couple extra locks while I was at it.

The room spanned the width of the house, and windows lined the upper halves of three walls. The front wall snugged up to a hill, so there was no front entrance to the basement except the stairs from the kitchen above. I walked the perimeter, checking the lock on each window. I hadn't bothered with curtains or blinds, wanting as much natural light as possible during the workday. Tonight I felt the eyes out there; not benign nighttime critters going about their business, but threatening, malignant eyes. I shrugged off my heebie-jeebies. A penchant for too much Stephen King combined with finding a dead man—granted, a particularly gruesome-looking dead man—and there I went getting all spooked by the dark like some neurotic schoolgirl.

I paused in front of the window by the back door. My smudgy reflection gazed back at me from the glass. Next to Meghan and Erin, it's like I'm from a different planet, one with a stronger gravitational field. I feel stout and unwieldy, blonde and big-boned. In reality, I'm not any of those things, except blonde. At five foot six, I do have bigger bones than the Bly family—but so does a good-sized crow. When I'm out among normal people, I'm an attractive enough woman in my mid-thirties, with my long hair in a practical braid down my back and a tendency toward simple Eddie Bauer-esque clothing so I don't have to think too hard about how to put myself together in the morning.

Tonight all that showed in the glass pane was a wavering outline of my features and reflected glare from the overhead lights. And then it was Bobby Lee looking back at me, the same light hair, the same snub nose, the same genetic mix as mine, with the same sense of humor and way of looking at the world. For a moment his absence skewered through my solar plexus, and I began to close my eyes against it.

But I blinked and stood up straight again as my eyes refocused on a bright rectangle across the alley. While seeing a light on in someone's window on a dark October evening isn't unusual, this one was: this light shone in Walter Hanover's cottage.

Flipping off the switch for the tracks overhead, I peered out at the night. Definitely Walter's.

My father always left the lights on when he exited a room. So had my husband. Apparently our handyman had managed to live up to his Y chromosome, as well.

Opening the door, I stepped outside. Walter had told us he hid his spare key under a flowerpot on the windowsill. There couldn't be a better time to use it. The wind kicked up, and, as I ran through the chilly darkness, fallen leaves swirled around my tennis shoes and whapped at my legs like faint hands.

At the back door to the cottage, I saw I didn't need the key after all. Walter hadn't pulled the door closed all the way, and the wind had nudged it open a crack. Inside, I turned to shut it behind me, and my elbow hit a pile of old magazines stacked on an end table. They slid in all directions, slapping onto the floor like wet fish. I picked them up, restacked them on the table, and then gave my attention to the rest of the room.

This was the first time I'd been inside Walter's house, and I found myself at the rear of the living room. And it looked like he had done a lot of living in it. The open space formed a stubby ell around the enclosed kitchen. The front door opened into a small tiled entrance. One doorway to the kitchen opened off the tile, and the second, ahead and to my right, allowed access to the kitchen from the other end of the ell. In the dim light I could just make out the shadowy plane of a countertop.

Straight ahead of me a sagging and dusty sofa hunkered under the window facing the street, the claret-colored plush rubbed off the arms and seat cushions, leaving behind pink swaths like exposed skin. A coffee table squatted in front of the sofa, its faux-wood surface punctuated with dozens of sticky fingerprints between the piles of magazines and several half-full water glasses. Built-in shelves marched down the wall to my right, their original light wood darkened by age and neglect. Behind me, an ornate floor lamp with silk tassels hanging from its dingy shade emitted the light I'd spotted from my workroom. The cottage was silent except for the loud ticking of an old black-and-white clock like the ones that had hung above the classroom doors in my high school years ago.

I took a few steps down the short hallway, flipped on the light, and peered into the bedroom. Nothing to see. A row of work clothes hanging in the closet. An unmade bed. Next to it, a grungy-looking bathroom smelling of mildew and Old Spice.

Back at the built-in shelves, I poked at the sparse detritus. Pictures and office supplies, a signed baseball, a bowl of soggy peppermint candies, junk mail, catalogs, a stuffed bear wearing a Santa hat, three screwdrivers, a pack of gum, a wooden duck decoy, a chunk of petrified wood, an electric razor with bare wires sticking out the back, a stained pad of fishing flies, a book on baseball collectibles, a Bible, and among it all, the ubiquitous magazines. Walter had subscribed to everything from *Newsweek* and *Popular Science* to *Sports Illustrated* and *Nature*, and it didn't look like he'd thrown a single issue away. Ever. Dust streaked everything, a mottled, fuzzy coating as if the items had been handled and returned to their spots with most of the dirt intact.

One of the framed photographs showed an elderly woman, dark gray eyes looking out of a face encased in crepe-paper wrinkles and topped by a thick white braid coiled into a crown on her head. She sat in a wheelchair, scowling, while someone in a poor excuse for a rabbit suit leaned over and put a fluffy pink arm around her shoulders. **HAPPY EASTER FROM CALADIA ACRES** was stamped in dark pink metallic type across the bottom of the photo. Caladia Acres was a nursing home on the north side of town.

Other pictures revealed a much younger Walter than the one I'd known. In one, he looked about ten, laughing open-mouthed as a beagle puppy slurped his chin. In another, Walter and two other boys who looked like him—brothers, I assumed—posed with a humongous fish, grins all around. Four earlier pictures of the gray-eyed woman, black-haired and sans Easter bunny, convinced me she was their mother. One picture showed four teenagers: Walter, two boys, a girl—sister?—his mother, and a man I assumed was his father.

His baby picture, a sepia-toned, formal studio portrait, perched on a shelf by itself. He'd been a beautiful baby, and I don't mean that in the all-babies-are-beautiful sense. While I could easily see the resemblance to the man I'd known, age and alcohol, if what Erin had said at dinner was true, had imposed their effects on his features. Nice as he may have been, I'd never considered Walter to be a good-looking man.

I knew I should turn off the light and go back home, but my curiosity proved more powerful than my guilt. Next to the shelves, a card table covered with a mountain of loose paper beckoned to me. A metal folding chair invited me to sit down. Seconds later I'd dived in, rifling through an amazing array of unorganized information. Someone would have to step in and take care of things like the funeral. His mother might still be in the nursing home, but I saw Walter every week, sometimes every day, and he'd never mentioned her. Maybe she'd predeceased him. If not, I wondered whether she knew he was dead. Of course, the police had all sorts of ways to find out about next of kin, and they would have told her.

Many of the smaller slips were receipts. I found a few from the previous year for Caladia Acres, but the others had me stumped. They were receipts for donations. Walter had given money to the March of Dimes, Save the Children, Children's Miracle Network, and half a dozen other charities. This inexplicable generosity both shocked and touched me. I added up the cluster of figures in my head. The total came to over $300,000, and I doubted I'd unearthed all the receipts.

The crash of breaking glass in the kitchen wrenched me to my feet, heart pounding. I whirled, squinting into the dark. From my vantage I could see only the faint outlines of counters, the gleam of the white refrigerator. Something on the floor glittered. Feeling like the girl in the slasher films you know is going to die because she's too dumb to run when the background music sounds like that, I moved to the doorway of the kitchen, tiptoeing as if the carpet wouldn't effectively muffle my footsteps. I must have looked like an idiot.

But I stopped berating myself when I heard the front door open and then close on a muffled oath. A shadow passed outside the kitchen window. Groping along the wall, I found the kitchen light switch and fumbled it on. The sink overflowed with dirty dishes. The counters were cluttered with everything from cereal and cracker boxes to coffee mugs and empty soup cans. An explosion of glass shards littered the yellowing linoleum floor, dull reflections in the weak overhead light. A shiver skipped across my shoulders.

"Police. Turn around slowly."

My heart, already hammering away quite nicely, thank you, took another leap in my chest. I turned to find the sandy-haired officer from that morning standing in the doorway off the alley. His hand hovered near the gun in his unsnapped holster.

"Miz Reynolds?" His palm relaxed away from his hip, and I found myself able to breathe again.

"I just saw him go by the kitchen window. Maybe you can still catch him," I said.

His voice took on an edge. "What're you doing in here?"

I gestured toward the floor lamp. "Saw the light on. Doesn't matter. But someone was in here with me, and they just hightailed it out the front way. C'mon!" I moved toward the entryway, motioning for him to follow. He didn't budge.

"Who was it?" he asked.

"I don't know. I didn't see them."

"Then how do you know someone was here?"

"Oh, for heaven's sake! I was sitting at that table and heard a crash in the kitchen. When I went to look, the front door opened and closed. Then you sneaked up behind me, which, I can tell you, did nothing for my nerves."

"So this was just before I came in."

"Yes! You saw me looking in the kitchen, didn't you?"

"Sure. Standing there in the doorway looking around. Tell me again why you're here?"

"I saw the light was on and came over to turn it off."

"Ah. And perhaps you couldn't find the switch and thought the instruction manual might be among Mr. Hanover's papers." He pointed to the card table and then to me. I looked down and realized I still clutched several receipts.

I dropped them on the table like they were on fire. "What are you doing here, Officer? Isn't your shift over by now?"

"We're shorthanded—I'm working a double. And we got a call that someone was moving around in the house."

"See! Someone *was* here."

"Yes. Someone was." Sarcasm laced his smile. I counted myself lucky he hadn't shot me out of youthful enthusiasm.

"Listen, Officer—what's your name, anyway?"

"Owens."

"Well, Officer Owens, I saw the light and came over. It's not like I broke in. The back door was open when I got here. And Walter didn't talk about family much, so I don't know who'll be taking care of the funeral arrangements. When I saw his paperwork, I thought maybe I could find out. We were friends, Officer. And he died a horrible death in my workroom today."

"I'm sure I locked that back door when I left this afternoon."

But I thought I saw a spark of doubt in his eyes. "You were in here?"

He nodded.

"Well, if you locked the door, then someone broke in before I came over."

"Or someone had a key," he said, with a look that said it would be nice if I produced said key immediately.

"Or someone had a key." I sighed. "Look in the kitchen."

He did. I followed behind him.

"Was that broken glass all over the floor earlier?"

"No. So your intruder did that, huh?"

I could tell he thought I was responsible for the mess. But I was too distracted by the sudden, strong smell of peppermint to bother defending myself.

He switched off the lights and shuffled me out the door.

"Have you informed his mother already?" I asked once we were outside.

"They told her late this afternoon," Owens said as he carefully checked that the back door had latched behind us. "She'd probably welcome your help with the arrangements. Maybe it'll help you feel better about it, too. That lye you use is pretty nasty stuff."

The last comment made me want to kick him in the shin. I contented myself with a withering glance in his direction. He didn't seem to notice.

Walking across the alley to our backyard, Owens assured me he would check Walter's front door lock. Maybe take a look around the neighborhood for the person I'd heard in the house.

Yeah, right.

Back in my workroom, I checked the windows again. The exposure to the darkness outside spooked me on a deeper level now, and I didn't like the sensation. In the space of a day, the feeling of safety I'd felt in my own home had vanished. I'd smelled peppermint mixed in with the lye Walter had spilled on my floor. Then that same smell in Walter's kitchen, left by someone who shouldn't have been there.

I didn't like the coincidence, didn't like it at all.

Could Walter have been driven to commit suicide?

Or perhaps, just perhaps, his death was something else altogether.

Maybe his mother really would like some help with the funeral arrangements. I'd make a trip out to Caladia Acres in the morning to see her—maybe Mrs. Hanover could tell me where the money for those donations came from.

Groaning at the thought, I realized I absolutely had to do some work tonight if I planned to take time out tomorrow to visit Walter's mother. Not down here, though. Not tonight. I loaded a large basket with bars of cut soap, handmade papers, and labels. The scent of lavender would soothe, so I'd package those first, then move on to the bars from which my special citrus blend wafted. An old movie on cable and a nice cup of chamomile tea would see me through.

FIVE

I found Meghan sitting on the couch upstairs. She had lifted Brodie onto the cushion next to her and was stroking the corgi's soft ears with one hand while she stared out at the occasional car going by on the street. A small fire crackled in the fireplace, and smoke from the well-seasoned apple wood faintly flavored the air.

"How's Erin?" I asked.

"She's asleep. She'll be okay. Just needs some time."

"Yeah. Us, too."

Meghan nodded.

"I was just over at Walter's." Wrapping the colorful paper strips around the bars of soap and affixing each with the appropriate label, I recounted my recent adventure across the alley. When I'd finished, I said, "I wish I knew what's going on."

She looked resigned, though to what I didn't know. She smoothed the fur down Brodie's back.

"He had a ton of money and he just gave it away. I don't think he spent any of it on himself. Could have bought himself a new truck, junked that old Scout. He babied that thing along for years," I said.

"Maybe giving the money away was his way of taking care of things, before he died. People who decide to kill themselves often give away their possessions as they get closer to doing it," she said.

"He seemed happy enough."

She shrugged. "I always got the impression Walter was a sad man. He smiled and carried on conversations, but he always seemed to bear an underlying, I don't know…sorrow, is the only word I can think of."

"Well, maybe you're more sensitive to that kind of thing than I am. I think he went through funks like anyone else. That's not enough to kill yourself over."

She gave me a look. "Is this really about Walter?"

"Of course it's about Walter."

"You told me once you never knew why Bobby Lee killed himself, that you couldn't understand it. And that really bothered you."

I picked at the edge of a label. Pieces of the handmade paper broke off, fluttered to the floor.

"He had a reason, he had to. I was at school, so I wasn't around. We talked on the phone some, but that's not the same thing. Mom and Dad didn't want to talk about what happened, though they seemed as bewildered as everyone else. But he was eighteen, and he'd certainly stopped confiding in my parents by then."

"Walter had a reason, too," Meghan said.

"What if he didn't do it?"

"What do you mean? Of course he did it. You saw him."

"But what if he didn't…kill himself?"

She stared at me. "You're kidding, right?"

"That peppermint I smelled in his kitchen. I smelled it downstairs today, too. So did you."

"So? Peppermint's in all sorts of things."

"I've never heard of peppermint-scented lye."

"Neither have I. But your workroom often smells like peppermint, and what you smelled at Walter's was probably tea or soap or air freshener. It could have been anything."

"I don't think so. It was too strong."

She shook her head, picked up a label and a bar of soap, then threw both of them back in the basket and sat back on the couch with her arms wrapped around herself as if she were cold. Neither of us said anything for several minutes.

Finally I spoke. "Even if he did kill himself, I'd like to know why."

"And you think finding out what made him do it will somehow change the fact that you don't know why your brother killed himself?"

"No—will you drop that? I told you, this has nothing to do with Bobby Lee. But doesn't it bother you that someone swallowed lye—lye, for God's sake—in our basement? Don't you see how wrong that is? And now someone was in his house tonight. Do you think that was a coincidence? Something was going on with Walter, something pretty major. Something other than a bad case of the blues."

She turned to face me. "You were in his house tonight, too. And for a perfectly innocent reason. Whoever else was there could have just as valid an excuse. And even if they didn't, it's a bit of a leap to conclude it had something to do with his death. Don't make this into something it's not."

"I'm not making it into anything. It's already there. He died in your house. Don't you want to know why?"

She sighed. "Not the way you do."

"He tried to stop it, at the end. After it was too late."

"What?"

"The front of his shirt was all wet, and his cuffs. He'd tried to splash water in his mouth, drink it from his hands. That's why he died right in front of the sink."

She looked horrified. Swallowed audibly. "Maybe…maybe he didn't know it would hurt so much."

"I just…"

"I know."

"It's not about Bobby Lee."

"Okay."

We sat in silence, the scent of lavender doing nothing to smooth my nerves, the crackle of the fire offsetting the faint sound of the wind outside.

Meghan gathered Brodie into her arms and rose. "I'm going on up to bed."

"His mother lives at Caladia Acres," I said. "I'm going to go see her tomorrow morning about helping with the funeral. Want to come?"

"I can't. I'm booked solid all morning. But I guess I could try to fit in a phone call to the funeral home."

"Okay. Thanks."

Her small smile accentuated the dark circles under her eyes. "Sure." She turned toward the stair. "Goodnight, Sophie Mae."

———

I finished wrapping the lavender soap and started in on the citrus blend, relinquishing the idea of a movie. Soft sheets and my feather pillow beckoned. Forty minutes later, I lugged the basket down to my stockroom, then went straight up to my bedroom. I donned a pair of flannel pajamas and brushed my teeth in the hall bathroom.

Once snuggled under my down comforter, I worried that sleep would elude me, what with the image of Walter's dead face burned into my brain. But I was tired and beginning to drift—when I thought of something else. Getting out of my toasty bed, I put on a robe and a pair of tennis shoes and went back down to the basement.

Outside, the wind had died down and clouds blotted out the stars above. I made my way across the alley again to Walter's back door, hyperaware of every patter and rustle around me, jerking in alarm when a cat ran across the neighbor's yard. Lifting the flowerpot, I looked underneath. The key wasn't there.

I hadn't thought it would be.

SIX

FRIDAY THE RAIN RETURNED. In the Pacific Northwest we have a continuum of terms describing the precipitation, from "misting" to "toad choker." The morning after Walter died, tiny droplets spit from on high seemed suspended in the air, unaffected by anything so mundane as gravity and giving the illusion that if I would just stop driving into them they wouldn't gather on my windshield. But the moisture collected at a high rate, requiring the steady swish of the wipers as I drove my little Toyota pickup north on Avenue D and took a right on Thirteenth. Caladia Acres sat at the north end of Pine, their land petering out into trees at the edge of town.

The closer I came to the nursing home, the more I wondered if I'd lost my mind. How could I have thought this would be a good idea? Okay, so I felt terrible about Walter, and I wanted to do something about it. I wanted to help, and if I could find out more about him, all the better. But what on earth would his grieving mother think? She had to be in her eighties or nineties—what if she wasn't all there? But the dread in my stomach came more from the fear that she was still perfectly sane and functioning. I don't like the idea that it's better to hide from the truth than to face into it, but I had to concede in this case ignorance might be bliss for a mother outliving her son.

I pulled into the small parking lot and turned off the engine. Drops, larger now, pattered against the windshield, gathering together in bleary runnels, blurring the long, low building ahead. I got out of my truck and walked up the curving sidewalk to the front door. A man stood under the shelter of the awning with his shoulders hunched; his frame seeming to have collapsed in on itself over the years. He wore a red-and-black quilted plaid shirt as a jacket over a green flannel shirt and black slacks. In the weather-induced twilight, the skin on his bald pate shone dimly in the yellow illumination from the automatic porch light above the sliding glass door. Pungent smoke trailed up from the unfiltered Camel smoldering between the fingers of his left hand.

Greeting me cheerfully, he stepped on the pressure pad to open the door for me and waved me inside with a gallant gesture. I thanked him, braced myself, and entered the reception area.

I hate nursing homes. Not that anyone likes them, nor plans to end up in one. I'm not talking about senior apartments or even assisted living. I'm talking about nursing homes, where the care goes beyond "assisting." Even the best have about them an air of finality. This is the end of the line; for most there's only one way out. People change once they move in. Some of that change is because their world closes in around them, and some of it because they've already begun to change—that's why they come to live where they can receive around-the-clock care in the first place. Some of it has to do with a conglomeration of concepts like hope and independence and connection and interests and purpose and self-respect that mingle together to create an alteration that goes beyond physical circumstance. It's like being forced to give up.

The scent of pine oil hit me as I walked to the front desk. Dinner-plate-sized dahlias were clustered in a huge vase on the deep-green Formica reception counter, towering over my head like a multi-colored tropical tree. The white-clad woman at the desk wore a name-tag that said her name was Ann, and she came around to take me to Mrs. Hanover herself.

"Tootie doesn't get a lot of visitors," she said.

"Tootie?"

"Her name's Petunia. Can you imagine naming a child that?"

I shook my head no.

"Well, she hates it, so she's been Tootie her whole life."

"She knows about her son?"

Ann nodded. "Such a shame. I'm not sure how surprised she is, though." Her bland face didn't reveal what she meant, and I didn't ask.

We went past a TV room where two women watched from wheelchairs and a man with sunken cheeks slumped in an armchair, asleep. Past an empty dining room, the tables covered with light-green cloths and set with white dishes and more dahlias, smaller ones, bunched in vases. Down a hallway, past murmuring sounds from open doorways: radios, televisions, conversations, and from one room soft snoring. Ann stopped before a half-open doorway near the end of the hall and motioned for me to wait. She slowly pushed the door inward, saying "Tootie?" in a quiet, quizzical voice.

The only light in the room came from the gray day outside the window. A tall but stooped silhouette leaned forward, right hand resting on something in front of her. The image of the bent form among the shadows in the half-light was spare, desolate, lonely as a scratchy record playing through tinny speakers at two a.m.

"Hon, there's someone here to see you. A friend of your son's."

The figure turned toward us. "Please, come in." The voice was deep. Strong.

Her arm moved and I heard a click and suddenly a lamp came on, dispelling the grays and shadows and replacing them with vibrant jewel tones. Two wingback chairs upholstered in gold and maroon sat opposite a daybed made up under a dark-blue coverlet with matching gold and maroon pillows plumped along the edges. As I stepped inside the room, my feet sank into a thick wool rug in the same colors. Ann stood aside as I walked past her.

"This is Sophie Mae Reynolds," she said.

"Hello, Mrs. Hanover."

Walter's mother stood taller, pushing herself erect with a silver-headed cane. Her back rigid, she gestured me further into the room. Her black slacks would have been slinky on a younger woman, loose swinging fabric draping long legs, but on her they simply looked damn good. Her silk tunic top in a deep plum color was well suited to the space, another jewel in the setting. And above her patrician face, that lovely white braid swirled into a precise crown. I had expected a cranky old bat at best, a grief-stricken mess at worst, but not this.

No little knickknacks for Tootie Hanover, no porcelain figurines or collections of spoons or thimbles. Other than the sheer abundance of color and texture, the only decorative touches in the room were two oil paintings, both dark, broody landscapes, and a silver tea set on a cherrywood side table. The air carried a hint of jasmine perfume.

"At least sit down, Tootie," Ann admonished. "Have you taken your pill?"

Walter's mother ignored her. "Miss Reynolds, please. Have a seat."

I chose one of the wingbacks and found the seat hard as wood. As I watched Tootie ease herself into the other one, I realized a cushy chair would have been more difficult for her to rise from; she moved with caution, and the careful poker face almost covered the pain it cost her to move at all. Arthritis had caused my grandmother to move like that, hunched under the additional illusory weight of osteoporosis. In the photo with the Easter Bunny, Tootie Hanover had been in a wheelchair. This was one stubborn woman.

The nurse left. Tootie watched me with calm anticipation. She inclined her head toward me a fraction.

"You were a friend of Walter's?" she asked.

Of course, that was when my inconvenient habit of becoming tongue-tied at the worst possible moment settled over me. My mind went blank and I tried to think what I could say to this woman who had just lost her son because he had gone into my basement, swallowed a glassful of lye, and then made the futile attempt to undo that fatal swallow with water from the industrial sink he'd installed for me just months before.

"Miss Reynolds—or is it Mrs.?" she prompted.

"Sophie Mae," I said.

"And you must call me Tootie."

The name didn't fit her at all. "All right, Tootie. I, uh…Walter and I were neighbors. He did some work for me and for my housemate Meghan, on occasion. Like he did for other people around town. In my mind we were friends. I'm so sorry for your loss." I hated the last words the second they flew out of my mouth, so trite and pat. But what else could I say? Sorry your son's dead? Sorry he did it at my house?

She considered me. "Thank you. But the way you put that—'in your mind you were friends'—I get the feeling you're not sure Walter thought of you as a friend."

"I didn't mean it to sound like that."

"So why are you wondering if you were really friends now that he's dead?"

So much for worrying that Walter's mother might be a bit vague. I made a decision.

"I went over to his house last night." I told her about the door being open, about discovering her picture there, the intruder who got away, and about Officer Owens finding me. I told her about finding the receipts for the donations. I ended with, "So I guess I was thinking that there's an awful lot I don't know about Walter. It's not that I expected him to tell me every detail of his life or anything. But frankly, what I'm the most surprised about is that he didn't tell Meghan or me about you. I'd think he'd mention his mother to his friends."

Tootie's gaze had dropped to her lap as I spoke, and when she raised her head I saw tears in her eyes. "We weren't on the best of terms."

Oh, God. "I'm sorry."

"So am I, though I doubt he'd believe it." She stopped speaking, and I had no idea how to fill the silence. So I just waited while she gazed into space, remembering. Or regretting. Then her eyes found mine again.

"When the police told me he died, I wondered how he'd done it. Not whether, but how. A bullet? A bridge? Or had he finally managed to drink himself to death? Now you come and tell me about an intruder in his house. About his money, which he apparently had even more of than I was aware." Bitterness grated through her voice, delivered from a throat constricted by grief. "But I didn't think he'd drink drain cleaner. Probable cause of death was esophageal asphyxiation, they said, when I pressed. They were afraid an old lady wouldn't want to know the details. I had to insist."

"Perhaps they wanted to spare you."

Her narrowed eyes told me what she thought of that notion. "Miss Reynolds—Sophie Mae—I understand that you knew him, but really, what is your interest in my son's death?"

I opened my mouth to tell her how I wanted to help with the funeral arrangements, but found myself saying, "Walter died in my workroom. I found him. He drank lye in my workroom, and I want to know why."

Her brow furrowed. "Your workroom?"

I nodded and explained about my soap making and about finding Walter, couching things as gently as I could while trying not to insult her obvious intelligence. Her impassive face revealed no reaction to my words, and my voice gradually trailed off.

This is ridiculous. What are *you doing here, Sophie Mae?*

"I think I understand," she said.

Maybe, but I doubted it. I didn't even know if I understood.

I stood up. "I'm sorry. I never should have come here. I thought you could tell me something about Walter that would shed some light on what happened, but I was wrong, so wrong, to ask you…please forgive me."

"Sit down."

Reluctantly I perched back on the edge of the chair. I wanted out of there as fast as possible.

"I don't know if I can help," she said. "As I mentioned, Walter and I were not on the best of terms. I had judged him for years, blamed his unhappiness on his own weakness, his insistence on living in the past, and his drinking. Eventually he visited less often, and six years ago he stopped drinking and also stopped coming to see me. Which I've come to accept was the best thing. For him, I mean." Her eyes filled, and she looked away.

"But I don't have the right to burden a perfect stranger with my…with that. But I can tell you Walter had grief in his life that coagulated around his heart, and he shielded himself from everyone. You need to understand that it wasn't personal; it was just his way.

"He was the last of my children. One son died of cancer, and another in a horrible accident. Walter was my baby." Now tears spread across her cheeks, running together in the mass of fine wrinkles. But her voice remained strong.

"As for the receipts that you found, I knew he'd come into some money, because he called and offered to put me in a condominium with a private nurse about three years ago. But I said no. I like it here. The staff is kind and I trust them. I get good, respectful care, and I like having other people around. I wouldn't want to live alone anymore. He said he understood, and he bought Caladia Acres some pieces of new medical equipment and furniture. When I asked him where he got the money he said he'd made an investment that had paid off. I'm glad to hear he gave so much to the children's charities. He loved children."

An investment. Well, it was certainly possible.

"Meghan's ten-year-old daughter, Erin—she and Walter were great friends."

"That's good." Tootie suddenly seemed very tired.

"I'll let you get some rest. But there is another reason I came. Meghan and I'd like to help with the funeral, if you'll let us. We can phone the funeral home today."

Her smile was thin. "Thank you. I'll take you up on that."

I stood up again. "Thank you for talking with me."

"Will you let me know what you find out about my son?" The tentative way she asked the question, so different from what seemed to be her inherent self-possession, broke my heart.

Tongue-tied again, I nodded, then managed to get out a promise to call her the next day about the funeral. I was almost to the front door when I turned and went back. Tootie's eyebrows rose in question when I reentered her room.

"I was wondering if you know of any friends Walter might have had, other people I could talk to."

She shook her head. "He used to do some of his drinking at the Gold Leaf Tavern down on First Street. But I doubt that he'd gone in there for a long time."

I thanked her again and left. The rain hung like a curtain in the air as I drove back home.

SEVEN

I SPENT MOST OF that afternoon meeting with my teenaged helper, Kyla, about Winding Road Bath Products' participation in the upcoming holiday bazaars. I hate bazaars and farmers' markets; spending the day hawking my soap and other products makes me itch with impatience. But selling retail garners me three times as much profit as wholesale, so it's worth it. Last summer I hit on the solution. Since I made so much more by cutting out the middleman, I could afford to hire someone to do the hawking and make the obligatory appearances for setting up and breaking down the displays.

We had participated in three farmers' markets each week over the summer: one each on Saturday and Sunday, and another on Thursday evening. I paid Kyla an hourly wage and a small percentage of what she sold. Her genuine fresh-faced interest in people, coupled with that vital, dewy beauty possessed by those under twenty—in her case nonexistent pores, shining brown hair, and a metabolism that could have burned jet fuel—attracted customers.

She liked talking with them and thoroughly enjoyed herself, while I escaped the tedium and still turned a decent profit.

I'd applied to and made it through jury selection for five major holiday bazaars in November and December, one each weekend for five weeks straight. Kyla had some great ideas for giving our usual display some Christmas pizzazz, and I had a few new products I wanted to try out on the public to gauge response. One was a fizzing peppermint and rosemary foot soak. The few people I regularly used as guinea pigs liked it so much I knew we'd need more. I added it to my list of items to make.

"Can you work more hours after school?" I asked Kyla.

She shook her head. "Mom doesn't want me to. Grades."

"Well, she's right." Keeping the grades up was more important. I was just going to have to get used to a few more late nights. The money would be worth it. My annual product liability insurance premium, a hefty chunk of change, loomed ahead.

"What do you think about placing these tin snowflakes among the different items?" I asked.

We finally figured out what we'd need to make the adjustments to the display, and I sent her off to the craft store for supplies.

The door at the top of the stairs was open, and as I climbed I heard a man's voice in the kitchen. It was Friday and Erin's father, Richard Bly, had come to pick her up for their weekend together.

I entered the room to find both him and his girlfriend lounging against the counter, while Erin knelt on the floor, struggling to fit a book into her already stuffed bag. Meghan stood with her arms folded, watching her ex.

Richard wore a sweater with jeans and a sleek black leather jacket. A flip of dark hair curled against his forehead like John

Travolta's in Grease, and the rest of it fell in gentle waves to his collar in back. He had big blue eyes rimmed with lashes a model would die for, smooth tan skin, and lips that habitually curled in the slightest of sneers. He was one of the prettiest men I'd ever seen, if you go for that type. Meghan certainly had. Too bad the guy turned out to be such an asshole.

This girlfriend wasn't the one who had broken up his marriage. He always had one around, sometimes more. She fit the type he found comfortable: her face showed some hard living, her hair was brittle with bottled color, curling, and teasing, and her makeup had been applied with a palette knife. Skinny but flabby, she stood a little outside the family tableau and sucked her teeth, staring off into space.

For a long time I couldn't understand why he would screw around on a woman like Meghan. Then I figured it out. Attractive, smart, assertive, funny, kind, and practical scared the hell out of him. It was one thing to bed her in a college apartment, another to have her on his insecure hands day in and day out. He couldn't handle it. When I shared my theory with Meghan, she shrugged and said it didn't really matter now. She's good at moving on. I hope she finds someone wonderful who can not only handle her, but also appreciate her.

My love life? Not so hot. Maybe I wasn't as good at moving on. There had been a series of—what? Guys I dated, I guess. Calling them love interests would be going too far. And sure, I still missed Mike sometimes, but I'd recovered from his death. I just wasn't sure I'd recovered from our life together enough to try to start another one with someone else.

"Hi, Dick," I said.

Richard glared at me. He insists on being called Richard, never Rich or Rick, and never, ever Dick. So naturally I call him Dick whenever I can.

I turned to the woman and stuck out my hand. "I'm Sophie Mae."

She looked flustered and then took my hand. It was like holding a warm washcloth. "Hi. I'm Donnette."

Okay.

"I heard you had a little trouble here yesterday, Meghan," Richard said.

She gave him a warning look, indicating Erin with her eyes. All she said was, "Yes. We did."

"Terrible tragedy, something like that happening in the house. I hear it was lye he drank? Sophie Mae, you need to be more careful. I don't like the idea of you leaving dangerous stuff like that around where Erin and her friends could play with it."

Fury swept up Meghan's face, and her jaw clenched as she tried to contain it. That morning she'd mentioned to me that she had told Erin that Walter had drunk poison by accident, but not the particulars about the lye.

Erin grew still. She looked up at me, her duffle bag half zipped. I tried to meet her gaze with sympathy and regret, but some of my anger at her father must have seeped through. I didn't know what she saw in my eyes before she looked away. She finished zipping her bag and stood up.

"Will you be bringing her back on Saturday or Sunday?" Meghan asked her ex-husband.

"Sunday, of course. I want my sweetie with me as long as I can," he said.

She opened her mouth, then clamped it shut. As often as not, Richard brought Erin back home on Saturday so he could go to the casinos on Saturday night. But Meghan had made it a personal rule never to put her daughter in the middle of a fight with Richard, and she never bad-mouthed him in front of Erin. I marveled at her self-control.

"Um, we were thinking of taking Erin to a movie in Monroe tonight," Richard said.

"That sounds like a good idea," Meghan said. "Which one?"

"The new Disney movie. What's it called?" he asked Erin. She told us.

"You've wanted to see that, haven't you?" Meghan asked her daughter.

She shrugged. Meghan shot me a concerned look. This was the time for a serious discussion, not for Insensitive Dick to haul her away to a movie.

"Well, uh, those assholes at work haven't been paying me my commissions on time, so I'm a little short on money. I do so much work for them, and they shaft me any time they get a chance. I'm looking to move to a better job where they don't jerk their good salesmen around."

Erin was looking away from her parents, and I saw her roll her eyes.

"Really," Meghan said.

Donnette picked at a hangnail and looked bored.

"So you think you could manage a little cash for Erin's movie?"

"Just Erin's?"

Richard looked like a petulant two-year-old. "No, Meghan, not just Erin's. Unless you think we should sit outside in the car while she watches the movie."

That was exactly what I thought he should do, but I kept my mouth shut. I seemed to spend most of my time around Richard keeping my mouth shut.

Meghan sighed and went into the hall to get her purse. She came back and handed some bills to Erin. "Here, Bug. Why don't you take your Dad and, um, Donnette, out to a movie and maybe have some pizza afterward."

Richard didn't look happy as he watched Erin stuff the cash into the pocket of her jeans.

She smiled. "Thanks, Mom."

"You're welcome. Have a great time tonight."

The little girl hugged Meghan, mumbling something into her shoulder.

"I love you, too, Bug," she said, squeezing her daughter tight.

When Richard's car had pulled away from the curb, Meghan returned to the kitchen and sat down at the table. She rubbed her face with both hands as if trying to clean away the encounter with her ex.

"I put the kettle on for tea," I said.

"I hate it when she goes with him. I just hate it. I don't trust him."

I sat down. "Don't trust him how? You don't mean…"

"No, no, nothing like that. I guess it's that I don't trust him to be a good dad. To think about what he says or how she'll take it.

And he drinks a little too much for my comfort. I don't trust him to take good care of her."

"You think he might neglect her?"

"I'm being stupid, aren't I? I'm sure he feeds her all sorts of junk food—which she probably loves—and doesn't make her go to bed or brush her teeth. He gets to be the good guy, and I have to be the disciplinarian. I don't like that he tries to be her pal instead of her dad. Damn it, she needs a dad." She added, "And he's not even that good at being a pal."

"I know. But you have to remember that Erin is part of the equation, too. She's one of the smartest kids I know. No, she's *the* smartest. She's not taken in by her father's constant excuses. She loves him, but she understands what's going on, and she's dealing with it just like you are."

Meghan groaned. "God, that doesn't make me feel any better!"

The kettle began to whistle on the stove. "What kind of tea do you want?" I asked.

"I don't want tea," she said.

"Coffee? Wine? Scotch?"

"I want a beer."

"Well, that we don't have."

Meghan grinned. "Well, let's go get one, then."

"And dinner."

"Yeah. And dinner. Greek food."

"Mmm. That sounds great. I'm starving."

Pushing her chair back, Meghan stood. "Go get changed. We're leaving in ten."

EIGHT

I HURRIED UPSTAIRS. GOT out of my scrubby work clothes and into a freshly washed pair of jeans and a forest-green, long-sleeved knit shirt. I zipped on a pair of black ankle boots, applied a little eyeliner and lip gloss, and smoothed my hair back from my forehead, patting the thick braid down my back to make sure it hadn't come loose.

Downstairs, Meghan waited for me in the living room. She wore the same clothes—khakis with a button-down white shirt—and had run a comb through her curls.

Cadyville isn't exactly a rocking town. It shuts down early except for a few restaurants and taverns, and the latter don't serve any hard liquor, only wine and beer. We headed to the Greek and Italian place on First Street, where I indulged in souvlaki and Meghan had the spanikopita. We almost always ate at home, both to save money and because of Erin's schedule, but we both loved Greek food. Well, truth be told, I love most any kind of food.

While we ate, she updated me on what she'd learned from the funeral home. Then I told her about my visit with Tootie Hanover.

"So he told her he'd made an investment that turned out well?" Meghan asked.

I nodded. "And he gave it all away. You'd think he would have spent some of it on himself. Forget a new truck, I never saw so much as a new shirt."

"How do you know he gave it all away?"

"I guess I don't. Do you think there's more?"

"Could be. The investment could still be paying off," Meghan said.

"But he didn't tell anyone about it," I said.

"No, Sophie Mae. He didn't tell *you* about it."

After we had shared a piece of decadent pumpkin cheesecake for dessert, I sat back and took a sip of fragrant after-dinner coffee.

"So, do you still want to go have a beer?" I asked.

"Yeah. You?"

"I'm up for it. How 'bout we go into the Gold Leaf?"

Meghan wrinkled her nose. "I was thinking more along the lines of Eldon's."

"But Walter didn't used to hang out at Eldon's."

"Ah. But he did used to hang out at the Gold Leaf?"

"Before he stopped drinking. I hadn't realized Walter was an alcoholic until Erin said that the other night."

We shrugged into our coats and went outside. The pavement was wet, but for the moment it had stopped raining.

As we walked down the block to the tavern, Meghan said, "Walter moved into that cottage soon after we bought the house. He seemed pretty functional, but his daily window of sobriety steadily decreased the first year or so that I knew him. Then all of a sudden he stopped drinking. He came and talked to Richard and me once, apologized for I don't even know what, and I figured he was working his way through a twelve-step program. He did the same with everyone else he had worked for in the neighborhood. As I recall, Richard was kind of an ass to him."

"Talk about someone who should be in a twelve-step program," I said.

Meghan grimaced. "If only."

The door to the Gold Leaf was open, spilling rock 'n' roll onto the quiet street. Inside the doorway, a large tattooed man perched on a stool far too small for his behind. He checked our I.D.s more from habit than necessity and waved us inside.

Layers of blue-gray smoke drifted on the air, gathered into clouds on the ceiling. On our left, three pool tables marched down the length of the room. The muted clacking of the balls underscored the music and the voices, most of them male, which rose and fell in conversation. Ahead, a wide aisle divided the pool tables from the bar running parallel on our right. Here and there, small round tables held pitchers of beer and half-full glasses for the pool players. The whole place smelled of cigarettes and microwaved hotdogs. A shout of laughter erupted from the end of the bar, and as two men moved away, Meghan and I slid onto the stools they had vacated. On Friday night the place was hopping.

"Getchoo?"

"What?" I shouted.

"What. Can. I. Get. You?" the bartender repeated. He was nice looking, with long hair pulled into a ponytail and friendly green eyes. He smiled when he spoke.

Meghan ordered a Red Hook Hefeweizen, and I asked for the bitterest thing he had, which turned out to be the Red Hook India Pale Ale.

When he brought our pint glasses, I asked him, "Does Walter Hanover still come in here?"

He reached under the counter, and a moment later the volume of the music lowered an iota. A guy at the other end of the bar protested, but the bartender ignored him. No one else seemed to notice.

"Walter Hanover? What's he look like?" the bartender asked.

"In his sixties, gray hair in a ponytail, always wore yellow suspenders."

"No…wait a minute. Walt! Never knew his last name, but, yeah, he shows up every once in a while, has a cup of coffee. Used to come in a lot, but then he quit the booze. Good thing, too. You lookin' for him?"

"You've worked here that long?" I asked the bartender.

"I own the place. What're you looking for Walt for?"

"Well, I'm not, exactly. I'm looking for anyone who might have known him, and I was told he used to hang out here."

"The way you're talkin'—something happen to ol' Walt?"

I nodded. "He died yesterday."

"That's a damn shame. Walt was a nice old guy. Heard he'd come into some money."

I leaned in. "We heard that, too. Any idea where it came from?"

"No idea."

"Well, thanks anyway."

"Hey, if you're looking for people who knew him, check out the coffee shop two doors down. I saw him in there a lot of afternoons."

"Thanks," I said again. "So you own this place, huh?"

He started to answer, but there was a shout from the end of the bar, where a man stood holding an empty pitcher in the air. "Listen, I gotta go see to business. I'm real sorry to hear about Walt." And then he was taking the pitcher from the guy, saying something that made the scowl on his face change to laughter. As I watched, he took three other drink orders and had a glass of wine poured before the new pitcher had filled. He started another one while he took money and made change. His hands were a blur, but I was pretty sure there wasn't a ring on the left one.

"…go to Beans R Us. Am I right? Sophie Mae?" Meghan's voice penetrated.

I turned to her. "What?"

Her eyes flicked from me to the owner of the bar, now laughing with an older couple, and back to me. "I said, I suppose you want to stop by the coffee shop on the way home."

"We can finish these and head over there," I said.

A voice behind me said, "No way. You can't go yet. Come shoot some pool with us."

I turned to find two men in their twenties wearing jeans and long-sleeved waffle-weave underwear shirts with T-shirts over them. One had a Mariner's baseball cap jammed over his blonde hair, but the other's crop of dark curls was uncovered. The blonde one grinned and gestured to one of the pool tables. I glanced at Meghan, who raised one eyebrow in question. I nodded.

"Girls versus guys?" I asked them.

The blonde smirked and said, "If that's the way you want it."

We followed the guys to the table, and I heard the other one say, "Man, you're so dumb. We're gonna get our asses whipped."

Blondie won the break, but all the balls stayed on the table. Meghan walked around the table once before calling the three ball in the corner pocket. It bumped in, smooth as butter, as did three other solids before she miscalculated the angle on the five. She joined me where I leaned against the wall working away on my IPA.

"I'm a little off tonight," she said.

"We haven't played for a while," I told her.

"True," she said.

Looking grim, the curlyhaired one approached the table, chalking his cue until blue dust began drifting to the floor. He indicated the ten in the side pocket and grinned at the satisfactory *thock* as it dropped in. That left him with several impossibilities and a tricky bank shot, which he managed with aplomb. I smiled and gave him a thumbs-up when he looked over, and Meghan told me to stop being condescending. But he missed the next, much easier, shot by a hair. A little condescension can go a long way.

I mopped up the rest of the game, pocketing the eight ball in the corner with an easy bank off the side. Blondie walked away in disgust, but his friend grinned and offered to buy Meghan and me a round. We'd had enough, though, so we thanked him and left. It had begun to rain again, little spits that were just enough for us to raise the hoods on our jackets.

We hurried down to the Beans R Us Coffee Shop and ducked inside. The bell over the door jingled, and a woman with short spiky black hair and an eyebrow ring came out of the back, untying her apron. I recognized her from the few times I'd been in for a double tall nonfat latté.

"I was just getting ready to close up. I've got some decaf on the burner if you want it for free."

I looked at Meghan. She shrugged. "Sure," I said. The woman reached for two paper cups with one hand and the pot of coffee with the other."

"Sorry I can't get you a latté or anything," the woman said. "I already put everything away."

"No problem. We're not here for coffee, actually," I said.

She stopped pouring. "So what are you here for?"

"Do you know Walter Hanover?"

She nodded. "Sure. He comes in afternoons a lot. Hangs out with Debby and Jacob. Plays backgammon. Sometimes cribbage." She pointed to a cluster of tables in the corner with games sitting on a shelf nearby.

"Debby and Jacob?" I asked.

She nodded again. "Why? What's this all about?"

Meghan said, "We're trying to find people who knew Walter to let them know he died yesterday. The owner of the Gold Leaf said he'd seen him in here a lot."

The woman's hand flew to her mouth. "Ohmygod."

"Debby and Jacob a couple, then?" I asked.

Meghan gave me a look that bordered on a glare. Apparently, I wasn't being sympathetic enough.

"Um, oh, I don't know. They just all come in here together," the barista said.

"What time? We'd like to pass on the information to his friends."

"Oh, don't worry. I'll tell them." She said it with such relish I could imagine her rubbing her hands together in anticipation. In the blink of an eye, she'd recovered from the shock and was getting ready for the gossip circuit.

"Come on," Meghan said and opened the door.

"Wait a minute! What happened to him?" the woman called from behind us. "Hey, don't you want your decaf?"

We walked the five blocks home at a fast clip, both happy to reach our front door. But I wasn't sure whether we should be happy or not when we heard the message Detective Ambrose had left on the answering machine, asking me to call him at the station the next day.

NINE

On Saturday morning, I got Ambrose's voicemail. I dutifully left my name, number, and the time I called, hung up and dialed Caladia Acres. They transferred me to Tootie Hanover's room, and she answered on the second ring.

I asked how she was doing.

"As well as can be expected, I suppose." Her voice was dull, the delivery flat.

"I have some information from the funeral home," I said.

"You're very efficient."

"Well, Meghan is, really. And we're happy to be able to help. But they can't have a funeral until the morgue releases…" I took a breath "…well, releases Walter."

"It's all right to say it."

"I know. I'm sorry." Another deep breath. "The mortuary anticipates it will be at least a week and could be more than two weeks before they can do that, so the funeral may have to wait."

"Oh, no."

I hated this to drag out for her and had said as much to Meghan when she'd told me about the delay. She'd mentioned a possible alternative that might afford Tootie some modicum of closure. After determining that neither she nor Walter had any particular religious affiliation, I suggested a nondenominational memorial service on Monday, two days away. She agreed and said when the time came she wanted her son cremated. That brought up another thorny subject.

"Do you know if Walter had a will?"

"He never said anything about it to me."

"Maybe I should look for one? I can go through all his things if you'd like. My housemate would help. Box up what's useable and donate it, save anything you might want."

"I don't know," she said.

I couldn't really blame her for being reticent. "I understand. You barely know me."

"It's not that. You're a good girl. I can tell."

That made me squirm. I didn't feel like a good girl. I felt like someone who wanted to find out as much as I could about Walter while I still had the chance. But no matter how I felt, if we didn't clean his place out, his landlady, Mrs. Gray, might just bring in someone to haul everything away, including photos and other mementos Tootie might want.

"It's too soon," I said. After all, Walter had only been dead two days.

After a long pause she said, "No, of course not. You go ahead and take care of it, if you don't mind. I'm not as mobile as I once was, and I'd rather someone who knew Walter went through his things."

"If you're sure, I'll talk to his landlady and have her let me in. If she has any questions, she'll probably call you for confirmation."

"That'll be fine. I'm pretty easy to reach." Her thin, dry laugh sounded forced.

"One last thing," I said. "Meghan said the funeral home would place the obituary with the local papers, but neither of us knew what information to include. May we tell them to contact you for that information?"

When she spoke, there was even less energy in her voice than before. "Yes. Of course. I'll expect the call."

———

As soon as Meghan's client left, I checked her office. It was empty, so I went in and sat down on the loveseat opposite her desk. Minutes later, she came in from the massage room, rolling her shoulders.

"That," she said, "was a big guy. A big, tense guy."

"Get your workout for the day?"

"I'll say. Hey, I don't have any more clients until this afternoon—you want a quickie?"

Meghan's massages turned me to mush. "Love to, but I've got too much to do."

I updated her on my conversation with Tootie Hanover.

She turned in her chair and took down two thick white towels from the shelf behind her. "I'm still surprised you told her about someone being over at Walter's that night."

She'd told me over dinner the night before that I shouldn't have given his mother something else to worry about. But Tootie was stronger than Meghan realized and certainly more interested in the truth than in being kept in the dark for her own good just because she'd passed a certain age.

"You have to meet her."

"I hope to, soon."

"She gave me—us, actually—permission to go through Walter's things."

"Have you called Detective Ambrose back?" she asked.

"He wasn't in. I left a message."

"The police might not like it if we go through his stuff."

"Why? They sure as heck don't seem to be doing anything to find out what happened to Walter."

"I thought you wanted to do this to help his mother."

"I do. But do we have to wait? I mean, is it actually illegal?"

She looked unhappy. "I don't think so. It's not like his house is a crime scene. They may have told Mrs. Gray not to let anyone in, though."

"Well, I'm going over there and find out."

"Now?"

I nodded.

She rose. "Sparrow's coming at one, but I guess I could help until then." Sparrow was a regular client, a champion dressage rider who believed in massage for her horses as well as for herself.

I'd planned to go down to the coffee shop later to see if any of Walter's friends showed up. The day was dribbling away already, and I wondered how to make up the time. I still had so much to do to ensure Winding Road did well during the upcoming holiday season.

We went to the main house to see Walter's landlady, Mrs. Gray. The police had said nothing about staying out of the cottage, and she was only too glad to give us the key. Meghan insisted that Mrs. Gray also get direct permission from Tootie Hanover, and I dialed the nursing home for her. Minutes later, we were entering Walter's cottage—this time through the front door.

Meghan went into the bedroom to start with Walter's clothes, and I headed straight for the kitchen.

The floor was clean. The broken glass was gone, and if I stood where the light fell at an angle, I could see the edges where a freshly scrubbed spot of linoleum stood out from the rest of the floor. The scent of peppermint I'd remembered had been replaced by the nasty smell of rotting garbage coming from the overflowing pail under the sink. Whoever had taken Walter's key had returned and cleaned up their mess. Too bad they hadn't bothered to tidy up the dirty dishes and food-strewn counters.

Dumping the garbage into the can in the alley, I watched for glass fragments, wet paper towels, any evidence of the magical floor cleanup. Nothing. Whoever had removed the broken glass from the floor hadn't left anything behind.

Somehow, I doubted the intruder had been compulsively tidy. Something about broken glass and peppermint had been important enough to break back into the cottage after almost being caught the first time.

Shaking my head in puzzlement, I opened Walter's cupboard doors until I found a cluster of cups and glasses. There I found five more tumblers like the one he'd dropped on my rag rug across the alley. Why had he brought his potion over there? Maybe he'd been afraid he wouldn't be found for a while if he died alone in this little cottage.

No, no, that couldn't be the reason. What if Erin had found him at our house? He adored her, and I couldn't imagine he'd risk her discovering his dead body. There had to be another explanation.

I didn't find any lye under the sink or in any of the cupboards. Of course, the police may have taken it when Mrs. Gray let them in after Walter died. He hadn't used any of my lye, so it had to come from somewhere. Could that be what had broken on the floor last night? The peppermint smell was the same.

Sighing, I headed back across the alley to raid my supply of shipping boxes and grab a tape gun. Soon Meghan and I were boxing things up like mad. We started with every shred of paperwork we could find, glancing through a handful at a time in hope of seeing something that looked like a will and then cramming it all in the cardboard cartons. As soon as a box was full, I'd cart it across to our house and come back for another. But our cursory review revealed no will. Meghan went back to work on the bedroom, and I started on the shelves in the living room.

"Hey! What the hell is going on?"

I whirled from where I was wiping the dust off several pictures I'd gathered together for Tootie and found a dark-haired woman with corpse-pale skin standing in the front doorway.

"Where's Walter? What are you doing with his stuff?" Her little-girl voice scarcely contained her anger. When I didn't respond right away, she said, "Don't just stand there gawping, answer me!"

Meghan stepped forward. "You wouldn't happen to be Debby, would you?"

For a moment the woman looked afraid. "Why?"

Holding her hand out, she said, "I'm Meghan Bly. This is Sophie Mae Reynolds. We live across the alley there." She indicated the direction of our house with a wave of her other hand.

The woman's icy glare returned. "Good for you. So why are you ripping Walter's house apart?"

"First, tell us who you are," I said.

The woman's head swiveled toward me. She came further into the room, moving like a skittish cat, ready to leap at the slightest provocation. Meghan's hand dropped to her side, unshaken. A man, short and wiry, followed the woman in, his mouth agape as he took in the mess we'd made. Both wore jeans, he with a long-sleeved plaid flannel shirt, and she with a black tank top.

She folded her thin arms over her chest. "Okay, I'm Debby. And this is—"

"Jacob," Meghan and I said together.

"What, are you two a coupla psychics or somethin'?" Jacob asked, but the joke fell flat. His questioning eyes knew something was wrong.

"Don't be stupid. Walter told them about us, is all."

Jacob shook his head. "Nuh uh. I don't think so, Debs. Somethin' happened to Walter, or he'd be here. Is he in the hospital or somethin'?" He directed this last to me.

I looked at Meghan and took a deep breath. "I'm sorry to have to tell you this. Walter died the day before yesterday."

Debby put her hand to her mouth. Her eyes filled with tears, and she made a gurgling sound. The blood drained from Jacob's face.

"Would you like some water?" Meghan asked.

Jacob, who had seemed paralyzed by the news, now frowned at her words. "Water? What good would that do?"

He helped Debby to the dark-red sofa, where she folded into a shuddering heap, wrapping those skinny arms around herself.

"I told you something was wrong when he didn't show," she said to Jacob.

He perched on the arm next to her. "How'd he die?"

Before I could say anything, Meghan spoke. "There was an accident."

Debby raised her head. "What kind of accident?" she managed to get out.

"Well, uh, it was poison," I said.

"Poison? By accident?" She looked back and forth between us.

I was silent. Meghan pressed her lips together.

"You two know more than you're telling me," Debby braced her hands on the sofa seat as if readying to launch herself at us. "What happened to my Walter?"

My Walter? The phrase—and the way she'd said it—evoked an image that made my mind reel.

"He drank it," Meghan said.

Jacob's brow wrinkled. "What was it?"

"Lye," was my short reply.

"He drank Drano? Ohmygod." Debby wrapped her pale arms around herself again and rocked back and forth. The sofa bumped gently against the wall. "I can't believe it. He'd say that, sometimes, but I never thought he'd do it."

"Do it?" I looked at Jacob. His eyes were red and his hands trembled. "Do what?"

He looked down at the woman. Took a wobbly breath. "Kill himself. With Drano."

"He told you he was planning to drink drain cleaner?" Meghan asked.

Jacob patted Debby's shoulder. "Nah. Not like you mean. He used to joke about it. You know, like when someone says 'If such-and-such happens I'm just gonna shoot myself,' only he said he'd drink Drano. We never thought he was serious."

"Especially now," Debby said, almost too low for us to hear. She fumbled in her purse, extracted an orange prescription bottle. Suddenly Jacob changed his mind about the water. He hurried into the kitchen, came back with a glassful, and helped her to hold it steady as she gulped down the little white pill. Liquid sloshed down her chin, but she didn't seem to notice.

"Why especially now?" I asked.

Debby sniffed, a horrible gurgling sound, and stuck out her hand like a paw to be shaken. On her third finger, a sizeable diamond glittered amid a circle of smaller ones.

"We were gonna get married."

TEN

HOLY COW. As I tried to wrap my head around that one, Meghan walked over to admire the ring. Debby thanked her and snorted wetly.

"It must have been expensive," Meghan said.

I joined them. Up close, I saw Debby was older than I had first thought, probably in her late fifties. Hard to tell with the mascara streaking down her face. She'd kept most of her figure, but her blue-black hair came from a bottle, and the years had engraved a healthy set of lines. The extreme pallor seemed to be her natural coloring, and I wondered for a moment whether her real hair color had been red or even a whiter blonde than my own.

"Yeah," I said. "That's a nice ring. Must have set Walter back a bit."

Debby nodded. "He said he wanted to get me a big diamond, and then he went and actually did it." She said it like she wasn't used to people following through on what they said.

"Well, at least you got that, Debs. You got that t' remember him by." Jacob's words had a bitter edge to them. His face held sorrow, but as he gazed at the woman beside him on the sofa there was something else as well. He reached out and brushed a strand of hair out of her face. She pushed his hand away.

"We're so sorry," Meghan said.

He nodded and fished a crumpled bandana out of his pocket, handed it to Debby. She honked into it.

"I don't know how to ask this," I said, "so I'll just come right out with it. Do you know anything about the investment Walter made that turned out so well?"

"Investment? Oh!" Jacob's smile looked tired. "The money. He'd call it that sometimes, if he talked about it at all."

Meghan and I waited.

"Ol' Walter won the lottery a few years back. So's I guess the investment he told you 'bout would be the ticket."

"Well, it's nice he spent some of it on that beautiful ring," I said, trying to bring Debby back into the conversation. All it earned me were fresh sobs, which Meghan's glare told me I deserved for trying to extract information from a grieving fiancée.

"He spent precious little, I dare say. Gave it all away to strangers, when he coulda done some good with it amongst people right here." Jacob looked at Debby as he spoke.

She dug the heels of her hands into her eyes and hiccupped. "He didn't like anyone to tell him what to do with his money."

"How much did he win?" Meghan asked. Okay for her to do it, I guess.

"Don't know for sure. A whole shitload. And then he went and started giving it all away," Jacob said.

"All of it? Wow," Meghan said.

He looked away and shrugged, his eyes darting to the woman beside him again. "Don't know if he was scrapin' bottom yet, but he was workin' on it."

"Any idea why?" I asked.

Debby turned her wet face to me. "What do you care?"

"Just surprised, I guess. He still did work for us on a regular basis and for other people in the neighborhood. From what I can tell, he didn't really have to, or he wouldn't have had to if he'd kept his winnings."

Neither of them spoke. The silence lengthened. Meghan broke it.

"There will be a memorial service at Crane's Funeral Home on Monday at two o'clock."

A stubborn expression crossed Debby's face. "Moved kinda fast, didn't you?"

Meghan sat down beside her on the sofa. Our eyes met and an unspoken understanding passed between us. "Not really. He died on Thursday. We didn't know you'd want to be involved, and his mother wanted to go ahead with the service."

Debby snorted. "His mother. Right. Didn't care much when he was alive, did she?"

"Will you come?"

"'Course we'll come," Jacob responded for them both. "Debby here's just a little overwhelmed by all this. We wouldn't miss Walter's send-off for nothin'."

Meghan scanned the woman's pale face. "Debby?"

"I'll be there. It would have been nice to have a say in things, is all, seeing as how I was his fiancée."

"Well, there are a few details to work out yet. For example, we haven't chosen hymns yet, and no one has selected a cinerary urn."

"Hymns. Right. Like I know anything about hymns. And what's a ciner...cin...whatever you said?"

"It's where you keep the ashes after someone is cremated."

"Oh. So the old bat wants to burn him up, is that it? Figures. She always said he was going to hell."

I doubted those were her exact words, but perhaps Tootie had understated the schism between Walter and herself.

"She said he was claustrophobic as a child and wouldn't want to be buried," I said.

"Oh. I didn't know that." She looked around. "But you can't just come in here and take all his stuff."

Meghan said, "Right now we're just boxing up some things for the Salvation Army, and whatever mementos we thought his mother might want to keep. Is there anything here you want?"

Debby got up and walked to the set of shelves we hadn't started on yet. She picked up the signed baseball and turned it in her hand. Her face crumpled. Jacob scurried to her side.

Meghan said, "This'll wait. We can put it all on hold until after the funeral."

"I think that'd be best," Jacob said and led Debby to the door. She went through, fingering the leather of the ball and sniffing loudly, but he turned in the doorway. "I want to know how you knew who we were."

"The barista down at Beans R Us told us you were friends of Walter's," Meghan said.

"Oh," he said, and looked to his left, into the kitchen. "That where he did it?"

I tried not to sigh. "No. Not there."

He looked hard at me. "Where then?"

"In my workroom." I swallowed. "Across the alley."

"Jacob?" Debby's tiny voice drifted in from the front sidewalk.

He licked his lips, like he wanted to say more, then suddenly turned on his heel and walked out. Meghan closed the door, looking grim.

"I know, I know," I said. "But what did you want me to do? I couldn't lie, and besides, I didn't want to. Walter didn't have very many friends, and I'm not going to lie to the few he did have just because the truth is uncomfortable for me."

"Well, it's not like how Walter died is a secret."

"At least now we know where Walter's money came from. And that he had a fiancée—can you believe it?"

"She's something, isn't she?"

"I noticed you didn't exactly warm up to her," I said.

"I was nice."

"You were very nice. You're always very nice. But something struck you funny about her, didn't it?"

"Something, yeah. It did you, too. Something about the lottery money?"

"I'm not sure. I got kind of mixed signals from her."

"Not the best time to try and get a read on someone, right after they learn their fiancé has died," Meghan said.

"And we know of one possible problem Walter could have had besides the money."

"What're you talking about?"

"Jacob, of course. Walter's rival for Debby's affections."

Meghan looked skeptical

"Didn't you see the way he looked at her?"

"That doesn't mean he was a rival."

"Doesn't mean he wasn't, though, does it?"

"You don't have to look so happy about it."

"Sorry. Have we done enough for now? It's almost time for Sparrow, isn't it?"

Looking at her watch, Meghan ran her fingers through her curls. "You're right. I have to get back." She looked around the room. "We said we'd leave it until Debby could help, anyway."

And the paperwork was already over at our house. I had two or three days to sort it out for Tootie, though I had to wonder how helpful it would be if I couldn't find a will. I'd hoped to discover where Walter's money was coming from, but now we knew. Still, the boxes might contain an insurance policy or other financial information. And I wanted to take another look at those donation receipts.

I hesitated, then grabbed the open carton of mementos I'd collected so far. Tootie should look at them first and decide what she might want to keep, since I was here at her request. Debby could have second crack at them. Meghan locked Walter's door, and we walked back across the alley to our house.

ELEVEN

THE LIGHT ON THE answering machine blinked; Detective Ambrose had returned my call. As I punched in the number for the police department, Meghan laughed.

"You look like you're about to take a spoonful of cod liver oil."

I grimaced. No doubt she was right. The thought of speaking to Ambrose made little fluttery things flap around in my stomach.

This time I didn't get the good detective's voicemail. The man himself was on the other end of the line in less than ten seconds.

"Ms. Reynolds," he said. "I'd like you to come down and see me, if you would."

"Um…is something wrong?"

"It's about Walter Hanover's death."

No kidding. "Well, I sort of figured that. Did I leave something out of my statement?" I asked.

"Not that I know of. Why, did you remember something you'd like to add?"

"No. I'm just wondering why you want to talk to me. Can we do it over the phone?"

"I'd rather it was face to face."

"Well, Detective, let me see…today isn't good, and I'm pretty busy tomorrow as well. Perhaps on Monday…oh, that won't work either. Walter's memorial service is that day…"

"I'll be in my office this afternoon between two and four. Come by then, Ms. Reynolds." His tone didn't invite argument.

I tried again anyway. "I have a very busy afternoon planned—"

"I can always ask a patrolman to give you a ride, if you'd rather."

So. It was like that.

I sighed. "All right. This afternoon."

"Looking forward to it," he said.

I bet he was. My teeth clenched as I thought about our brief conversation. Power-hungry egomaniac.

So the afternoon I'd thought was salvaged when Debby and Jacob conveniently showed up at Walter's, saving us a trip to Beans R Us, now would be wasted listening to Ambrose's diatribe about God-knew-what. Lovely. I went downstairs to see how far behind I was.

One problem with working at home is people don't think you really have a job. Meghan understands, of course, because she's in the same situation. But others think because you have a flexible schedule, which is, let's face it, a perk of being your own boss, your work is more like a hobby than a job. But you still have to put in the hours. In fact, you have to put in more hours, because if your week isn't productive, no one will be writing you a paycheck on Friday.

After looking over my notes, I determined that evening I'd make three hundred lemon lip balms for the holiday bazaars. My inventory already included two hundred of the peppermint and the same number of lavender, but lately lemon had been my best seller. Since they make great stocking stuffers, they'd go pretty fast, and I wanted to have enough.

I gathered the ingredients together on the counter by the old range and put the lip balm tubes in closed baskets in the sterilizing dishwasher. I filled the rest of the racks with glass bottles for the oatmeal-milk bath salts I planned to make the next day and started it up.

Walter's collection of paper had filled three medium-sized boxes, which still sat in the front hallway by the staircase. I lugged them upstairs and stowed them away in a room Meghan had always planned to make into another spare bedroom, but, until we got around to it, was the junk storage room. The cartons looked right at home, stacked between a bentwood rocker with a split seat and Erin's old hobbyhorse. I put the open box of mementos on the floor under the window.

Next, I packed up the two wholesale orders of soap that should have been sent out the day before, created invoices, packing lists, and mailing labels, and ran over to the UPS drop-off counter. Buzzing back home, I drove a reckless thirty even though the Cadyville traffic patrol was known for being sticklers about the twenty-five-mile-an-hour speed limit.

Back in the basement, I wiped down the workroom with a vinegar solution. Bleach might be okay on occasion, but I preferred the vinegar; it's a great disinfectant and smells much better than chlorine. When everything was tidied and clean and ready to go,

I gathered the ingredients for the oatmeal-milk bath salts and the apparatus to combine the mixture: a heavy-duty paint mixer attached to a drill, and four plastic five-gallon buckets, one for each scent. Kyla had called the day before, wondering if she could work on Sunday. I guess her mom was okay with her working more on the weekends, if not afternoons after school. Once I'd mixed the product, she could spend tomorrow afternoon bottling it.

Feeling a little more in control, I left for the police station at two-thirty. Sparrow had booked a full hour-and-a-half massage, so I didn't have a chance to talk to Meghan before leaving, but surely I could handle one little conversation with Detective Ambrose without being prepped by my lawyer housemate.

The rain from the day before had abated, though leaden clouds still hung overhead. Like a down comforter, they provided insulation from the cold. A mild breeze brushed against my cheek, and the thermometer on the front porch read sixty-one. The air smelled sweet and spicy, laced with the faraway smoke from burning leaves. Inhaling deeply, I decided to walk to the station.

Cadyville was abuzz with families and couples from Seattle and elsewhere who turned the downtown into touristville on the weekends. Most of the visitors concentrated on the antique stores and restaurants along First Street or ventured out to the fruit and vegetable stands for fresh produce. With Halloween just over a week away, many were shopping for potential jack-o'-lanterns in the local pumpkin patches. Northwesterners would have to give up on having weekend plans at all if we gave in to the weather, so gray or rainy skies rarely disturbed the flow of people. A steady stream of traffic accompanied my walk.

I strolled along, telling myself I was enjoying the chance to be outside and the bustle of the weekenders, while knowing I was really delaying the encounter with Detective Ambrose. Something about the man, the way he carried himself, expressed himself, felt familiar. Not don't-I-know-you-from-somewhere familiar—I was sure I'd never met him before. But something. Was it his voice? Maybe. Yes, just maybe I heard a faint edge of midwest cowboy there.

But that day I'd been so freaked out about finding Walter I'd probably imagined it, that ease of communication, as if there existed points of commonality we hadn't yet discovered, because now I didn't have a clue why Ambrose had ordered me to come to his office.

The police seemed willing to chalk up Walter's death to suicide. And since it wasn't Ambrose's job to find out why he'd do such a thing, he wouldn't know life had been treating Walter pretty darn well lately.

Well, he *should* have been looking into what happened, should have cared enough to make it his job.

By the time I reached the police station, my blood had reached a low simmer. Inside, a uniformed cadet escorted me to Ambrose. It was a good thing he didn't try to make me wait, in some pathetic attempt to gain the upper hand. I might have boiled over altogether.

We didn't go to the same room where I'd given my statement two days before, but to an open area delineated from the reception counter by a long shelving unit, where the tidy spines of technical manuals and law books crowded together. Desks with computer workstations lined the room, and the cadet took me to one in the corner, apparently Ambrose's own.

I'd expected clutter, a work space overflowing with stacks of papers and reports, coffee rings on all available surfaces, files sliding to the floor, the constant ring of the phone. Instead, I found it tidy and organized. Two file cabinets sat against one wall, and his dust-free desktop held only a closed laptop computer, multiline telephone, legal pad and pen, and on one corner a geode the size of a man's fist, cracked open to reveal the crystals within. The walls above the various workstations sported calendars and family photos, but opposite Detective Ambrose's chair hung a rather nice oil painting in the style of Frederic Remington.

Detective Ambrose sat with his back to us. He looked around when we approached, then stood and pulled over a chair for me to sit in. Today he wore khaki slacks and cowboy boots, a deep-blue shirt, and a silver bolo tie with a hunk of turquoise in the middle of it. A sports jacket was draped over the back of another chair. We were the only ones in the room. Everyone else must have been keeping an eye on all those rowdy tourists.

"Do you want anything, Ms. Reynolds? Coffee?"

"No. Thank you."

He sat back down and considered me. I considered him right back. Feathers of gray curved through his chestnut hair and one dark strand swept down over his eyebrow. His irises were a darker brown, with mocha-colored rings around the pupils. Probably one of those men who spend hours in front of the mirror, fussing to look like they didn't. He blinked, slow, like a cat.

He said, "I understand Officer Owens found you in Walter Hanover's place Thursday night."

I raised my eyebrows.

He raised his.

"I'm sorry. Did you ask me a question?" I asked.

Brief anger flashed across his features before being replaced by an expression of bland amusement. "What were you doing there?"

"Didn't Owens—sorry, *Officer* Owens—tell you? And did he bother to mention someone else was in Walter's house that night as well?"

Another slow blink. "I'd like you to tell me what happened. If you would."

I settled back in my chair. "That evening, I was in the basement gathering some things to take upstairs. Work that I needed to finish but didn't feel like doing in my workroom that night—it gave me the creeps down there, if you can imagine *that*." He cocked his head briefly, acknowledging my sarcasm but not interrupting. "While I was downstairs, I noticed a light on across the alley, in Walter's window. Since he wouldn't be coming home to switch it off, I went to turn it off myself." I paused.

"How did you get in?" Ambrose asked.

"The door was open."

"Unlocked?"

"No, open to the elements, though just a crack."

"Did he leave it like that a lot?"

I shrugged. "I really don't know."

Ambrose nodded, reached for the pad and pen.

"So you went in."

"I did."

"And?"

"And…I…well, I snooped a little. Okay? Happy?"

He leaned back in his chair. "What were you looking for?" His tone was mild, curious.

I opted for the truth, since I didn't have anything better. "I don't know. I guess at first I just wanted a better sense of the man. You'd asked me all those questions that afternoon—about his family, his friends—and I realized I hardly knew him. Yet he died where I work…and live. I wanted to know why. I still want to know. And then I saw family photos and that card table with files and papers, things he'd accrued simply as a consequence of being alive. It made me wonder who would take care of him, you know, funeral-wise. I started going through the papers, trying to find names of family, anyone I could contact about his death. And I wanted to know if they'd tell me more about him."

"The papers or the people?"

"Well, both."

Ambrose tapped his pen on the desk, never breaking eye contact. If I'd lied, he'd have known. He just would have. I didn't understand why I knew this, but I did. The cockiness I'd felt when I first entered the police station had deserted me.

I held up my palms. "So? Was that so bad?"

"Nnoo…" He drew the word out. "I suppose I can understand it."

"And I found all sorts of receipts for donations—Walter had tons of money. And that's not all."

"So you were looking through Hanover's files when Officer Owens found you?"

"Not exactly. When Officer Owens came in I was busy trying not to have a heart attack."

He smiled. "Is this where the other intruder you mentioned comes into it?"

"He *didn't* tell you! That little...I swear..."

"Didn't tell me what, Ms. Reynolds?"

"Will you please stop calling me Ms. Reynolds? My name's Sophie Mae."

"Sophie Mae, then." He made a get-on-with-it gesture.

"Someone else was in Walter's house when I was there. He must have been hiding in the kitchen and accidentally knocked a glass or something off the counter. When it broke, scaring me *spitless*—you can't imagine how loud something like that is, when you think you're all alone—he skedaddled out the front door before I could see who it was."

"So you didn't actually see anyone?"

"I saw a shadowy figure—I know, what a cliché—go past, outside the kitchen window. And right before that, I heard the front door open and shut as I was going to look in the kitchen."

"You went to look in the kitchen, thinking someone was in there?" His look said it all.

"Pretty dumb, huh?"

He laughed. "Well, for someone who goes around sticking her bare fingers in lye, I suppose it's par for the course."

"Hey!"

He made a note on his legal pad. "So you told Officer Owens about the other person—it was a man?"

"I assumed a man, but now that you put it like that, I'm probably being sexist. It could have been a woman. And yes, I did tell Officer Owens, but he was far more concerned with hustling me out of there and giving me friendly advice about how to assuage my guilt about Walter's death."

"Assuage your guilt?"

"He seemed to think I felt responsible for Walter dying in my workroom, implying he had used my lye. Which I already know he couldn't have, as I've told you ad nauseum. He told me to go talk to Walter's mother!"

"Did you?"

"Did I what?"

"Go talk to Mrs. Hanover."

"Oh. Well, yes, actually, I did. Yesterday."

"Feel better?"

I bit down on the rude retort that came to mind, and he flashed a quick grin. For a brief moment I got a good look at the man behind the profession, and that glimpse gave my hormones an unexpected jolt.

Schooling my face to hide my reaction, and at the same time knowing the effort was futile, I said, "No, actually, I feel worse. She's a nice lady, but she and Walter hadn't been getting along. Now he's dead, and she has to live with that. But she's strong, and she'll be okay. Don't you think?"

Official demeanor back in place, he made another note. "I haven't had the pleasure. Yet. I'll see her this evening."

"Oh. You weren't the one who told her about Walter?"

He shook his head. "Let's get back to your curiosity about your neighbor. Tell me more about why you've developed this sudden interest in him."

"I told you—"

"Ambrose!" Sergeant Zahn stood in the rear doorway, looking very unhappy.

"Excuse me," the detective said, and rose. Zahn took a couple steps toward him, and they spoke in low voices. Affecting disinterest, I examined the painting of men working a herd of cattle and listened as hard as I could.

"Why is she here?" Zahn asked in a low voice.

"Just finishing up a few loose ends," Ambrose said.

"Like what?"

"She saw someone over at Hanover's place the night he died."

Out of the corner of my eye, I could see Zahn glance at me. I ignored him.

"Did she see who it was?" he asked.

Ambrose shook his head. "No."

"Anything missing?"

"Not that I know of." Ambrose said.

"Then forget it. The guy killed himself. End of story. Stop trying to make it into something more. We don't have time to investigate a homicide that didn't even happen. I need you back on the mayor's case."

Stop trying to make it into something more. Meghan had said those same words to me. Was Ambrose looking into what had happened to Walter after all?

TWELVE

Detective Ambrose sighed as he sat down again. "I think we're done here. Thanks for coming down."

"Walter was murdered, wasn't he?" I whispered.

He looked uncomfortable. "We have no evidence of that."

"Did you find a note?"

He shook his head. "Not in his house or his vehicle."

"What about the lye—did you find any at his house?"

He hesitated, then shook his head again.

"Okay," I said. "So he didn't leave a note. Lots of people don't, so that doesn't prove anything. But someone was in his house the night he died, and he had a pile of money and a new fiancée, neither of which tends to make someone want to kill himself. And both of which could be a motive for murder."

Sergeant Zahn walked by.

Ambrose said, "I'll walk you to your car."

"No! You can't—"

He grabbed my arm and hauled me to my feet. As we approached the entrance, he said, "I'll be back in a few minutes," to the officer manning the front desk.

Outside he asked, "Where's your car?"

"Wait a minute!"

"Where is it?"

"I walked."

His hand firmly gripping my elbow, he guided me to the sidewalk that ran along the side of the long, low police station.

"What's this about a fiancée?" he asked.

"You don't already know?"

"If I did, I wouldn't ask."

"But you know about the lottery?"

"Yeah—got his bank records yesterday."

I told him about meeting Debby and Jacob, wondering if I was getting her in trouble. But if Walter had been murdered, Ambrose needed to know about her.

"What are their last names?"

"I don't know. But they hang out at Beans R Us."

"So you were in Hanover's place, moving things around?"

"This morning. Boxing things up at his mother's request."

He muttered "shit" under his breath.

I raised my eyebrows.

"Sorry."

I laughed. "We stopped in the middle of cleaning out the place. Walter's fiancée wanted to help go through things, after the memorial service."

"That's on Monday?"

"In the afternoon."

He looked thoughtful. "You still insist the lye wasn't yours."

"Yes! But why would someone kill Walter in my…" I trailed off. Swallowed. "Am I a suspect?"

He looked disgusted. "At this point no one is a suspect." All of a sudden, he looked me in the eye and gave me that grin. "But I suppose you'd be as good as any."

"That sounds just a tad unprofessional, Detective Ambrose," I said.

"Just a tad." He blinked that slow cat blink again.

"So why doesn't Sergeant Zahn want you to investigate Walter's death? Don't you guys usually keep at it until you know for sure what happened?"

The grin slid off his face. "It looks like suicide. And I can't point to any physical evidence to the contrary, just an odd set of circumstances that makes my gut twist. I don't know, maybe he's right. It's true enough that I've got other cases that deserve my attention. But I can't seem to let it—" Suddenly he looked chagrined, and I knew he wished he hadn't said anything.

"Is whatever you're working on for the mayor more important than catching a killer?"

Ambrose looked at the pointy toes of his boots. Ground one against the cement. He sighed.

"Well, for what it's worth, I agree with your gut," I said. "But how do you *make* someone drink lye?"

He shoved his hands in his pockets and looked across the street. "I'd like to know that myself. Is there anything, anything at all you haven't told me?"

I shook my head. Then, "Wait a minute. There is something else." I told him about the intruder coming back to clean up his mess.

"Don't go over to Hanover's again. I need to take another look around over there before you disturb anything else." He closed his eyes and rubbed the bridge of his nose with his thumb and fore-finger. "Listen, I don't know exactly what happened to your neighbor, but whatever it was, you need to stay clear of it. You're too involved."

"To your benefit," I said, indignant.

He dropped his hand. "I would've found out about the fiancée and her friend soon enough. Now I need you to back off until I can get the situation sorted out."

Back off? I'd already found out more than this cowboy had. "And how are you going to, uh, sort it out if you're not allowed to officially work on the case?"

He ignored the question. "Do I have your word you'll leave it to me?"

"Um…"

A deep-red flush swept up his face and he leaned over me. I felt a little shudder of fear, and maybe something else, travel up my spine, but I stared back, defiant. When he spoke, the words were measured and low.

"I'll find out what happened to Walter Hanover. My job. *Not* yours."

He turned and took a few steps, then turned back. "I can't have you interfering in this investigation. It's too dangerous."

I rolled my eyes. "But I helped."

"Maybe. Maybe not. You may have already compromised any information we could have gained from Hanover's home, tainted interviews, who knows what else. And Sophie Mae? When I indicated you don't appear to be a suspect now, that doesn't mean if there's evidence that implicates you, I won't dig it up."

With that, he strode back inside.

And I walked home, contemplating why men seem to have such tender egos.

THIRTEEN

As BAD AS I felt when I came into the house, someone else felt worse. Erin was curled on one end of the sofa, rereading *The Wolves of Willoughby Chase*, one of her favorite books. Brodie lay with his head in her lap, watching her face.

Dickhead had done it again. He couldn't even keep his daughter for a full twenty-four hours. And this time he'd come right out and assured us all he would see the weekend through.

"Hi, Bug," I said, trying not to let my anger show.

She looked up, misery shining from her eyes. "Hi."

I sat down next to her on the sofa and put my arm around her. She leaned into me and sighed.

"Where's your mom?" I asked.

Erin shrugged against me. "Don't know. No one was here when I got home."

"He…Did your Dad know that?"

She nodded. "I had to get the spare key to get in."

We kept the key under a particular rock in the garden on the west side of the house. I'd have to mention to Meghan that Richard knew where it was now. I couldn't believe he'd left Erin alone like that, not knowing when we'd be home.

"You okay?" I asked.

A little nod. Then, "Sophie Mae? Why's everything else more important than me?"

That bastard. I kept my answer light. "Actually, Bug, I think you have that backwards. 'Cuz you're more important than everything else."

"I mean at Dad's. It's like I'm…" She twisted her head to look up at me. I let her know with my eyes I wanted to hear whatever she had to say. She snuggled back into my side.

"It's like I'm a pet or something. Like we are with Brodie. We love him and feed him and snuggle him and play with him. He's around all the time, keeping us company…" She shrugged and stroked the dog's velvet ear. "I guess it's not like I'm a pet." There were tears in her voice.

How do you like that, Dick? Erin thinks she treats her dog better than you treat her.

I hugged her closer and spoke into her hair. "It's okay, Bug. It's just the way he is. It doesn't have anything to do with how he feels about you."

She sniffed. I could tell she didn't believe me, and I couldn't blame her. It sounded lame, even to my ears. How could I convince her without making her dad out as a creep? He was, no doubt about it, but I didn't have the right to tell her that. Especially not after Meghan had been so careful about that taking-the-high-road thing.

I heard the front door open and steps in the hallway. Then Meghan stood in the doorway, two bags of groceries in her arms. She took one look at the three of us on the couch and Erin's wet face, and anger flared bright behind her eyes. Without a word, she went into the kitchen and started putting groceries away. We heard a cupboard door bang shut. Erin dragged her sleeve across her cheek and pulled away, giving me a worried look.

"Mom's mad, huh?"

I nodded. "She'll be back in a minute. She's cooling off."

"I know," Erin said. We waited. The cupboard noises stopped in the kitchen. After a few minutes, Meghan came back in and sat on Erin's other side.

"What was his excuse this time?" she asked her daughter. Her tone was neutral, but I was surprised she put it so baldly.

"He, uh, said something about someone he had to meet who could get him a job," Erin said.

"What happened to the job he had?" I asked.

"He quit." Erin's body tensed in anticipation of the storm.

It didn't come. "I see," Meghan said. "Well, if he had to go, then I'm glad he brought you home instead of leaving you alone this evening. Sophie Mae and I were talking about renting a movie tonight—"

I broke in. "But then I decided I had too much work to do, so now your mom won't have to watch it all by herself."

"I went to a movie last night," Erin reminded her mother. Meghan was fairly strict about rationing TV and movie watching.

"Oh, c'mon. Like I don't know you'd be watching TV all afternoon at your dad's if you were over there. I doubt a movie two nights in a row will hurt you. Much." She smiled.

Erin clambered off the sofa. "What movie?"

Meghan stood up and held out her hand to her daughter. "We hadn't decided yet. So now that Sophie Mae has to work, you have to help me pick. Let's go now, before dinner. But first, put your bag up in your room."

Erin started to pick up her coat, which lay over her duffle on the floor. Then she came back and put her arms around me.

"I'm glad you live with us, Sophie Mae," she whispered.

"Me, too, honey."

I cleared the lump out of my throat, and she started lugging her bag up the stairs. I turned to my housemate.

"How do you do that? She was so upset when I came home."

"I think it's like taking a stubborn lid off a jar: you got it started and I just finished it. Besides, she's ten. I have a feeling it won't be so easy when she's fifteen."

I remembered my teenaged relationship with my mother. "I have a feeling most things won't be easy when she's fifteen."

"I guess we'll find out," Meghan said. "Wait a minute. She was here when you came home?"

I told her what Erin had told me, and that Richard now knew where we hid our spare key. Her lips pressed together for a moment before Erin came back into the room. Then she smiled at her daughter and jingled her keys in her pocket.

"Ready, Bug?"

Erin nodded and they left. Richard was going to be hearing from Meghan about this one.

And I was itching to tell her I wasn't the only one who thought Walter might have been murdered. Tonight I'd have to try to grab her away from Erin for a few minutes.

That night while I measured and melted lip balm ingredients, then painstakingly filled three hundred little white tubes, I thought about who would want to kill Walter.

Murder. How odd: even though the concept was far more frightening, it was easier for me to think about than suicide. The specter of Bobby Lee had promptly receded to the shadows at the first suggestion Walter may have died by a hand other than his own. And I didn't miss the heavy weight of that presence at all.

Shrugging off that bit of introspection, I returned to theorizing. Love and greed were supposed to be the two most common motives for killing someone. Debby and the lottery. Or something else? What about an insurance policy? Walter wasn't someone I thought of as having life insurance. I'd have been surprised if his old International Scout was insured for anything beyond liability, never mind his own life. But I hadn't thought of him as someone who would win the lottery and donate the winnings to charity, or be engaged to the charming Debby, either. And those two things together could be a reason for him to have life insurance he'd want to pay out. If he'd given all the money away from the lottery and then it turned out he had someone to take care of, he might be prompted to take out a policy.

I warmed to the idea. Was there an insurance policy in the boxes upstairs? Meghan and I could have missed it while packing up Walter's papers, all our attention focused on finding his will. We could have missed the will, too, considering how fast we'd packed the boxes. And a will would open up a whole new bag of possibilities, greed being what it was.

So how did the person who had been in Walter's house play into this? Had I been alone with a killer? My stomach quivered at the thought. Could it have been a coincidence, a break-in? Unlikely. When Mrs. Gray had let us in, the front door hadn't looked like it had been forced open. Debby could have a key. Or, Jacob might have dropped by, though neither of them had given any indication of having seen me before. But I hadn't seen whoever was hiding in the kitchen that night, so maybe he—or she—wouldn't recognize me either. In fact, I sincerely hoped not.

But if someone had used a key, why was the key under the flowerpot out back missing and the door still open? And if you had a key, why would you take the one under the flowerpot? To divert attention away from yourself. To confuse the issue. Because you didn't have your key with you. Or maybe the key hadn't been under the flowerpot for a long time—Walter had told us about it a year ago or more—and maybe he was the one who left the door hanging open when he left that morning, as I had first believed. The key, or rather the absence of the key, might not mean a thing. Come at it from another direction.

If Walter did have a policy that named Debby as the beneficiary, she could have wanted the money, since any hope of getting her hands on his lottery winnings after they married faded with each check he wrote to charity. Jacob could have killed him because he wanted Debby. And either or both of them could have known about my soap-making business and the lye from Walter himself.

I stopped still. Had someone intentionally tried to frame me? I lowered myself slowly to a stool, setting the lip balm tube I'd been filling on the counter in front of me. Crap. Oh, crap, crap, crap.

I'd involved myself in finding out what had happened to Walter because I wanted to understand his need to kill himself, and that desire had segued into wanting to know why someone else would want to kill him. But, I realized now, a lot of my interest came from the fact that he'd died right here, *right here*, on the floor under this very stool. This was the first time it had occurred to me that I, personally, could have been on someone's mind as they thought about needing Walter to be dead.

Could I really be framed for killing Walter? Was there some manufactured evidence waiting for the police to find it?

I felt a little nauseated and walked to the back door, opening it and walking out into the backyard. The air was cool and damp and I sucked it into my lungs, trying to steady my sudden onrush of nerves.

Oh, for heaven's sake, Sophie Mae. Stop being so paranoid. Sheesh.

How exactly do you make someone drink lye? At gunpoint, maybe? Only if the victim is stupid or believes they can survive the lye, but not the bullet. Or, you might threaten something, or someone, they wanted to keep safe. I could see Walter drinking lye to save someone else. Debby. Or—I had a horrible thought—Erin. Or maybe it would be possible to trick a person into drinking lye. Disguised as water?

When lye is first mixed, the chemical reaction results in heat. The lye on the floor had been room temperature, so it had been mixed long enough before to allow for cooling. How long was that? A couple hours, I thought, maybe more. I hadn't really paid attention. And, of course, you could speed it with ice, but not too much or the granules would precipitate out of the liquid. Also, the volume of the mixture would affect how quickly it cooled. So, the fact the lye had cooled to room temperature didn't mean anything more than it had been mixed at least some time prior to Walter drinking it. No, it didn't even mean that. Maybe he drank it hot, and it had then cooled on the floor before I got home and found him.

I grimaced. The only thing worse than drinking lye would be drinking hot lye. Still, it was a possibility.

I went back inside and continued filling lip balm tubes out of sheer stubbornness. My eyes were bleary as I finished the tedious and exacting process, and it was after eleven by the time I poured the last one. My bed beckoned, but I wanted to make a start on Walter's paperwork. On a tea run upstairs, I'd managed to pull Meghan aside and tell her Ambrose had at least implied Walter might have been murdered. Her face had pinched at the news, the fear of lawsuits replaced with a more primal one.

Settling cross-legged onto the wood floor of the spare room, I dumped one of the boxes of papers out in front of me. As I sifted each individual piece out of the jumble, it received a thorough perusal and my judgment regarding any relevance to anything. All I ended up with after an hour was a pile of charity receipts held together with a stray paperclip and a box full of unmitigated junk. Sure, a particular check stub or movie theater ticket might provide the telling clue, but not with the dearth of information I had. I'd be happy to turn the whole lot over to Ambrose.

Just as soon as I went through the other two boxes.

FOURTEEN

I WAS HAVING ONE of those crazy dreams that you can't describe when you wake up but you know was crazy because you remember something about Captain Kirk and a pecan orchard and someone losing a piece of Swiss cheese. The siren in the background fit well enough, and it took me a while to realize it wasn't in my dream. Brightly revolving lights flashing through my window added to the surreal effect when I got around to opening my eyes.

Groggy, I dragged myself out of bed and looked out. My bedroom was at the back of the house, overlooking the backyard and the alley and Walter's little house. Which now had flames licking out the windows.

I threw on my robe and a pair of tennis shoes and ran into the hallway. Erin stood in her bedroom doorway rubbing sleep from her eyes, Brodie woofing low in his throat beside her. Meghan rushed past me to her daughter.

"It's Walter's place," I said. "Fire."

She nodded and began speaking to Erin. I went past them and down the stairs, through the living room and kitchen and down to my workroom. I unlocked the back door and trotted out to the alley.

The smell hit me like an open-handed slap. Bitter, harsh, and acrid, it was nothing like the pleasant wood smoke from a friendly hearth fire. This reek contained destruction. Wisps of ash floated down like snow from hell, settling on my shoulders and in my hair. My eyes started to burn.

Two figures in bulky fire gear appeared, lugging a huge hose around the corner of the little house. Another appeared behind them, speaking into a radio. They aimed, and a column of water gushed forth. They trained it on the roof. The hose seemed to flex and pulse with a life of its own.

Walter's old International Scout, painted the same bright yellow as the suspenders he'd always worn, flared like a torch. The firefighters, concentrating on the house, let it burn.

None of the windows had glass in them anymore; fire shot out of one, and black smoke poured out of the others, accompanied by flickers of flame. One of the firefighters shouted something, and the other one nodded. They shifted the plume of water to the left. The flames roared, as if trying to fight back, but the abundance of water tamed them somewhat. The roofing sputtered and steamed as water worked into the burning interior.

Up and down the alley and on the street in front, neighbors stood around watching in their varied night garb. Sensing movement behind me, I turned to find Meghan approaching, Erin's hand clasped tightly in hers. Erin wore sweat pants, and a coat over her nightgown, though heat shimmered through the air and made them unnecessary. She wrinkled her nose and blinked rapidly.

There wasn't much to say. We stood and watched as the firefighters worked to contain the fire, to keep it from spreading to any of the other homes. There was a bad moment when the siding on Mrs. Gray's house flared up near the roofline, but the men extinguished it in seconds. The whole thing took less than two hours, and half of that was spent soaking the dying embers. Walter's house was a complete loss, a charred skeleton reaching up from the soggy black mess of scorched furniture and unrecognizable flotsam and jetsam.

Meghan took Erin back to bed after the worst was over and came back to stand by me for a while. Then she left again. I couldn't seem to go inside, though. A gawker knot had gathered around Mrs. Gray at one end of the alley, but I ignored them, more stunned than morbidly curious. I was sure this fire hadn't been an accident any more than Walter's death had been.

I picked my way through the sodden detritus in the alley, walking to where the firefighters were packing up their equipment. After a few moments of watching them, I decided on who looked to be in charge. I walked toward him, but another man ran in front of me, shouting.

"Chief Blakely. Please, Chief, what can you tell us about this fire?"

Us? I looked around. A sudden flash of light blinded me, and I put a hand over my eyes. Squinting, I lowered my hand, and another flash went off.

"Stop that!" I said.

The photographer, a tall angular woman with short blonde hair, ignored me, turning to take a couple shots of the chief talking to the man I'd figured out was a reporter. I waited until she had moved on to the smoking mess behind me, then walked toward the fire chief.

He was saying, "I have no comment, Randy. You know it's too early for me to be able to tell you anything more. We have to complete our investigation."

"Anyone inside?"

"Nope. We didn't find anyone, and the owner confirmed it was empty."

"Can you speculate on what caused it?"

"C'mon. You know better than that. Check with Lucy in a couple of days. We'll know more then."

"That's past my deadline—we go to print on Monday night," the reporter said. He must have been from the *Cadyville Eye*, our local weekly.

The fire chief shrugged. "Sorry. Not a lot I can do about that."

"Crap. All right, then. Can't blame me for trying. See you on the next one."

"I'm sure I will."

As the reporter picked his way to where the photographer stood arguing with another firefighter, the chief looked up and saw me.

"And what can I do for you, ma'am?" He sounded tired, and I could tell he wanted me to leave.

I said, "I'm from across the alley there, and I saw how hard your crew worked to keep this house fire under control. I just wanted to let you know how much we appreciate it."

His expression softened. "Well, that's real nice of you. Offsets the three complaints I've heard so far about how we disrupted someone's sleep."

"You're kidding." I shook my head. "Sometimes I wonder about people."

"You and me both."

"So the house was empty? No one got hurt?"

Chief Blakely nodded toward the few remaining onlookers. "Lady who owns it says no one was in there, and from what we could find, she's right."

"The man who used to live there died last week, and my house-mate and I had been helping his mother by boxing up his things. You never know, though."

He nodded slowly. "I'd like to get your name, if I can. Since you've been in the house recently, I might have some questions for you in the next couple of days."

"Happy to help. My name is Sophie Mae Reynolds, and I live in that house right there." I pointed.

Taking a battered notebook out of his pocket, he scribbled a couple lines. "What's your house number?"

I told him, then asked in the most casual voice I could muster, "How did it start? Since no one was there, it was probably some-thing electrical, right?" I looked at the charred remains of the wine-colored sofa in the halogen lights, spongy brown stuffing erupting from the cracked upholstery.

"We don't know yet," he said.

Pulling my gaze away from the wreckage, I met his eyes. "Was it arson?"

He crossed his arms and leaned against the side of the ladder truck. "What makes you say that?"

I checked to make sure the reporter and his obnoxious photographer were still out of earshot. "Because, unless it was electrical, I can't think what else it would be. No one was smoking in bed, no one spilled grease on the stove, no one *did* anything to cause the fire by accident, because the house was empty. I suppose the gas furnace could have blown up or something, but we would have heard the explosion next door, and I think the fire would have looked different."

"Um, Miss…"

"Sophie Mae," I said.

"Right. Sophie Mae. We don't know what happened here. It warrants an investigation, but we can't start until the place has cooled down. And until we have some daylight, as well. So I can't answer your question."

I persisted. "All I want to know is whether we need to worry about some pyro running around the neighborhood."

"Is that really all you want to know? Not just a bit curious?"

"Not like you think. There are…questions about the occupant's death last week. I'm worried."

He raised his eyebrows. "What kind of questions?"

"Let's just say it was suspicious."

"I see. Well, I still don't like to comment on what started a fire until I have some evidence."

I was too tired to feel the full brunt of my own frustration. I nodded and turned toward my waiting bed, then turned back. "I meant what I said about being grateful for the job you and your crew did tonight."

Chief Blakely gave me a nod. "I'll pass it on."

At home, I went in the bathroom to wash off some of the grime I had managed to collect on my hands. Looking up, I saw my reflection: green eyes practically glowing within their red rims, hair escaping its braid in a dozen places, and a nice big black smudge across one cheek. Given the addition of my striped pajamas, robe, and tennis shoes, I was surprised Chief Blakely hadn't run after the first glance.

I rubbed the charcoal off my face and faced the fact that unless I wanted my bed to smell like smoke for a month, I had to take a shower. Afterward, I slid my scrubbed, weary self between the sheets and plunged into a dream even crazier than the last one.

FIFTEEN

SUNDAYS ARE MADE FOR sleeping in, but I dragged my sorry butt out of bed at seven a.m. Kyla was coming at nine, and I needed to be ready for her. Discovering I still smelled faintly of smoke, I showered again and dressed in jeans and pulled on a soft old sweatshirt. If I had to be awake, at least I'd be comfortable.

Erin sat at the kitchen table with a bowl of Cheerios and the *Seattle Times* Sunday comics. I paused in the doorway to finish braiding my still damp hair. Her mother would still be in bed, lucky woman. I made coffee and asked Erin about the movie they'd watched the night before. She replied that it was a fluffy comedy, a "chick flick with hokey dialog." We talked a little about the fire, then I poured a cup of fresh brew, grabbed a pear, and told her I'd be downstairs.

Her next words stopped me. "Walter's obituary is in the paper."

"Where?" I turned back and Erin handed me a carefully folded section she'd put to one side. I sank onto a chair opposite her.

"It doesn't say much," she said.

And it didn't. One short paragraph. Survived by his mother, Petunia Hanover, preceded in death by his father and two brothers. No indication of military time, a brief reference to his work in the local sawmill, no mention of marriage or children, and no information about how he died. At least Crane's Funeral Home had added the time and place of the funeral service. Saddened by the paltry death announcement, I continued downstairs.

I'd mixed two batches of oatmeal-milk bath salts, one scented with rosewood essential oil and the other with a combination of orange and sandalwood essential oils, by the time Kyla showed up. Pure sandalwood would have been nice, too, but the real oil is so expensive I'd have to charge more for that variation than for the other three in the series, and I'd never dream of using the fake oil. Real essential oils not only impart more intense and evocative scents, but the customer gets the additional aromatherapy and herbal benefits as well.

Kyla started capping the lip balms I'd made the night before while I started on a batch of the bath salts in balsam peru, another of my favorite scents. It's like a rounder, denser form of vanilla, definitely a blue scent in my mind, so I chose blue for the label. The rosewood label is a rich taupe, the sandalwood/orange combination a dark peach, and the fourth scent, fir needle, is a gray-green. I'd saved the fir-needle batch until last because it's so invigorating, and I knew I'd be ready for a boost.

But Kyla had brought me a double latté, and between that and my usual morning cup of plain old coffee, I was soon buzzing around like a manic bee. We went to work on opposite sides of the table, chatting about the fire, the upcoming bazaars, and Kyla's latest boyfriend while she funneled the bath salt mixture into sterile six-ounce glass jars and passed them to me to wrap with raffia and affix the hanging tag. Kyla filled faster than I labeled, so when she'd finished a hundred bottles, she started popping cellophane bands over their tops and shrinking them to fit with an old hair dryer I kept for the purpose.

When the oatmeal-milk bath salts were done, she agreed to apply the labels to the lip balm tubes, an operation that required a precision I didn't feel up to that day. I began carting bottles of oatmeal-milk bath salts back to my storeroom. It smelled like heaven in there, and I lingered to take another inventory of the soaps stacked neatly along the shelves. I had plenty of everything except the emollient cocoa butter soap, which a recent order had depleted somewhat. If I ran out, I ran out; there wasn't time enough for another batch to cure properly before the bazaars, and I didn't want too much extra inventory on hand at the end of the year.

I'd make some holiday-themed glycerin soaps, which need very little curing. Glycerin soap is fast and easy, so I could do a couple of small batches and see how they moved at the first two bazaars. I called to Kyla to make sure she planned to come in on Tuesday; she could wrap them then. She shouted back that would be fine.

Kyla's voice came from the other room again, and I stuck my head out to ask her to repeat what she'd said but discovered she wasn't talking to me at all. Lugging a forty-pound bucket of melt-and-pour glycerin soap out of the storeroom, I nodded to Chief Blakely standing in the doorway.

"We tried the front door, but no one answered."

"Couldn't hear you down here. And Meghan's with a client, so even if she did hear you, she wouldn't have interrupted a session to answer the door. Who's 'we'?"

He entered. "Meghan? That must be your housemate, the one Ambrose told me about. What kind of work does she do on a Sunday?"

"She's a massage therapist, and she works whenever her clients are available," I said. "Are you here about the fire?"

"I mentioned last night I might need to ask you a few questions. I'd like to do that now, if you don't mind."

"Let's go sit outside at the picnic table." I gestured toward the cedar plank table in the backyard. "Want something to drink?"

"Nah, I'm good," he replied. If he'd talked to Ambrose, he probably feared I'd spike his coffee with sodium hydroxide.

I closed the door behind me, shutting the very curious Kyla inside, and followed him out.

"Hey, what the heck…?" I strode over to where I'd parked my truck on the grass verge between our yard and the alley.

Ambrose stopped poking at something in the bed of the truck and craned his head to peer through the passenger side window.

"What do you think you're doing?"

"Just taking a look."

My paranoia skyrocketed. What did he expect to find? A book of matches from the Pyro Club? A copy of *Arson for Dummies* on the front seat?

"I see you've been talking with Chief Blakely."

He straightened. "Hanover's place burning down right before I get in there to look around again? You bet I have."

And I'd known he planned to go in Walter's house again. Great.

I started back to where Blakely sat at the picnic table. To my relief, Ambrose followed me.

Sun broke through a jagged hole in the clouds, and sudden warmth struck my face. Blakely perched at one end of the table. He wore a uniform, but Ambrose wore slacks with a sports coat again, this time with an olive green shirt and a copper bolo tie in the shape of a steer's head. I sneaked a look at his feet as I sat down opposite him. Uh huh—cowboy boots.

"We need to know how you left the Hanover place." Ambrose asked the question before he'd even managed to slide his frame onto one of the picnic benches.

"You mean when Meghan and I were boxing things up?"

A curt nod.

"Well, everything was still pretty much a mess. We'd packed maybe ten boxes for the Salvation Army to pick up when Debby and Jacob came in. Debby wanted to help, so we decided to leave things until after the funeral."

Blakely leaned forward. "Can you remember where they were? How things were arranged?"

I closed my eyes, trying to remember. "There were two or three boxes in front of the sofa, which sat under the front window. They contained various junk from the shelves. I was sorting through pictures and trying to find anything Tootie—Walter's mother—might want. Meghan had spent some time in his bedroom, sorting through clothes, and the rest of the boxes were in there."

I opened my eyes. Blakely was taking notes. He looked up.

"Any piles of stuff in the living room?" he asked.

"No. Not really."

The two men exchanged a look.

"No piles of old newspapers, magazines, that sort of thing?"

"There were some papers. Lots and lots of magazines," I said. And three boxes worth of miscellaneous paperwork I should probably mention about now.

"Where were the magazines placed?" Blakely asked.

"Placed? Well, most of them were on the shelves and some on the coffee table, another pile on an end table. We were going to see if the library wanted them for one of their book sales."

"Not all of them in one big pile in the middle of the living-room floor, then."

"Huh uh. Is that what started the fire?"

Blakely nodded. "It looks like it. We'll test for accelerants to make sure, but my guess is someone piled the magazines all together, poured gasoline on them, and tossed a match on it."

"Not that there's any evidence of a break-in left," Ambrose said.

"They didn't have to break in," I said. "They had the key, remember?" And then I remembered: I had forgotten to tell Ambrose about the missing key. I explained about it now.

"If it was the same person you say you heard in Hanover's house," Ambrose said.

"'Say I heard?'" I repeated.

He held out his palms. "All right. The person you heard in Hanover's house."

"Thank you. But you think the arsonist was someone different?"

Ambrose shrugged. "Can't jump to conclusions."

I stood up. "If that's all, then, I have to get back to work."

Blakely said, "Yeah, we're done."

Ambrose studied me like a particularly thorny algebra problem, then abruptly rose and followed Chief Blakely around to where they'd parked on the street in front of the house.

———

Kyla went back to labeling the lip balms, and I finished taking inventory. Or tried to. Halfway through counting something, I'd find myself speculating about what nasty surprises might be in store for me in the near future if someone was really trying to frame me. I wracked my brain for anyone who might hate me that much. It didn't take long to decide the idea bordered on ridiculous. I just wasn't that important in the scheme of things.

Enough with the persecution complex.

After a while, I gave up and went to find Meghan. I found her at the kitchen table, paying bills. She didn't look pleased.

"What's wrong?"

She just shook her head.

"Where's Erin?"

"She went over to Zoe's to play."

I slathered peanut butter on a piece of bread for my lunch and poured a glass of milk.

"Can I help?"

"Not unless you can make that asshole pay his child support on time."

I sat down and munched, watching her. "It's never going to happen, Meghan."

She sighed. "I know. Getting mad doesn't change anything. I could just kill him for dumping Erin off like that yesterday, though. How could I have been so stupid?"

It took me a moment to figure out what she was talking about. "You mean marrying him?"

She groaned. "Of course that's what I mean."

I cocked my head. "Why *did* you marry him?"

"Oh, I don't know. I mean, I thought I loved him, of course. Maybe I really did. At least I'd have the love-is-blind excuse." She leaned back in the chair. "But he had that thing, you know. That boy thing. It's horribly appealing."

"Tell me you're not talking about what I think you're talking about."

"What? No! He had a kind of little boy…vulnerability, I guess. You know what I mean."

Actually, I had no idea what she meant. Richard seemed anything but vulnerable. "Well, at least you got Erin."

"I know. I guess she's yang and he's yin. I can't have one without the other."

"Well, it does work. He's an asshole and she's an angel."

She laughed. "Yeah. At least I get the angel most of the time. I'd really hate it if it was the other way around."

I grinned and nodded, unable to speak. I'd eaten my peanut butter too fast and had to drink most of the milk to unglue my mouth.

"How much do I owe you?" I asked once I could talk again.

She told me, and I got out my checkbook and started writing. I tore out the check and handed it to her. "When do you want to go over to the funeral home?" I asked.

Meghan stuck a stamp on an envelope and gathered the rest of the paperwork into a pile in the middle of the table.

"How about now? I'd like to get it over with."

I agreed.

SIXTEEN

Down the hall from the funeral director's office, organ music echoed in the chapel. Mr. Crane, dressed in a tasteful dark suit, leaned over his desk and informed us in quiet tones that Walter's body definitely wouldn't be released from the morgue in time for the memorial service. However, they would let us know when they had access to the body in case anyone wanted to be present for the cremation. Crane himself offered to perform the honors at the service; he was an ordained minister and officiated over many of the nondenominational funerals. Sounded good to us. We chose a couple hymns and tidied up a few other details.

When we rose to leave, the director asked us whom he should bill. Meghan and I looked at each other.

"Send it to me," I said.

He nodded and made a notation, and we left.

On the short drive home, Meghan asked, "Do you really want to pay for Walter's funeral? There must be some other way."

"Maybe I'll get reimbursed. I imagine Walter had enough left to pay for a simple service and cremation. And what was I going to do, tell Mr. Crane to send the bill to Tootie? Or Debby?"

She was silent. Then, "If he left everything to Debby you might find yourself out of luck on the money."

"It'll be fine. I can juggle some things around and cover it if I have to." And maybe I'd find a will, a safe deposit receipt, a reference to a lawyer, *something* in the two remaining file boxes to tell us Walter's financial wishes.

"I'll help. If you get stuck with the bill."

"You don't have to," I said.

"I know."

We were almost back home when I thought of dropping by Caladia Acres for a few moments to check in on Tootie. She could meet Meghan, and we could fill her in about the fire. Meghan turned her Volvo around, and we headed toward the north edge of town.

"Didn't the police tell her about the fire?" she asked.

"Detective Ambrose didn't mention it. After all, the house didn't belong to her—or to Walter."

"Are you sure you want to be the one to tell her?"

"You want her to read about it in the paper?"

"No. You're right. I have to say, after all you've told me I'm looking forward to meeting this lady."

We parked and went in. The dahlias on the reception counter were the same ones from Friday and beginning to look a little tired. No one was behind the desk, so I led Meghan down the hallway to Tootie's room.

The door was open a crack. I knocked. A quiet response from inside bid us to enter, so I pushed the door open. Tootie Hanover sat in a wheelchair in the center of the room. Daylight streamed through the windows, illuminating the colorful carpet, the rumpled bedclothes, and Tootie's vibrant-green silk dressing gown. Her white braid hung down over one shoulder and curled in her lap. The disarray of the room and dishabille of the woman surprised me, but her drooping posture and tired eyes shocked me. She waved us toward the two wingback chairs. Meghan sent me a questioning look as we settled into them.

"Tootie, this is my friend and housemate, Meghan Bly. She's been helping with the funeral arrangements and with packing up Walter's things. In fact, she knew Walter longer than I did."

Walter's mother nodded to Meghan. "It's so nice to meet you, dear. I want to thank you for all your help." Her voice, so resonant the day I'd met her, emerged today as a dry murmur.

"It's lovely to meet you, as well, Mrs. Hanover. And I've been very happy to help in any way I can during this difficult time."

We sat for a few moments, Tootie with apparent indifference, Meghan trying to reconcile my description of Walter's mother with the woman she saw before her, and me, completely at sea.

After about a hundred years, I said, "We came to tell you about the memorial service—the last details that we worked out with Crane's."

"All right, dear," she said.

Meghan jumped in then, sparing us all my awkward stabs at conversation, and filled in the particulars. When she'd finished, I asked if Tootie had heard about the fire at Walter's. She hadn't, but she barely blinked when we told her.

"We'd already removed some mementos for you to go through, as well as his files. The fire was unfortunate, but nothing was lost that we wouldn't have been boxing up for the Salvation Army anyway, and I'm sure the owner was insured," I said.

"Well. I'm glad of that." She nodded to herself. "Yes. Good."

I said, "The police may want to look through the papers."

"All right."

"Tootie? Didn't Detective Ambrose come to see you yesterday?"

She sighed again. "He came. He had so many questions."

But apparently he hadn't told her he thought her son had been murdered. Well, for once I'd keep my mouth shut.

Meghan leaned forward. "Mrs. Hanover, are you going to be all right? Is there anything we can do for you?"

Tootie shook her head a fraction. "No, dear. I'm fine."

I stood, at a loss. "I suppose we'll see you at the service tomorrow, then."

"Yes." She gazed at the silver tea set on the side table, her voice rustling just above a whisper.

Meghan stood. "It was nice to meet you, Mrs. Hanover. Please take care of yourself."

Tootie nodded without attempting a smile and raised her hand in farewell. I hurried Meghan to the front desk, where Ann, the nurse from my first visit, now sat.

"Hi! Are you here to see Tootie again? I'm sorry, I don't remember your name."

"Sophie Mae Reynolds. We've already been to see Tootie. What's wrong with her? Is she drugged?"

"Um, no. She's not drugged. But she has changed, hasn't she? Listen, can I talk to you a minute?" I didn't like the expression on her face.

"Of course."

Ann led us to a sofa against one lobby wall and sat down. Meghan and I sat on either side of her. She lowered her voice, so that we both had to lean in to hear her.

"Tootie isn't doing so well."

"We noticed," I said.

"In the last few days, she's gone downhill. Physically, I mean. But I think it's more than that. She's giving up."

I shook my head. "I don't know her that well, but she immediately struck me as a woman who was very…determined."

"And she was. She overcame a great deal of her pain through sheer willpower for years. And never with a word of complaint or bitterness. But her son's death, well, it appears to have sapped her vitality, drained away whatever it was that made it possible for her to meet each day with such resolution."

"Is it that bad?" I asked in alarm. "You make it sound like she's at death's door."

Ann stood up. "No, no, nothing like that. At least not yet." At my look of distress she said, "She may recover. They sometimes do. But I've seen grief wear away at others until they just don't care anymore. And not caring is a giant step toward dying."

"I…I don't know what to say."

"I'm only telling you because she doesn't get very many visitors, and she seems to like you. I thought you'd want to know."

"Of course." A part of me didn't want to know, though. Because with knowledge came a kind of responsibility, a feeling I should step in and try to stop Tootie's downward spiral. But what could I do? I stood staring after Ann until Meghan took my arm and steered me toward the door.

———

Back at the house we started dinner. Meghan arranged garlic and chives, lemon slices, and cracked pepper on a salmon fillet, which she then wrapped into a foil packet and placed in the oven. I snipped sun-dried tomatoes into jasmine rice, added some vegetable stock, and put the pan on the burner. Meghan dumped a package of frozen peas into a colander in the sink and defrosted them under cold water, while I lined the olive and toasted sesame oils, a jar of crushed ginger, and salt on the counter for her. She juiced a lemon and began mixing the cold pea salad, while I sliced green onions and dug the pine nuts out of the freezer to add to the rice when it was done cooking. Erin came in halfway through our preparations and chattered about her afternoon. I was glad to see her so cheerful.

After eating, Erin and I cleaned up.

"Monopoly?" Meghan called from the living room. Her voice sounded muffled. I peered around the corner and saw why: her head was buried in the trunk where we kept games and puzzles, and all I could see was her behind sticking in the air.

"And Clue," Erin said from beside me.

We gathered the games and spent most of the evening playing them at the kitchen table. When Erin went to bed, Meghan began to make her daughter's lunch, and I went upstairs to continue going through Walter's papers.

Two hours later, I'd discovered Walter took blood pressure medication, had gone to the Evergreen State Fair in August, had no credit card records, paid his utility bills on time, and seemed to use a prepaid calling card for any long distance phone calls he made. But, other than those gems of information, I didn't find anything worth a darn.

SEVENTEEN

I spent Monday morning swirling together white and blue peppermint soap and white and red cinnamon soap, leaving them to harden in the molds while I ran upstairs to don my funeral clothes. Erin had insisted she wanted to come, so Meghan had taken her out of school for the afternoon. We left a little early, in case the funeral director needed to talk to us about anything before the service began.

The chapel wasn't crowded when we arrived. Two women whom we'd seen at the funeral home the day before sat in pews halfway back. I wondered if they were seat fillers for what could be a poorly attended memorial. The tempo of the invisible organ music slowed our steps up the central aisle, and the three of us slid into the second pew. Then Tootie Hanover came through the door. Ann pushed her wheelchair to the front and helped her get settled.

Tootie turned and nodded to us. She looked better today, wearing a simple navy dress and low-heeled pumps, her hair coiled atop her head again, powder and rouge on her cheeks. Her dull expression still alarmed me. But when Meghan introduced Erin, warmth sparked in Tootie's eyes. Perhaps I expected too much from a grieving mother.

Rustles and shuffles at the rear of the chapel made us turn our heads. The pews began filling up. On the other side of the aisle, a dozen people in garb from suits to jeans clustered together, the good-looking owner of the Gold Leaf Tavern and the spike-haired woman from Beans R Us among them.

The seats behind us were filling as well. I recognized many of our neighbors and a few people I'd seen here and there around town. Walter had worked for them all on one project or another. Building a fence or a patio. Cleaning up after a windstorm. Installing a sprinkler system. Helping with a renovation or caring for the yard when someone was on vacation. Walter had been one of a dying breed, the all-around Jack of all Trades.

Behind them, Detective Ambrose slipped into a corner seat.

Just as the director/minister began adjusting the microphone sprouting out of the podium, Debby and Jacob hurried in. She wore a long black dress that tucked in the right places and flowed in the right places to accent her figure, but the black fabric combined with the heavy eye makeup, the black hair, and her ghost-white skin made her look like an over-the-hill goth. Jacob wore a black suit with a white shirt and a bow tie. He looked like he wanted to scratch.

The service itself was generic and short. Mr. Crane didn't know much about Walter, so his comments were by necessity impersonal. When he asked if anyone wanted to get up and talk about Walter. I looked at Debby, but she shrank back.

One of the two women I'd thought were pew fillers got up and sang the hymns. Her voice, pure and sweet, brought unexpected tears to my eyes. Both Erin and Meghan cried, too.

After *Amazing Grace* we shuffled outside, blinking like moles in the brighter light. Above, clouds scudded across bits of blue, in thrall to the whim of the wind. I didn't see Ambrose; he'd slipped out as unobtrusively as he'd come in.

"I wonder if Debby and Jacob know about the fire," I said, searching the small crowd milling on the lawn in front of the funeral home.

"Down there," Meghan said, pointing down the street. The two figures in black were already a block away, leaning together and not looking back.

"Well, I'm not chasing after them," I said, not sure what to make of their hasty departure.

Ann assisted Tootie into an old mint-green Buick in the parking lot and walked around to the driver's side. We went over to say good-bye, but Walter's mother was obviously exhausted so we cut the conversation short.

As we approached Meghan's Volvo, which was parked on the street, Erin tugged on her mother's sleeve. "Hey, look. There's Dad."

Richard drove slowly past, gesturing as he spoke to the woman beside him in the white Camry. She wore a green coat over a black turtleneck and looked to be much older than Dick, despite the unnatural red of her hair. They appeared to be arguing.

"Was he at the funeral?" I asked.

Meghan said, "I doubt it. Richard hates funerals. He was probably over at the hardware store." She gestured down the block. His car turned and accelerated away.

"Who's that woman with Dad? It wasn't Donnette," Erin said.

Meghan frowned. "I don't know. I feel like I should know her, but I can't place her. Probably someone he works with." Then she grimaced, and we exchanged glances, remembering Richard had quit his job again.

We arrived home about four. Erin trudged up the walk behind us. Poor kid. She'd been through a lot the last week. Meghan started to push her key into the lock, but the door swung open at her touch.

She turned to me. "I must not have pulled it shut all the way."

In my mind I saw Walter's open back door. Thought of Walter's intruder. Following Meghan inside, I tried the knob as I closed the door behind me. Locked. An itch skittered across my shoulders. Meghan and Erin went upstairs.

I wandered through the house, opening doors and glancing behind furniture. My inspection was deliberately casual—I didn't even want to admit to myself what I was doing.

And I found nothing.

Upstairs I changed into jeans and a sweater, and was groping through my drawer looking for a pair of matching socks when I spotted something on my dresser that made my heart stutter. More precisely, I *didn't* spot something.

"Meghan!" I yelled.

I heard her footsteps in the hall while I stared at the empty space where my jewelry box usually sat.

"What?"

She leaned against the doorframe and raised one foot to slide on her loafer. I moved so she could see and pointed to the dresser top. She blinked twice, then whirled and ran back to her room. I followed. She let out a whoosh of air at the sight of her own jewelry box. She hurried over and lifted the lid.

I felt sick. Insurance should cover the few valuable pieces from my grandmother. And then there were the bits of silver jewelry picked up over the years, mementos of places I'd been and moments I'd wanted to remember. I'd miss them. But I would have dumped it all in Puget Sound myself if I could have kept my engagement and wedding rings. Not that I wore them anymore—though at the moment I fervently regretted that—but I knew they were there. And right next to them, Mike's platinum wedding band. For a year after he died, I slid the circle of smooth metal onto my thumb each night before I turned out my bedside lamp, slept with my hand curled to my chest until morning. Even recently I'd sometimes taken it out, held it in my palm like a talisman.

"My mother's ring is missing. So's the engagement ring Richard gave me." Meghan looked grim.

We went through the rest of the house. Erin helped. We couldn't find anything else missing, though Erin said some items in her room had been moved.

"I don't know how you can tell, Bug. You haven't cleaned your room for over a week," Meghan said.

"I can tell," Erin said, and crossed her arms.

We called the police. An officer we'd never seen, thank heaven for small favors, came within thirty minutes to take our statements.

"We'll do our best to find the thief," Officer Danson said. She reminded me of a young Kathy Bates.

"But it's not very likely you'll recover our jewelry, is it?" My voice came out a depressed monotone.

She grimaced. "Jewelry is pretty easy for a thief to get rid of. I wish I could be more encouraging."

"We understand," Meghan assured her. And we did understand why it would be hard to catch them. What I didn't understand was why someone did it in the first place. They'd taken more than just stones and metal; those rings were my only connection to a person—and a time—now lost. I blinked back tears, took a deep breath.

"Why did they only take the jewelry?" I asked. "Why not the television, or the stereo? Meghan has a laptop in her office, and I have a computer downstairs as well. Why'd they leave those behind?"

The policewoman said, "Time. A quick in and out before they could get caught."

"Well, they got lucky. We both work at home, and it's pretty rare that someone isn't here during the day."

She looked thoughtful. "That's interesting. It sounds like someone knew you'd be gone. Any idea who knew you'd all be at a funeral?"

"Anyone who knew about Walter—the man who died. Which turned out to be a lot more people than we thought," I said, thinking of the full chapel.

"So someone burglarized the house when you were all gone—and you just happened to leave the door unlatched at the same time?"

"They must have broken in," I said, "then didn't pull the door all the way closed when they left."

"The lock doesn't look forced," Officer Danson said.

"So they picked it," I said.

Meghan's eyes narrowed at the woman. "Are you implying something?"

The officer shook her head, expression still pleasant. "Just getting the facts straight."

It took me a few seconds. "You think we arranged this? For insurance or something?" I was incredulous. "I can't believe you people. You're supposed to protect and serve, right? I used to think we needed more police. Voted for more funds, believed the rhetoric. But if all you do is hassle the victims, we'd be a helluva lot better off with fewer of you! What a useless…"

"Sophie Mae," Megan said.

"…bunch of ineffective—"

"Sophie Mae!"

The policewoman's jaw set. Brodie, leaning against Meghan's leg, whined low in his throat.

Meghan continued in a gentle voice. "Just because they don't always recover stolen jewelry doesn't mean they won't find ours. You still might get your rings back. Mike's ring back."

I started to cry.

The officer mumbled something placating, reminded us to be careful about making sure the door was closed and locked, and told us she'd let us know if and when they found anything out. She looked back at me once from the open doorway, then made her getaway, while I stood in the middle of the living room sniffling like a fool.

EIGHTEEN

MEGHAN SAID SHE'D MAKE grilled cheese sandwiches and tomato soup for dinner since we could all do with a little comfort food. Upstairs, I splashed cold water on my face, feeling drained and so tired I was sick to my stomach. The empty space on my dresser seemed to throb like an ache. Trying to ignore it, I went back downstairs.

At the bottom of the stairs, the image of Erin's duffle bag came to mind. Another thought followed it, and another. I went out the front door and around the side of the house. Picking my way in the dark, I groped for the rock in the garden where we kept the spare key. Lifting what I hoped was the right one, I patted the damp ground beneath. My fingertips registered the coldness of metal, and I was about to dig into the mud when a light flared on over my head. I looked up, squinting.

"Erin?"

Wordlessly she shone the narrow beam onto the patch of ground. The house key glinted back at us. I put the rock back and stood up.

"I thought maybe we had latched the door when we left, and someone found this and used it to come in," I said. "Guess I was wrong."

Erin's eyes looked black in the half-light from the flashlight. "Unless they put it back," she said. She squatted and picked up the rock, training the light on the glittering key. Standing again, her shoulders sagged. "And that's what he did."

I noted the male pronoun. She was thinking the same thing I was.

Making my voice light, I said, "But we can't really know, because the key's there. If it were missing, that'd be another thing. But since it's there, it may never have been moved. Your mom probably didn't pull the door all the way shut."

Erin sighed. "Nice try, Sophie Mae. But it has been moved. I know, 'cause when I put it back on Saturday, I pointed it away from the house."

"How could you possibly remember that?"

"Because I pointed the end to where the small end of the rock goes. I always do. I don't know why." She sounded defensive.

Stooping again, I saw what she meant. The rock in question narrowed at one end. It had settled into a distinct depression in the ground, a teardrop-shaped hole for a teardrop-shaped stone. I angled the light to the side and squinted. I could make out another imprint in the wet soil under the key; an imprint that matched the way Erin said she'd replaced it when Dick dropped her off early on Saturday.

The key felt gritty and cold when I picked it up and put it in my pocket. As we walked back to the front door, Erin said, "It was Dad, wasn't it?"

I didn't know what to say, so I didn't say anything.

Inside, Meghan stood ladling the soup into bowls. A stack of sandwiches sat on the table, cheddar oozing from between slices of golden bread. The smell of warm bread and cheese, the click of the ladle against the bowl, the rustle of Meghan's apron, all combined to say "home."

"Where have you two been? I thought I'd have to..." Meghan trailed off when she saw our faces.

"What's wrong?" Her expression said "what now?"

"Sophie Mae and I think Dad came in and stole your jewelry," said Erin. Her voice was serious and matter of fact, but when she finished that bald statement her elfin features crumpled. Meghan shot a look at me.

"It's okay, Bug," Meghan said to her daughter. "I'm sure Sophie Mae's wrong this time." Her tone barely contained her anger.

Erin shook her head. "No, she's not. I put the key back the one way and he saw me and now it's different, and all your nice stuff's gone and I'm sorry, Mom." She choked out the last words. "I'm really sorry."

"Oh, Erin!" Meghan hugged her, then walked her out of the room, murmuring. She didn't even spare me a glance.

I slumped onto a chair and watched the cheese stop oozing and start to congeal.

Disgusting.

Meghan returned to find me with my head lying on my crossed arms, eyes closed. The cold food had become too much to look at.

"Sorry," she said, leaning against the counter. "Erin told me she figured it out herself. Sometimes she's a little too smart for her own good. When I suggested she might be mistaken she was quite offended. But I told her the key being moved didn't prove anything. Anyone could have found the key."

"Maybe," I said, raising my head and sitting back in the chair. "But it was probably Richard. You know he's always looking for money. He either owes it to someone or thinks he's found a sure-fire bet. We have to tell the police."

Meghan showed an inordinate interest in the kitchen floor.

"We have to, Meghan. If he did this, we can't just let him get away with it."

Her eyes moved toward the stairs, and I knew she was thinking of Erin. "If he did it."

"Of course, if. But how can we know unless they question him?"

She pressed her lips together. "I don't want Erin to think her father is a thief."

"She already thinks he's a thief. Can it be that much worse if it turns out he really is?"

"But…"

"But nothing. If Dick stole my stuff I'm not letting it slide. I know you want to protect Erin. But she's not stupid, far from it. It might be better if she knew what her father is really made of."

Meghan rubbed her face with both hands. "God, I hate this." She looked over her fingers at me. "You really think he did this, don't you?"

"Well, I don't have a better candidate. He'd know we were at the funeral, and he knew where we kept the key. Which we don't keep there anymore, by the way," I said, taking the key out of my pocket and handing it to her. She dropped it in the front of the silverware drawer.

"I could have left the door unlatched," Meghan said.

"But the key *was* moved. I saw the old indentation where Erin put it."

"We saw Richard right after the funeral."

"But we didn't see him in the chapel. He could have been here during the service."

"What about Debby or Jacob, or both of them? They didn't like it when we were going through Walter's things the other day. Maybe they thought we took something." She paused. "Which we did."

I shook my head. "They were at the funeral, right where we could see them."

"They came in late."

"Okay. You're right. Who else?" I asked. I didn't point out that Jacob and Debby didn't know where we kept the spare key. But we hadn't hidden it in the most original spot, now that I thought about it, and it was possible that they, or someone else, could have found it.

"A stranger. Or someone who reads the obituaries and plans burglaries for when friends or family will be attending the funeral."

"They'd have to know we were friends."

"What about someone from the funeral home? I'd like to know if there've been any other break-ins when someone was at a funeral," Meghan said.

"I'm sure the police would track that kind of thing."

"Oh, fine. Now you think they're perfectly competent."

"Sure," I said, "except when they're accusing me of murder, arson, or stealing my own jewelry. Then I think they're damn incompetent. But seriously, in case you're right I'll be happy to ask about other funeral-related crimes when I tell them about Dick tomorrow."

Meghan sighed. "Okay. I can't stop you. But you won't be paying the price if you're wrong. I will. And so will Erin."

"I don't think I'm wrong," I said.

"You never do," she said, and got up to try and salvage some dinner for Erin to eat.

I headed upstairs. Might as well haul Walter's paperwork downstairs so I wouldn't forget to take it to the police station in the morning. Oh, by the way, Detective Ambrose, here's a bunch of Walter's stuff I forgot to mention. Now, would you mind running out and finding my wedding ring?

Opening the door to the spare room, I flipped on the light. A moment later I was back in the kitchen.

"I was wrong," I announced.

Meghan turned from where she was slicing an apple. "What?"

"I was wrong. It wasn't Richard. Someone else used the key. And the jewelry they took was just icing on the cake."

"The cake being?" She looked like she didn't really want to know the answer.

"Walter's papers. They're gone." It hadn't occurred to either of us to look in the junk room after discovering the burglary.

Her face cleared. "Richard wouldn't want those. Why would someone else take them, though? I thought you told me they were useless."

"But whoever took them couldn't know that. Maybe they thought there was something incriminating in those boxes."

"But you didn't find anything?"

I shook my head. "Huh uh. But there's something they don't want discovered. That has to be why they burned down his house."

She took a bite of apple and chewed it slowly, swallowed. "Ambrose won't be very happy about the papers being missing."

"I'm not going to tell him," I said. "If we hadn't brought them over here they would have gone up in flames. So it's a moot point."

"You know, I bet he'd disagree with that." She walked to the doorway with a plate of food for Erin, then turned. "How could anyone know we had the papers?"

I shook my head.

But I thought about it while I did the dishes. At least two people might have noticed the files had been removed. I'd already hauled the boxes over to the house before Debby and Jacob had shown up at Walter's that day. They'd both seemed upset, Debby especially, and with good reason as Walter's fiancée. But I couldn't quite get a handle on either of them. And I wanted to know more about the relationship between her and Jacob.

My head had begun to throb, but I made a cup of tea and went down to my workroom anyway. I'd thought of a couple things I could do to try and find the thief—and Walter's murderer if they were one and the same. I had to finish the soap for Kyla to wrap when she came after school because I wouldn't be around tomorrow afternoon.

I released the bars of glycerin soap from the PVC half-pipes I used for molds and was slicing them into generous slabs when I realized I'd have to check with Meghan to see if she'd be here when Kyla came. The spare key wasn't outside anymore. I'd told my helper where it was, and she'd actually used it once or twice.

Kyla wasn't behind the theft. I was sure of it. She wasn't that kind of kid, and besides, she wouldn't have any more reason to take three boxes of paperwork than Richard would. And I didn't think she'd have told anyone about the key. Or would she? I reminded myself to ask her tomorrow, just to make sure.

The soap looked good. Streaks of blue swirled in pure white in the peppermint, and I'd mixed a little copper metallic soap colorant in with the red that swirled in the cinnamon, so it glittered when turned in the light. If these proved popular with customers, maybe I could add green and white bayberry, or orange and white sandalwood.

I lined the fifty or so soaps on the clean counter to cure overnight, tossed the molds in the dishwasher, and set it going. Checking the lock on the back door, I found myself looking out the window at Walter's, half expecting to see the light burning in the window. Only the dark hulk of the charred remains greeted my eye.

It was almost ten o'clock. Trudging upstairs, I could hear mother and daughter talking in Erin's room, lower- and higher-pitched murmurs down the hall. Erin usually didn't stay up this late, not on a school night, and she'd probably be crabby in the morning. Light peeked out from under the closed door to the spare room; I'd left the light on in my haste to tell Meghan about the missing boxes.

I opened the door and went in, inspecting the floor between the rocker and the hobbyhorse. Nothing. Nada. Zip. Then I spied the box under the window. Either the thief hadn't noticed it, or hadn't deemed it worth carrying downstairs. I lifted it to an open space and began pulling out the contents.

In addition to ten or so framed pictures, I'd thrown in a ceramic bank shaped like a chicken, a locket that seemed to be rusted shut, an old Bible, a book on baseball collectibles, a field guide to Pacific Northwest birds, and three otter figurines formed of Mount St. Helen's ash. That was it. Sighing, I placed the items back into the box. I'd take them by Tootie's this week.

On impulse, I grabbed Walter's baby picture, flipping the light off on my way out. In my bedroom, I propped the photo in the gaping emptiness on my dresser. Serious eyes gazed back at me, strange in the infant's face.

"Sorry about all this, Walter," I said. "But I will figure out what happened. I promise."

NINETEEN

I SHUFFLED INTO THE kitchen Tuesday morning, still in my pajamas. Meghan and Erin greeted me with broad smiles on their faces. So much for the ill temper I'd expected from both of them; apparently I'd been the sole recipient of the morning grouchies. They kept sneaking glances at each other. Whatever was up, I could only hope it was something good.

Pouring a bowl of granola, I joined them at the table. Erin grinned around a mouthful of toast and peanut butter, and shoved the *Cadyville Eye* across the table to me.

"What's this?"

"Take a look," Meghan said, eyes wide and amused.

Unfolding the paper, I scanned the front page. For a moment I pitied that poor woman in the lurid black-and-white photo right under the headline. I'd already started to turn the page before I did the double take.

"Oh no," I groaned.

"How come you didn't tell us your picture was gonna be in the paper?" asked Erin, delighted at my expense.

"Because, smarty pants, I didn't know. And if I'd been asked, I'd have said 'no, thank you.'"

It had to be the second picture that damn photographer had taken the night of the fire. In it, I wore my white-and-blue-striped pajamas, the ones still waiting to be washed because they smelled like rotten smoke, and my fluffy blue bathrobe. The sprigs of light hair sticking out around my face stood in high relief against the dark, smoldering ruin behind me. My eyes, squinting against the light and smoke, were half shut and puffy, as if I'd been crying when that Valkyrie accosted me with her camera. It looked like I was reaching toward the lens in supplication, when in reality I'd been trying to shield my face from the glare of the flash. And let's not forget the crowning touch: the lovely smear of black charcoal across my cheek.

Maybe no one would recognize me.

Then I read the caption: "The blaze that burned a house to the ground Saturday night devastated neighbor Sophie Mae Reynolds." How had that blasted woman discovered my name? The story, as I expected, contained few details about the actual fire, though the reporter had connected it with Walter's death. The *Eye* called it suicide, so apparently that was still the official story from the Cadyville police department. But so much for anonymity.

"Why would they run this picture? I didn't even talk to the reporter. Oh, God. I look awful!"

"At least you weren't wearing those." Meghan pointed down at my yellow ducky slippers.

"It wouldn't have mattered," I said, irritated. "You can't see my feet." Like I'd wear my ducky slippers out in the mud like that. Sheesh!

Meghan tried to wipe the humor from her face and look sympathetic. "Pictures with people in them are more interesting than pictures without. And you do look rather, um, dramatic."

I glared. "That fire was plenty interesting—and dramatic—without any contribution from me."

Erin finished her breakfast and loaded up her backpack for school. Meghan put on her coat; she was taking Erin to school early, both to explain to the teacher why her daughter hadn't finished her advanced placement math homework the night before, and to give Erin a little extra time to work on it.

I flipped through the rest of the paper without really paying much attention to it. The *Eye* wasn't known for its stellar reporting, and since it was a weekly, all the stories were pretty much old news by the time it hit the streets.

But an article about the mayor caught my attention. I perused it, waving distractedly to Erin as she shouted good-bye from the hallway. When I was done, I put the paper down and sipped my coffee, considering.

Apparently, someone had been harassing the mayor. It sounded serious, except said harassment had taken the form of toilet paper streaming from the numerous maples towering in the front yard of his million-dollar home on the outskirts of town.

Could this really be the case Zahn wanted Detective Ambrose to work on instead of finding out what had happened to Walter? For heaven's sake, toilet papering trees was kid's stuff, not some terrorist activity. But it would explain the sheepish look on the detective's face when I'd asked what was more important than solving a possible murder. Yes, thinking back on it, he'd been downright embarrassed. Well, no wonder. God knew what would happen if they caught someone egging the mayor's car on Halloween.

I flipped the paper into the recycle bin and did my breakfast dishes. Then I took a shower and put on a pair of nice slacks and a crisp white shirt. Looking at myself in the full-length mirror in the hallway I thought about what jewelry would complete the look. Something understated, but classy. I stood in front of my dresser, looking at Walter's baby picture, before it hit me: I didn't have any jewelry, classy or otherwise. Just the pair of gold stud earrings I'd worn to the funeral yesterday and my watch. A wave of anger washed over me as I threaded the studs through my earlobes.

My goal was to appear professional, but approachable. First, I'd canvas the neighbors, find out if any of them had seen someone around—or in—our house yesterday afternoon during the funeral. Later, I'd head down to Beans R Us. We didn't know nearly enough about Debby and Jacob, and I needed their last names before I could find out more.

And maybe I'd stop at the Gold Leaf Tavern, say hello to the owner, the guy with the ponytail and the wonderful eyes. If I was thirsty. And had time…

Meghan had returned from dropping Erin off at school and had fifteen minutes before her first client showed up, so I told her my plan as she set out scented oils, lit candles, and plugged in the small fountain in the corner of the massage room. She frowned, but didn't try to talk me out of it.

"Be careful," was all she said.

I walked down the block until I had to crane my neck to see our front yard, and started knocking on doors. But at nine a.m., not many people were home. I didn't know the harried woman who answered my knock with a baby on one hip, a toddler clinging to her leg, and the television blaring behind her, but she couldn't help me. The retired couple who lived next to her came to the door together, radiating suspicion. Even after I'd explained about our burglary they thought I was trying to sell them something. Mr. Harpol, a widower who owned a Pembroke Welsh corgi like Brodie and sometimes stopped by for iced tea on summer evenings so the two dogs could socialize, had been at Walter's funeral, too. So had our friend Bette, a potter by trade, who answered her door in canvas pants and a ratty old sweater, both liberally splattered with clay slip. Both expressed horror at our break-in, and promised, after lengthy conversations, to be extra vigilant.

I made notes of the people who weren't home. As my list grew, discouragement infiltrated the determined optimism with which I'd begun the enterprise. But I'd started, and I hate to leave something half done, so I worked my way back up the other side of the street. Only four people answered their doors; two had been at Walter's funeral, one hadn't been home the day before, and the last, glaring at me out of red-rimmed eyes, told me he worked nights and had been asleep. More notes, and then I went around to the street behind us. Our house was hidden from the view of most of those homes, but I plodded from one to another anyway, hoping I'd at least find someone who saw a strange car in the alley that afternoon. No such luck.

Walter's landlady, Mrs. Gray, I saved for last. She was a talker and had been known to take offense if you rushed off after initiating a conversation. Mrs. Gray fit her name to a T. Iron-gray curls clung close to her scalp, her pewter-colored eyes sparkled under long lashes, and she opened her door wearing one of her assortment of gray tracksuits.

Inviting me inside, she brewed tea while I told her about the theft.

"That's terrible!" she said when I had finished my tale of woe.

I nodded while stirring honey into my Darjeeling. "So I'm going from door to door this morning to see if anyone saw anything that might help us catch them. Him. Whomever."

"Well, I'm afraid I was at the funeral the same time you were," Mrs. Gray said.

"I know. But we left pretty early, and of course we don't know exactly when they were in the house. You didn't notice anything right before you left, did you?"

She shook her head. "I can't think of anything." Then, "Well, I do remember one thing. I can't see that it would be of any help, though."

I leaned forward, excited. "Please let me be the judge, Mrs. Gray. You never know what might help."

"I was doing my hair, and I heard a car in the alley out back."

Bingo.

"What kind of car was it?"

"Oh, I don't know. I was in the bathroom. I just remember thinking it was odd to hear a car, with Walter gone and the fire and all."

Then why, I thought, *didn't you go look*? Aren't little old ladies supposed to be inveterate busybodies? What I really needed was a nosy old bird who kept binoculars on her windowsill and spent all her time watching the neighborhood goings on. You just can't find a good stereotype when you need one.

"Did it sound like Walter's truck, or like a smaller car?"

"Um, more like a smaller car. I would have remembered if it had sounded like Walter's truck."

I took a sip of tea, thinking. "Did it keep going or stop in the alley?"

"I don't know. I'm sorry. I meant to look out the back window, but I got distracted."

"That's okay. Do you remember hearing any doors shutting? Like someone was getting out of the car?"

She frowned, squeezing the wrinkles in her forehead together. "I think I did."

"One? Two?" I knew I was leading the witness, so to speak, but couldn't help myself.

"Um, one. No, two. Well, one for sure."

Okay, now I had just forced this very nice lady who wanted to be helpful to remember something that probably hadn't happened at all. I dropped it.

But I'd drunk only half of my tea, and I wouldn't be allowed to leave until I finished it. Not that I wanted to. It was so pleasant and homey in her kitchen that the accumulation of the last few days sloughed away. And my feet hurt.

Settling my posterior more firmly in the old-fashioned, red vinyl kitchen chair, I asked, "How long did Walter rent that little house from you?"

"Oh gosh—I guess I rented to Walter for almost twenty years. But that little cottage? About six or seven years, I'd say. He moved in there shortly after the Blys bought that house where you live. He lived in a duplex I used to own over on Cedar, but he loved that little cottage, and when the other tenant moved out he asked if he could move in." She blinked back tears.

"That fire was just awful. I'm sorry you lost the cottage," I said. She nodded.

"Were you insured?"

"Oh, yes. Though I don't know whether I'll rebuild it or not."

"And twenty years is a long time to have a tenant. You've had a terrible week, haven't you?"

She sighed. "Yes. Thank you for not offering platitudes. Because this week has well and truly sucked."

Surprised, I laughed. She smiled, and those gray eyes brightened.

"You must have known Walter pretty well," I said.

"I knew the whole family."

"Really? I didn't get that impression from the way you talked with Tootie the other day, when you were getting her permission to let us in Walter's house."

"Tootie. Yes, well. I don't think she remembers me. Actually, that's not true. I'm sure she remembers me, but she remembers Mavis Smart, not the Mrs. Gray you introduced on the phone."

"Mavis Smart? Your maiden name, I take it."

"Yes. Mr. Gray's been gone for many years now."

"Why didn't you tell her who you were?"

Mrs. Gray was quiet for a minute, looking out the window at the brilliant autumn red of the burning bush in her side yard. "Let's just say her memories of me aren't the best. I don't see any reason to remind her of that time."

What on earth? But it was clear from the look she gave me that Mrs. Gray would not divulge more than she already had. I stifled my raging curiosity, took another sip of tea, and asked what she could tell me about Walter's childhood.

"He grew up like any normal kid," she said. "He had two brothers, and the three of them were close enough in age to spend a lot of time together. They'd roam around the edges of town—it was considerably smaller then—fishing and playing and getting into the usual sort of trouble boys get into. Nothing too bad, just boys being boys. Walter had a tendency to collect creatures. Frogs, snakes, the occasional wounded bird. I don't think his parents—his mother, really—would allow him to keep a pet, but he always had some animal or another out in the shed where they kept the tools. He was a nice little boy. I liked him."

"Tootie mentioned something about him having a lot of grief in his life. It was a bad time, and I didn't want to ask her about it. Do you know what she was referring to?"

Mrs. Gray nodded. "That was later. It started when he was a senior in high school. He took up with a girl from around here. I don't remember her name. Shelly? Sherrie? No—Cherry. Because of that hair of hers. Anyway, they were inseparable that year and the summer after they graduated. He asked her to marry him, and she said yes. But they both knew it would be a long engagement, since he was going to college in Seattle—he wanted to be a biologist—and wouldn't be able to support a wife until he'd finished."

"Walter went to college?"

"For a while. He ended up dropping out."

"Why?"

She gave me a look. I was interrupting her story.

"Sorry. Please, go on."

"Well, he went to classes, and she stayed home, living with her parents. Took a job working the counter at Cece's Variety." The store was still there on First Street, a retro hodgepodge of drugstore dry goods, children's clothes, and gifts.

Mrs. Gray continued. "It wasn't like now, when people think nothing of commuting from here to Seattle every day. The freeway hadn't even been built this far north, and there were only what we think of now as the back roads to travel back and forth on. So Walter lived on campus at the University of Washington during the week and came home on the weekends to see his family and his girl.

"After a couple of years she got pregnant. Walter dropped out of school and moved back to town. They got married, and he took a job working at the lumber mill. The baby was born healthy and happy, and while things weren't exactly the way he'd planned them, they were getting by okay."

Walter had a wife? And a child? And Tootie had left them out of his obituary. I had a bad feeling about what was coming next.

"They died," I said.

She shook her head. "No, they didn't die."

TWENTY

"Then where are they?"

"No one knows," she said. "Let me finish telling you what happened."

I nodded and shut my mouth.

"Like I said before, Cadyville was smaller then. Made it even harder to keep secrets. It came out that while Walter had been going to the university during the week, his girl was seen going around with someone else. He found out shortly after they were married. And naturally everyone wondered if the child was really his. I don't know what happened behind closed doors, but in public he never let on anything was wrong, and he was the best daddy to that little boy. He really loved Cherry. She swore to everyone she carried his child, that she hadn't cheated on him at all. And she explained who she'd been seen with. Of course, everyone else in town already knew."

Mrs. Gray paused and took a sip of tea.

"Who?" I prompted.

"Willy Hanover. Walter's older brother."

"But it was all innocent?"

"That's what Cherry told him. But when Walter asked his brother about it, Willy told him different. He said it had been far from innocent."

"Why would he do that? It just seems cruel."

"Willy meant it to be. He wanted Cherry, and she'd married Walter anyway."

"Because Walter was her true love."

"You're a romantic, my dear. No, because Walter had higher aspirations than his brother. Willy didn't go to college—started working at the mill right out of high school."

"But Walter worked at the mill."

"That was the irony. I don't know if Cherry loved either one of them. She wanted to have a better life than the one she grew up with. Her mama died when she was about ten, and her daddy started drinking, couldn't keep a job. He wasn't abusive, at least as far as anyone knew, but Cherry had to grow up in a big hurry. Maybe it was being so poor that made her harsh. Made her desperate. Maybe it was not having a mother. Anyway, she had big plans. Walter was going to be an important scientist, and they'd be able to move away, if only to Seattle. She wanted to leave Cadyville, and she wanted her husband to make money. And that meant Willy wasn't husband material."

"But Walter was. So who did the baby belong to?"

"No one knows for sure. Cherry said it was his, and Walter chose to believe her. He loved that little boy like life itself, and settled down to raise him here."

"I bet Cherry loved that."

"Indeed she didn't. As a teenager she'd had a bit of a sharp edge to her, but with a husband and baby to look after and no hopes for the kind of life she'd intended, she got to be downright mean. She made Walter's life miserable, berating him in public, scolding him about what she perceived as his failures, until he eventually came to believe her. After a while, she started throwing hints about her relationship with his brother in his face. He was a gentle man, and she completely emasculated him, stripped every shred of pride from him. Everyone in town knew she was a shrew, and they pitied Walter."

"Pity's a hard thing to take," I said.

"It was a humiliation piled on top of everything else."

"What about his son?"

"Whenever Walter wasn't working, he'd carry that little boy everywhere, in his arms, and then later on his shoulders. But Cherry ruined that, too. As the boy grew older and could understand, she tried to turn him against Walter with her venomous complaints."

"And it worked? Oh, poor Walter!"

"It would have worked, if things had continued like that. But Cherry reached the end of her rope. She just up and left one day. Took the boy with her. He was only four."

"She left? Did she go with Willy?"

"Not with Willy. I don't know if anyone knows where she went or with whom. But it would have been with someone, because she'd never done anything on her own. She knew how to use other people, though. She'd found some other sucker she thought could give her more."

"What about her father?"

"She never contacted him that I know of. He moved in with her younger sister in Yakima for a while. I heard he died about ten years ago."

"And Walter?"

"She left him a ruined soul. It was the loss of that little boy that really did it. Walter just kept working at the mill. Didn't talk to people much. Cut off most contact with his family, didn't have many friends. And he started drinking, just like her daddy had. After a while it got out of hand, and he lost his job."

I hadn't expected Walter's tale of woe to be so much about family. He'd always seemed so independent. Well, no wonder he'd become such a loner. ·

"He rented from you twenty years ago?" I asked.

She nodded. "Just before he lost his job. But he always managed to pay the rent. And I tried to keep it low. I was afraid Walter was the type that could have ended up down in Seattle, sleeping in a doorway in Pioneer Square. He'd just stopped caring. I think it was the work he did for folks around here that kept him going."

Mrs. Gray paused to drink some tea. "And then six, seven years ago he just up and quit drinking. Probably saved his life." An uncomfortable silence followed her last statement.

I broke it. "Did you know he was engaged?"

Mrs. Gray's eyes widened. "Really?"

"To a woman named Debby. You might have seen her around, along with a little wiry guy."

She wrinkled her forehead in thought. "I've seen a man and a woman at Walter's a couple of times. Is she, um, a little rough around the edges?"

I nodded, seeing how she'd strike Mrs. Gray that way.

"And Walter was engaged to her?"

"According to her. She's got a big ol' ring."

Mrs. Gray set her teacup down and leaned back in her chair. "Well, I'm both glad and saddened to hear that."

I knew what she meant. Nice things had started happening to Walter after years of difficulty, and he ended up dying. It felt horribly unfair.

Looking at my watch, I excused myself, thanking Mrs. Gray for the tea and the story. A red pickup with Cadyville Fire Dept. on the door was parked in the alley, and, knee deep in the blackened leavings of Walter's house, a man in navy coveralls cut out a piece of stained blue carpet pad and placed it in an aluminum can like the type paint comes in. I paused for a moment, but my stomach growled, urging me home.

TWENTY-ONE

BACK IN OUR KITCHEN, I grated cheese over leftover rice pilaf and popped it in the microwave. Walter's story kindled mixed emotions. First came pity, but I pushed that aside. He'd received enough of that in his life; he didn't need yet more of it from me now that he was dead. But I couldn't help feeling sorrow for a life wasted, for a gentle soul abused by greed and just plain nastiness. Anger at the selfishness and cruelty of his young wife. Anger, too, at Walter for being such a victim. His mother must have been frustrated by Walter's complete acquiescence to Cherry's early abandonment, his inability to get over it and get on with it.

After lunch I threw a load of laundry in the washer, then went down to my storeroom and turned on my computer. I found several soap orders from my website. Investing in the site had been a good business decision, and Erin had helped me put it together. Until now, filling my Internet orders once a week had been adequate, but now early Christmas shoppers had started checking items off their lists, and twice the usual number of orders awaited my attention. I'd have to check every day if I was going to be able to keep up with holiday orders. With so much to ship, I'd show Kyla how to pack up boxes and see about hiring some holiday help for the crazy time coming in December. In the meantime, I set to work processing credit cards and whipping out invoices and packing lists.

As I typed and printed, I fantasized about hiring an accountant. But even when I could afford one, I'd still have to do the order fulfillment paperwork, and today it seemed to take forever to process the orders from the site. Once I had the packing lists, I dropped each into an appropriately sized box and lined them on the counter by the storeroom, ran upstairs to switch laundry from washer to dryer and put another load in the washer, and hurried back downstairs to deal with my e-mail. Though I'd whipped through half of it by the time the laundry dried, queries from customers, entrepreneurial newsletters, and a request for follow-up from one of my suppliers still remained in my inbox.

They'd have to wait. At two o'clock I left Kyla a note to concentrate on packaging the holiday soaps, took the basket of laundry up and distributed clean clothes to each of our bedrooms, patted my hair down, and brushed my teeth. Halfway down the stairs I spun around and went back up to the bathroom, where I applied some eyeliner and lip gloss.

When I reached the bottom of the stairs, Meghan came out of the massage room, Brodie trailing behind her. If Erin isn't home Brodie follows Meghan around, waiting outside the door when she's with clients. If Erin is home, Brodie follows her. I rate only when I'm the only one around, and even then he usually lies in front of the door, waiting for one of his girls to return.

My housemate tried to keep the hour after Erin got home from school free so she could find out about her daughter's day and get her started on homework. I told her about Kyla coming, and she said she'd watch for her and let her into the workroom downstairs.

Cocking her head to one side, she gave me a look and asked, "Where're you going now?"

"Beans R Us. Like I said this morning, I want to know more about Debby and Jacob."

"Going to stop by the Gold Leaf?"

I shrugged. "I don't know. Maybe."

She smiled.

"What?"

"Nothing. You look nice."

"Shut up."

"Oh, stop it. You think the guy's cute. No harm in that."

I grabbed a rain jacket off the hook and grumbled my way out the door, embarrassed like some adolescent girl caught in a crush.

The sky scudded with clouds above, and rain spit unevenly toward the ground. I smiled to myself and tugged my hood up, hoping this kind of weather would drive some of Walter's cronies into the coffeehouse. Maybe I'd luck out and find Debby and Jacob themselves.

The scent of freshly ground coffee beans welcomed me into Beans R Us, causing an instant craving for a steamy latté. As the same spike-hired woman from the other night took my order, I surreptitiously examined her eyebrow ring. Eyebrow rings were okay, I mean, if you went in for that kind of thing. But the other stuff, the jewelry that can get all tangled up in bodily functions, like blowing your nose or eating spaghetti—or some things I chose not to dwell on right then—I just didn't get. But then again, the idea of committing to living with an image tattooed on your, well, anything, for fifty years I found nearly as unnerving as a marriage proposal or the little plus sign popping into view on a home pregnancy test.

While the milk steamed, I inspected the tables. Two women huddled together over notebooks and pamphlets. At first I thought they were students, until I spotted the Bible and overheard enough of the conversation to realize they were readying a presentation for their church. They both looked worried, so apparently it wasn't going so well. At a table by the front window, a man in a rumpled suit read the *Seattle Times* and slurped on a grande something-or-other. Abruptly reaching the bottom of the cup, he made an irritating sucking noise to get every last drop, rose, folded his paper, tossed the paper cup in the garbage, and exited.

Maybe this hadn't been such a great idea after all.

"Here you go," the barista said and handed me my latte.

"Do you remember me?"

"Yeah." She didn't seem happy about it. Too bad.

"You know Jacob and Debby?"

"Yeah."

"Can you tell me their last names?"

"No."

I sighed. "Please? I need to talk to them."

"Well, I don't know their last names."

"Oh." I thought a moment. "If I left a note, would you give it to whichever one comes in first?"

"I guess."

"Can I borrow paper and pen?"

"Sure, why not." Loaded with sarcasm, which I ignored. My confidence that either of them would receive the note I scribbled out didn't exactly soar.

Out on the sidewalk, latte in hand, I debated. How much did I want to talk to the cute bar owner? Well, he was good-looking and good at his job, which was admirable. No ring; not that I could count on that since some men don't wear them. But as I wandered down and sat on a park bench looking out over the river, I became aware that a kind of obligation compelled me to pursue this mild attraction. A sense of duty to…myself? Convention? The theft of my dead husband's ring had stirred up emotions I'd thought successfully tamped down for good. I'd played the grieving, relationship-phobic widow too long. Time to get on with my life. I didn't want to end up like Walter, wasting time on the past until it was too late.

Okay. Might as well go in and see what happens.

Inside the tavern two men sat along the back wall beyond the quiet pool tables, mesmerized by the sports news on the big TV in the corner and drinking beer out of pint glasses. And, I noted, the blonde-haired owner was standing at one end of the bar, sifting through receipts and making notations. He looked up when he heard the door open, smiled an automatic smile, and returned to his task.

"What can I get you? Oh, hi!" None other than Donnette, Dick's Donnette, stood behind me asking for my drink order. "What's your name again? I'm terrible with names. But I never forget a face."

People say that all the time, and I'm tempted to ask what good remembering a face is if you don't have any idea who it belongs to.

"Sophie Mae. And you're Donnette, right?"

"Right! You want a beer?"

"What do you have that's diet?"

"Coke."

"That's it?"

"Uh huh."

"I guess that's what I'll have, then." Not that I needed more caffeine after that double latte. What I would need soon was a restroom.

Behind the bar, she reached for a glass, scooped ice into it, and squirted Diet Coke out of a hose.

"Did you know Walter Hanover?" I asked.

"Who?"

"Walt. Older guy, gray hair in a ponytail, wore yellow suspenders all the time."

"Huh uh."

I handed her some ones. "I guess until about six years ago he was in here a lot."

"I've only been here a couple a months." Donnette stuck a straw in my glass and went into the back. I stared at Mr. Ponytail, willing him to look at me. Finally, he did. I smiled. He nodded. Raised his eyebrows a fraction. And waited. He had no idea who I was. Feeling like an idiot, I motioned him over. Putting down his pen, he walked to where I sat.

"I wanted to ask you a few questions," I said.

He frowned. "What kind of questions?"

"About Walter Hanover. Actually, I want to know more about his fiancée and a friend of his."

"Hey, you were in here the other night, right? Sorry—didn't make the connection."

"No problem," I said, trying for breezy. "What's your name?"

"Chuck. So do I know this fiancée?"

I described her, and Jacob while I was at it.

But Chuck shook his head. "Doesn't ring a bell. You sure they come in here?"

No, I wasn't. "Maybe not." And as I said it, I glanced outside and saw the pair in question walking by the window.

"Well, speak of the devil," I said. Putting my drink on the bar, I slid off the stool. "They just walked by. Probably going to the coffeehouse."

"Hey," he said, and I turned with my hand on the door handle. He held up a copy of the *Cadyville Eye*. "This you on the front page?"

I strode to the bar. "Can I have that? Thanks." His look of surprise followed me out the door. That he'd so readily recognized my currently coifed self as the wreck in the photo did little for my self-esteem.

As I entered Beans R Us, Jacob helped Debby out of her ratty jean jacket like it was a mink stole. They took a table by the window. The snotty barista saw me come in and made a show of taking my note over to them, saying something and nodding in my direction. Thanks for nothing, honey.

Jacob glanced my way without changing expression. Debby, on the other hand, didn't look very happy. Stepping over to them, I fumbled for what to say.

I started with, "May I sit down?"

Jacob surprised me by standing up and pulling out a chair. "You betcha. Take a load off, So-fee Mae." He said it like it was a nickname. "Your friend's Meg, right?"

"Meghan. Yes."

159

Debby finally spoke. "So what do you want?" Her skin hung on her face, slack and pasty. No makeup and red-rimmed eyes. Her hands trembled on the table. She saw me looking and clasped them together to make them stop.

I answered her question with another. "Did you hear about the fire?"

She blinked. "What fire?"

"The one at Walter's. Saturday night. We didn't get a chance to tell you yesterday at the service."

She shook her head, and her clenched hands turned white around the knuckles. "What happened?"

At the same time, Jacob asked, "Anyone hurt?"

The barista brought them coffees. The scent of hazelnut drifted from Debby's cup. Jacob took his black, and I bet he would have preferred to get it in a chipped brown cup from the diner down the street than in this joint.

I said, "The place burned to the ground. But no one was hurt."

"Wait a minute. Hey, Luce!" Jacob called.

"Yeah?" she responded from behind the counter.

"You gotta paper round here? The one came out today?" He turned to Debby. "I saw somethin' about a fire on the front page, walkin' by the newsstand."

"Here you go," I said, and handed him the one I'd confiscated from Chuck.

Lucky me, Luce brought a copy over, too. She looked at me. Looked at the front page. I closed my eyes.

"Nice picture," she said.

"We've got a copy, thanks," I said.

She shrugged and returned behind the counter, a little smile on her face. I was really starting to dislike that woman.

"What were you doing there?" Debby sounded suspicious.

"It was a huge fire, and we live right across the alley. Most of the neighborhood was there." But only I had been lucky enough to be around when that photographer from hell showed up. "I was trying to find out how it started when that picture was taken."

"And?" Jacob asked. Debby examined the photo and wrinkled her brow.

"They're still investigating." I figured it was safe to tell them that, even if one or both of them had set the fire.

"And there's nothing left," Debby said. Now her voice shook, too. Jacob watched her with concern.

"I'm sorry," I said. "I know you wanted the chance to go through his things."

Debby took a shaky swallow of coffee, holding the cup with both hands. Her fingernails were bitten to the quick, and dried blood crusted the cuticle of her thumb where she'd worried a hangnail too far.

"Well, thanks for telling us. 'Preciate it." Jacob was dismissing me.

"Can I get your phone number? Your last name?" I asked Debby. "So if I need to get in touch with you I can?"

"Why wouldja need to do that?" he asked.

The little guy was starting to get on my nerves. "Is there a problem, Jacob?"

Debby put her hand on his arm. "It's Silverman."

"Debby Silverman."

She nodded. "Deborah Silverman."

I looked at Jacob. He scowled.

"You'll find me with her," he said, thrusting his chin toward Debby.

"And I don't suppose either of you have a phone, do you?" I couldn't keep the sarcasm out of my voice.

She opened her mouth, but Jacob spoke first. "Nope. No phone. Sorry."

He had seemed downright nice when I first sat down. What had changed? News of the fire? Of the investigation?

"Jacob, stop being an ass," Debby said, and recited a phone number. I scrabbled in my coat pocket for a pen—realizing I'd kept the barista's after I'd written the note for these two—and scribbled the number on a corner torn from the newspaper. I folded the scrap and put it in the pocket of my slacks. The pen I put in my coat pocket.

"Okay. Well, thanks," I said.

I'd wanted to ask what they'd thought of Walter's memorial service, but Jacob was pouting like a child and refused to look at me, while Debby's attention seemed to drift far away from both of us as she stared out the window.

So I left.

Out on the sidewalk I pulled up my hood against the rain. Through the front window of Beans R Us, I saw Jacob reaching for Debby's hands.

TWENTY-TWO

I STOPPED IN AT Picadilly Circus, the British tearoom across the street from the Gold Leaf, to pick up some PG Tips, a strong black tea Meghan and I both favored in cold weather. Overhead the clouds had collected into thick clots, and it began to rain big fat drops as I started home. I pulled my hood further around my face and hunched my shoulders. The air had grown several degrees cooler, and a shiver worked its way up my spine. Walking quickly, with my head down, I thought about what my next move should be.

Detective Ambrose would say I shouldn't have a next move. Why couldn't I let this rest, leave it for the police to figure out? Why did I feel so compelled to find out what had happened to Walter? If it had been straightforward murder from the get-go, not an assumed suicide that pushed all my buttons about my brother's death, would I have felt so driven to discover the perpetrator?

Yes. I would. Since it had happened in my workroom, to someone I knew, I would feel the same need to discover the truth. Of course if it was deemed murder from the start, Sergeant Zahn wouldn't be trying to keep Ambrose from doing his job by making him work on the toilet paper terrorist case; he'd be facilitating the investigation and providing more resources.

How sure was I that Walter had been murdered? Pretty darn sure. Whatever Meghan might say about Walter's "underlying sorrow," it never sat right with me that he'd killed himself. Maybe it would have made some sense earlier in his life, but not once he had sobriety, money, and the girl. So to speak.

That earlier time was what Tootie had based her expectations on—what had she asked when they'd told her that her son was dead? A bullet or a bridge? But she must have known he'd quit drinking. If he'd gone through AA and seen fit to make amends—or whatever they called that step—with Richard and Meghan, and the other people he worked for in the neighborhood, surely he would have done the same with his own mother. Perhaps he hadn't convinced her. Or maybe her view of him had been too slow to change.

Even Jacob and Debby's assertion that Walter had joked about killing himself by drinking Drano fell short of the suicide theory. And there was that sense of aha! when I'd heard the word "homicide" in the police station. Ambrose was no idiot, and his gut was telling him the same thing.

So, back to the original question: what next?

First, we needed more information about the two I'd just left. Meghan would know how to access public records now that we had Debby's name. I briefly considered using the services of an online information broker. I'd looked my own name up once, and while it only showed the town I lived in, the advertisement that popped up on my computer screen said for a fee they'd tell me not only Sophie Mae Reynolds' address and phone number, but who her neighbors were, any criminal history, marriages, births, and a slew of other information I found profoundly disturbing to think about.

Maybe I could trade Debby's last name to Ambrose in exchange for whatever information they dug up on her. Yeah, right. Ambrose wouldn't welcome my help, probably considered me a suspect. I grimaced as I checked traffic and stepped off the curb.

I was reflecting on the unpleasant twist my last conversation with Ambrose had taken when I heard the squeal of tires on wet asphalt. My head jerked up just in time to see an old pickup bearing down on me. I twisted and jumped aside to avoid the rusty chrome grill, losing my balance and falling between two parked cars. My elbow hit one of the bumpers on the way down, shooting sparks up my arm. I lay there, gasping and listening to the faint sound of the receding truck engine. Every breath seared along my side. After a small eternity, I managed to push myself into a sitting position on the sidewalk. I ran my fingertips over my ribs. Nothing broken, it seemed, but I'd pulled a muscle in my side, and my hip throbbed where I'd landed on the curb. Severe bruising was in my short-range forecast.

"Jeez, you okay, lady?" A young man, somewhere in his late teens or early twenties, squatted on the sidewalk next to me. "Are you hurt? I can call 911."

I shook my head.

"You must be hurt. You're crying."

"Hit my elbow," I gasped. "Funny bone."

"Oh. Okay. You need to be more careful about crossing the street. I don't even know if that driver saw you."

"Oh, he saw me, all right. He was aiming right for me."

The kid gave me a funny look.

"Didn't you see what happened? There was no traffic when I started across."

The truck had pulled out and had gathered speed rapidly in order to reach me. But putting the pedal to the metal had made the tires squeal, alerting me…and saving me. I looked at the slight sheen of rain on the pavement. If it had been dry the tires might not have lost traction, might not have made a sound. And I'd be more than a little banged up.

I'd be dead.

"I walked out the door just as you went down," he said. Slight build, pointed features, glasses. He smelled like smoke.

"Cigarette break?"

He nodded.

"You work there?" I pointed to the insurance office behind us.

"Uh huh."

Looking around, I saw the rest of the street was empty. Where was the concerned crowd that should form after a near hit and run? Where were the helpful citizens that define small towns?

"What's your name?" I asked.

"Don."

"Don what?" I felt for the barista's pen, but it must have fallen out. I didn't see it anywhere.

"I don't want to get involved in any court case," he said. "It's not like I saw the license number or anything."

"I don't give a damn what you want," I snapped. "I can find out your last name or you can give it to me. Your pick."

"Plunckett." He spelled it for me. I recited it in my head so I'd remember. Sullen, he asked again if I was okay. When I said I was, he turned and went inside without another word.

I thought about calling Ambrose. Then I thought about the look he'd give me, that skeptical not-quite-believing look he'd directed my way before. Or maybe I'd get the policewoman who had responded to our break-in. She'd just love dealing with me again. Or better yet, they could send sandy-haired Officer Owens, who'd almost shot me that night at Walter's. I sighed. I didn't have a cell phone, and there wasn't a pay phone nearby. I'd have to go in one of the businesses and ask to use their phone. My slacks were torn, my coat a muddy mess, and my once-pristine white shirt— was that blood? A little, there on the cuff above a shallow cut on my wrist. No one had seen what happened, and Don boy wasn't going to be any help either, since all he saw was some middle-aged woman who didn't know how to cross a street.

The shivers, from the wet, the cold, the adrenalin shock, or more likely all three, started across my shoulders and arms and graduated to full-blown shudders racking my whole body. I needed to get home, take a shower to chase the soreness already settling into my battered muscles. Then I could decide whether to call the police. I pulled myself to my feet using one of the car bumpers, feeling about a hundred-and-fifty years old. I began plodding home through the rain, teeth clenched against chattering, eyes moving along the streets, watching for any lurking dark blue pickups. At least it had stopped raining.

"Hey lady, wha'd ya do, fall in a puddle?" This shouted from a carload of teenagers driving by.

Hot rage bubbled up, then dissolved into a pressing behind my forehead. With horror I realized I was about to start crying, right there on the street. Breathing through my teeth, I upped my limping pace, gritting my teeth harder as I finally started down my block. Using the railing, I pulled myself up the front steps and went inside.

I took off my muddy shoes, hung my jacket on the coat rack, and walked into the kitchen. Empty. I heard voices downstairs and wondered who was with Kyla. Sniffing, I went upstairs.

Erin sat on her bed, surrounded by stuffed animals, doing her homework. One of the animals raised its head as I walked by, and I saw it was Brodie, but Erin didn't notice me. I found Meghan in the bathroom, clad in rubber gloves and scrubbing the toilet. I made a sound in my throat, and she looked up. Dropping the scrub brush, she stripped off the gloves and came toward me.

"Good God, Sophie Mae—what happened? Are you okay?"

I opened my mouth to tell her, but all that came out was a sob. She put the scrub brush in its holder and closed the lid of the toilet so I could sit down. Perching on the edge of the bathtub, she put her arm around my shoulders and let me cry it out. At one point I saw her motion Erin out of the doorway.

On the miserable way home I'd very carefully avoided thinking about the fact that someone had tried to run me down. I could have died. Now, sitting in the safety of my own bathroom with my best friend, the fear I should have felt earlier came crashing through. Someone wanted me dead. Someone had wanted Walter dead, and he'd died, and now someone wanted me dead, too.

Meghan moistened a washcloth with icy cold water, wrung it out, and handed it to me. I scrubbed it over my face, gasping. The shock of it against my skin settled the last of the hitching sobs out of my chest. I unrolled a length of toilet paper and blew my nose.

"I'm so embarrassed," I said.

"That's dumb. Crying is good for you. You know it rids the body of stress hormones? That's why you feel better afterwards. They're released in the tears. So, having a good cry is a very practical thing to do when things get crazy. Remember Holly Hunter in *Broadcast News*?"

I stared at her. Trust Meghan to turn my humiliating breakdown into something downright necessary.

"Now," she said. "Tell me what happened?"

"Someone tried to kill me," I said.

"What!"

I told her about the truck, about falling, about the lack of witnesses. While I was at it, I told her about Debby and Jacob and Chuck, the very uninterested barkeep, and the snotty barista with the eyebrow ring. I told her about my unsatisfactory canvassing in the neighborhood that morning. And I told her Mrs. Gray's story about Walter and Cherry.

She let me run down. After I finally stopped talking, she said, "We need to tell Detective Ambrose about the driver of that truck trying to hit you."

"He won't believe me. I don't have any witnesses." I even sounded pathetic to my own ears.

"You look like hell—how could he not believe you?"

"Thanks a lot!"

"He needs to know."

"He already thinks I'm a royal pain in the ass."

"Well, he's right about that. It's one of your best qualities."

I laughed. A little.

"You can't take the risk of keeping a murder attempt to yourself. And I can't let you. This doesn't sound like someone just fooling around."

"Okay, I'll call him."

"No, I'll call him."

"Kind of like reverse psychology? Make him think I'm being stoic so he'll be more inclined to give me a break? Might work."

"You dope. You are being stoic. Mostly I don't want you to fly off the handle at him."

"Meghan! You make me sound like a raving bitch."

"Nnooo…but sometimes you're, uh, less than gracious under stress."

"Fine," I said, and began getting ready to take a shower. It wasn't until I was rinsing shampoo out of my hair that it dawned on me I'd just proved her point. I turned the shower faucet to the right, gasping in shock at the sudden change in temperature, forcing myself to stay under the cold needles long enough to bathe all my bumps and bruises.

TWENTY-THREE

DOWNSTAIRS IN THE KITCHEN, a powerful pot of Bewley's Irish tea brewed on the counter while Meghan stirred up corn bread to go with the chili bubbling on a back burner. As she poured the dark liquid into a stoneware mug, I realized I'd lost the box of teabags when I'd fallen. I drank the Bewley's black, no sugar, and the tea went down stronger than Starbuck's dark roast.

Ambrose hadn't been in his office when she'd called, so Meghan had left a message. I didn't hold out a lot of hope regarding his response once he learned of the afternoon's events, but we didn't have many choices.

I went down to my workroom to see if Kyla had managed to wrap all the holiday soap. The festive little packages sat in a neat pile in the center of the island in the middle of the room. Not only had she covered each in a tight skin of cellophane—we use plain old Saran wrap because it's best for keeping the volatile essential oils from escaping into the air—but had also scrounged up some labels preprinted with my company name and logo, but otherwise blank. She'd hand printed each with either "Peppermint Swirl" or "Cinnamon Stick" and the average weight of the soaps in ounces, and affixed them to the bars.

A note lay next to the soaps:

Hi Sophie Mae—You've seemed kind of busy lately, so I went ahead and made up the names and labeled the soaps. My sister Cyan came with me today and helped. We had some extra time, so I also staged the shipments you have lined against the wall. Hope that was okay. See you Thurs. Kyla. P.S. Cyan would like to help out to make some extra Christmas money, if you need her. Thanx. P.P.S. You're getting kind of low on lotion bars.

In front of each box lined against the wall was the packing list I'd printed, with corresponding soaps and bath products from the storeroom clustered on top of it. If she'd been standing there, I might have kissed that girl. All the work she'd done that afternoon was the only good thing that had happened all day. Plus, she'd found me another helper.

Meghan's voice floated down the stairs, angry and frustrated. I shut off the lights and went up to the kitchen. In the hallway I could hear her talking on the telephone, and for a moment I thought Detective Ambrose might have called back. But soon it became clear she was talking with Richard.

"No! I won't say it again. You can't take her out of school for something like that. That's the kind of thing you should be doing on the weekends you have her, instead of bailing on her like you did last week….Don't give me that crap, Richard! I couldn't care less about yet another one of your money-making schemes. Here's an idea for you—get a real job! Go to it every day, get paid, and then pay your bills—including Erin's support—*before* you drive north to the casinos….What? That's not my problem…Of course I know you're her dad. You're the one who seems to forget. Why is this so important, if your mother's going to be here a while?" Then her voice lowered, taking on a decisive chill. Brodie whined in his throat when he heard the tone.

"I said no, Richard. That's the end of it. And don't try an end run. I'm calling the school first thing in the morning."

The phone clanked onto its base on the hall table. After a few moments Meghan rounded the corner, high spots of anger on her cheeks. She didn't seem surprised to see me.

"How much of that did you hear?"

"The last bit. Sorry."

She waved my apology away. Not a lot of secrets in this house.

"So what did he want?" I asked. "And where's Erin?"

"She fell asleep upstairs on my bed. She's exhausted—I don't think she's been sleeping very well lately."

The timer on the oven went off, and Meghan took the pan of corn bread out of the oven. It smelled heavenly, and I was famished. Nearly getting killed is apparently good for the appetite.

Stirring the chili, I said, "And Dick? What does he want now?"

Meghan sighed. "He wants to take Erin out of school tomorrow to have lunch with his mother."

"His mother? Dick actually has a mother?"

A small smile passed over Meghan's face. "Yeah, if you can believe it. Lives in California, where he's from. I met her once before we got married. She doesn't like me much. Didn't come to the wedding."

"Why on earth not?"

"I got the impression she didn't think I was good enough for her baby boy."

"Oh. One of those. So why lunch?"

"No idea. I guess she's staying at Richard's; he said she flew in Sunday. Anyway, he said she'll be here for a week, so I don't see why Erin can't meet her grandmother on the weekend or after school."

"Was that her in the car with Dick after Walter's service?"

"Now that you mention it—"

But the doorbell cut off her words. Brodie barked, and Meghan shushed him, not wanting to wake her daughter upstairs. But Erin slept like only children can, and I doubted the ruckus would disturb her.

Through the window next to the front door I saw a police car parked out front. Opening the door, I expected to see Detective Ambrose, but instead found the patrolwoman who had come about our burglary the previous afternoon.

So Ambrose couldn't even be bothered to talk to me himself. A simple phone call would have sufficed.

"Ms. Reynolds," she said in a tone several degrees chillier than the outside temperature. What had Ambrose told her? For that matter, what had Meghan told his voicemail?

"Officer Danson," I said.

"Please come in, Officer," Meghan said from behind me.

We led the way to the living room and invited her to sit down, but she insisted on standing. Meghan sat on the sofa and I leaned awkwardly next to the fireplace mantle. I could already tell this wasn't going to go well.

"I know you're upset about what happened, Ms. Reynolds, but you have to leave the investigation to the police. Your interference has already made things more difficult."

"Of course I'm upset about what happened! And I have yet to see any evidence of an *investigation*. All I was doing was walking home—"

"Walking home? I don't think so. From what I've been told you were questioning people, and I'm sorry, but you may have muddied the waters by doing so."

Had Debby and Jacob told the police I'd been questioning them? I'd only asked how to get in touch with them. I opened my mouth, but Meghan spoke before I could.

"Officer, could you be a bit more specific about what Sophie Mae did?"

I swear the woman harrumphed. "She went up and down the street, talking to the neighbors, trying to find out if anyone saw anything during the time of your burglary." She turned to me. "Luckily, it doesn't sound like many people were home when you did your door-to-door this morning, but you've done enough damage."

Oh. That.

"A lot of people were at work," I said.

"Which is why I waited until this afternoon to check with your neighbors about what they may have seen. Please leave it to me. I know you have good intentions, but I really do know how to do my job. Better than you do, Ms. Reynolds."

"I thought you'd just fill out the case report and file it away. Last night you said it's nearly impossible to find household thieves."

"It's hard to find stolen items. Usually thieves sell them right away. But that doesn't mean we just file the paperwork and forget about catching the perpetrator."

"I misunderstood," I said. "I'm sorry."

Meghan stared at me. So did Officer Danson.

"What?" I asked, feeling a little defensive.

"So I can count on you to leave this burglary investigation to me?"

"No problem. I won't say another word to the neighbors. Are you working on this burglary alone?"

"A detective is also assigned, but right now he's busy with other cases. So I'm taking care of it."

"What's the detective's name?" I asked. Her face reddened, and she glared at me.

"The department has only one. Detective Ambrose."

No wonder he was so busy. But that didn't explain Danson's anger.

"But he does know about our break-in yesterday?"

"Well, technically it wasn't a break-in," she said.

"Does he know?" I asked again.

"He should, if he read the shift reports. He works days, and I work swing."

"So he might not be aware of it?"

"His sergeant would have passed it on, too." A stubborn expression settled on her face

"There was a death in our basement a few days ago," Meghan said. "Detective Ambrose came to investigate. And Officer—what was his name, Sophie Mae?"

"Owens," I said.

Danson didn't look happy. "I didn't realize that death occurred here. You think they're related?"

Before Meghan mentioned Walter's missing papers, I said, "If we did, we would have said something yesterday." Meghan's amused look assured me she hadn't planned on spilling the beans. "It's probably just coincidence. But Detective Ambrose should be made aware of it."

"Of course. I'll double-check with him."

She turned to go, and Meghan stood. We walked her to the door, Brodie's nails clicking on the tile entryway as he accompanied us. Before she left, she gave me a hard look.

"I have your word?"

"I said I wouldn't question the neighbors anymore. I won't."

She seemed satisfied with this and walked down the sidewalk to her patrol car. As we stood in the doorway and watched her drive away, Meghan asked me if I'd just lied to the nice policewoman.

"Of course not. I promised not to quiz the neighbors about seeing anyone here during the burglary. She's obviously already doing that and no doubt better than I could. But that's all I promised."

Meghan surprised me by saying, "Good. Because somebody needs to figure this out. If talking to Ambrose about your attempted hit-and-run doesn't work, then it's back to us."

"You really feel that way?"

"We can't just leave it hanging, not if it's hanging over our heads."

TWENTY-FOUR

In the kitchen I made a quick salad, chopped onion, grated cheese. Upstairs Meghan rousted Erin from her nap and led the yawning girl to the table. We ladled the fragrant chili into bowls, topped it with the onions and cheese and sour cream, and dug in. Someone said hunger makes the best gravy, and I heartily concur. I didn't think I'd ever eaten food that tasted so good.

The doorbell rang again as I was spreading a second piece of corn bread with honey-butter. I sighed. Well, at least tonight we'd actually managed to eat dinner.

Licking my fingers, I got up to answer the door, certain this time it was Ambrose. But on the doorstep I found Dick and a woman I assumed was his mother.

"Well, aren't you going to ask us in out of this rain?" This from the woman, in a querulous voice.

I stepped back from the door, suppressing a sigh.

"Meghan," I called.

"Here," the woman said, thrusting her umbrella and coat at me. If the rain was that bad, I wondered why she hadn't bothered to unfurl the umbrella. I took them and laid them across the back of the chair inside the door, a move that did not meet with the woman's approval, judging from the look on her face. Dick still hadn't said a word.

"Richard. And Grace, isn't it? It's been too long," Meghan said from behind me.

I wouldn't have been surprised to hear Dick's mom respond that it hadn't been long enough, but she just said "Meghan," and then, "Where's Erin?"

"She's in here," Meghan said, leading the way to the kitchen. "We're having dinner. Please join us. It's just chili, but it's good stuff."

How she could be so gracious was beyond me. In the bright light of the kitchen I saw it was nearly beyond her, as well. The strain played across her features as she turned to the cupboard to get more bowls and plates. I moved toward the silverware drawer. Under the table, Brodie growled low in his throat.

Dick said, "No, thanks. Mom's not much for chili. We're on our way to dinner. We were hoping to take Erin with us, but I guess it's too late."

Meghan stiffened, turned from the cupboard. She hadn't expected this particular kind of end run. I stuck my hand out to Dick's mom.

"Hi, Mrs. Bly. I'm Sophie Mae Reynolds. It's nice to meet you."

"Not Bly. Not for a long time. Thorson," she said.

I nodded and smiled. She eyed me for a long uncomfortable moment, then shook my hand. Her skin felt sticky with lotion, and her grip was brutal. I met her eyes and resisted the temptation to either shake out my hand or wipe it on the leg of my sweatpants.

Grace Thorson was waging quite a war with the natural aging process. Her hair color, while one found in nature—if you happened to be looking at a blood-orange—would have been more appropriate gelled and spiked on the lead singer in a punk band than puffed into this sculpted hairdo on a woman so obviously in her sixties. Maybe her seventies. I did some quick math and decided it could be either one. Long false eyelashes fanned from eyes pulled a bit too tight at the temples, and her makeup had been applied with a heavy, but expert, hand. She wore a black pantsuit, quite stylish but rather overdone for Cadyville, and high-heeled pumps that could have come from Frederick's of Hollywood. Even with the heels she was shorter than me, and scary thin.

Erin had stopped eating and sat watching all this without a word. It seemed strange behavior for a grandmother to ignore her granddaughter like that, even for the brief time we'd been in the kitchen. My grandma would have been all over me as soon as she walked in the room. Of course, mine wouldn't wait until I was ten years old to get around to meeting me, either.

"Erin, this is your grandma," Meghan said.

"Hi, Grandma," Erin said in a small voice.

And then, I swear to God, the woman reached down and pinched Erin's cheek. The effect was surreal; a hackneyed gooey-grandma move from this painted death's-head creature, far more creepy than affectionate. Erin pulled back and rubbed her face.

"You can call me Grace. I like it better than 'Grandma.'"

Amused, I looked at Meghan, who still stood by the cupboard. Any hint of a smile slid from my face when I saw her expression. My housemate was terrified.

"Well," Dick said to Erin, "Since you've already eaten, how 'bout you come with us anyway. You can have some big yummy dessert while we eat."

Erin looked between her parents. "Can I have chocolate cake?"

"Sure! Whatever you want."

"And ice cream?"

"Erin," Meghan said.

"Oh, get off her back. She can have whatever dessert she wants. C'mon, kiddo," Dick said.

"No," Meghan said.

Erin, already on her feet, paused.

"It's too late for her to go out."

Dick made a show of looking at his watch. "It's only six-thirty, for God's sake. Lighten up, huh? We're just taking her for dessert. You wouldn't let me take her out of school for lunch tomorrow—it was going to be a surprise treat, Erin—and Mother wants to spend some time with my little angel."

"I'm sorry. She hasn't been feeling well, and she still has some homework to do for tomorrow."

He rolled his eyes. "Homework. Erin, do you want to do homework? Or would you rather come eat chocolate cake with your grandmother?"

Erin's gaze shuttled between her mother and father, uncertain. I wished I could do something, but I couldn't think what.

Mrs. Thorson spoke. "This is ridiculous. We're taking you to a restaurant, Erin. Get your coat."

Erin responded to the authority in her voice and moved toward the coat rack in the hallway, albeit slowly.

Meghan shook her head and said firmly, "I'm sorry, but that's just not going to happen tonight."

"I'm leaving in two days and I'm going to spend some time with my granddaughter, whether you like it or not. It's my right. Richard, for heaven's sake, stop being such a wimp and stand up for yourself. Erin's your daughter. *She* can't tell you what to do with your own daughter."

Whoo boy.

And from under the table, Brodie let loose, barking and growling and lunging at Grace Thorson, snapping at the air around her bony ankles. She screamed and started swinging her purse at him. I yelled, but Meghan moved. She was calling him off and had hooked her fingers in his collar, when Richard pulled back his booted foot to kick the little dog. Erin screamed from the doorway.

"No, Daddy! No! Don't hurt him!" She ran into the room and flung herself on the floor between her dog and her father.

Irritated, Dick brought his foot back to the floor. "I wasn't going to hurt him. What's wrong with the little fu…guy, anyway? He always behaved when I lived here."

Meghan ignored him, calming Brodie in a shaky voice and leading him to the laundry room. He continued to grumble low in his throat.

"That beast is a menace and should be put down. Stupid beast tried to bite me, and biting dogs cannot be allowed to live. Richard, you must see to it." The crotchety old bat stuck her pointy little chin out to emphasize her point.

Erin, still sitting on the floor, looked terrified.

Meghan shut the door. "I think that reaction is a bit strong, Grace. Brodie didn't bite you—he's never bitten anyone."

Grace sniffed. "He's vicious. Any fool can see that. Now, Erin, get up from that floor. We're going for dessert."

Meghan's head whipped around, but Erin said, "No, thank you. I need to get my homework done for tomorrow."

"You can do your homework when you get back. You're in what, fifth grade? It can't be that hard. Come on."

Erin shook her head, still sitting on the floor. Meghan had moved to squat beside her. "I don't want to."

"What? I don't care if you want to or not! Children don't know what they want. Now stop this—"

Meghan stood up and turned on the older woman. "Get… out…of…my…house. Now. If you don't leave immediately, I'll call the police, so help me."

Dick stared at Meghan. His mother's lip curled, and she shook her head. She began to speak, but the doorbell interrupted her. Erin was on her feet and out of the kitchen in a flash. I followed her out to the hallway.

I was downright overjoyed to see Barr Ambrose standing in the doorway. "Come in, Detective!" I said, louder than warranted. He gave me a funny look and stumbled as I grabbed his arm and pulled him across the threshold.

"What—?"

"Shh."

I led him into the kitchen, where we found Grace and Meghan nose-to-nose, glaring at each other.

"I don't give a damn if some stupid judge gave you custody, missy, you don't have the right to keep Richard away."

Meghan's eyes flicked over the woman's bony shoulder to Ambrose and me. She said, "I don't keep your darling son from seeing his daughter. He's the one who brings her home early on their weekends so he can party and gamble. If he's so interested in being a good father, maybe he ought to try paying a little child support once in a while. Now, I told you I want you out of my house, and I'm not kidding." She shifted her attention. "Hello, Detective."

Ambrose had recovered from my brisk treatment. He smiled and inclined his head. "Ms. Bly."

Turning his gaze to Dick and his mother, Ambrose raised his eyebrows in an unspoken question. I had expected his presence to quiet things down a little, but I was unprepared for the look of horror that passed over Dick's face before he managed to squelch it. His mother remained expressionless, but that could have been as much due to botox as to self-control.

"This is Dick Bly and his mother, Grace Thorson," I said. "Dick, Grace, this is Detective Ambrose."

Dick didn't even take the time to shoot me the usual withering glance for abusing his name. His words came out in a rush as he put his arm around his mother's shoulder and guided her toward the door.

"I'm sorry we can't stay to chat, but we've got dinner reservations. Talk to you later, Meghan. Bye, Angel." This last as he patted Erin's head on the way to the front door. Grace didn't say a word, just clicked across the hardwood in her high heels. Dick grabbed their coats off the back of the chair, but they didn't pause to put them on before they left. Meghan, Ambrose, and I stared after them.

"What happened?" I asked.

TWENTY-FIVE

AMBROSE PULLED OUT A chair and sat down. "I wouldn't mind knowing that myself. What was that all about?"

Meghan sighed. "My ex-husband. His mother's in town, and they wanted to take Erin out for dessert. I didn't want her to…where is she? Erin?" I heard panic in her voice.

"It's okay. She's getting Brodie from the laundry room," I said.

Erin came into the kitchen, the little dog padding behind her as if nothing had happened. Then he saw Ambrose and ran over to him, wagging his whole behind since he didn't have a tail to do the job. Ambrose bent down and scritched him behind the ears, laughing.

"I'll go up and do my homework," Erin said. Her eyes were red.

Meghan picked up Brodie. "Then I'll bring your little buddy along for company."

I was left with Ambrose. "Want some chili?" I asked.

"It smells pretty good," he said, craning his neck toward the stove.

I got up and ladled him a bowl, and he started loading it with condiments. I cut him a slab of corn bread, and, on second thought, cut myself another piece, too.

"Things always so crazy around here?" he asked between bites.

I shook my head. "Never. Well, hardly ever."

"Hmmm." He ate some corn bread. Watched me. Waited for me to fill the silence, maybe explain about the message Meghan had left him. I ate, too, keeping my mouth full so I wouldn't have to talk as I tried to decide the best way to tell him about the pickup trying to run me down. Should I tell him about the missing paperwork? He'd hit the roof.

Before I'd decided whether I wanted to weather that storm, Meghan returned, saving me from having to eat a fourth piece of corn bread.

"Erin okay?" I asked.

"No. She's not," Meghan said, sounding defeated.

"She's bound to be upset."

"She doesn't want to talk about it."

"Give her a little time," I said.

When Meghan didn't respond, Ambrose asked, "Why didn't you want her to go have dessert with them?"

I'd been wondering the same thing. As nasty as Dick's mother had been, Meghan's vehement reaction surprised me. Meghan swallowed, then reached out a trembling hand for her water glass. She held it in both hands and took a sip.

She said, "I know it sounds stupid, but when they showed up like that and wanted to take her out, I just knew they weren't going to bring her home."

No wonder she'd been so scared. Ambrose swallowed a mouthful of chili, leaning forward. "Why? Have there been incidents in the past?"

Meghan shook her head. "Nothing. He's a flake, and he's irresponsible, but I never thought before that he might take her. I mean, so often he brings her back early when he does have her that it never occurred to me he'd try to keep her until tonight."

"So what was different this time?" Ambrose asked. His tone was conversational, nonjudgmental, inviting. Part of me wanted to tell Meghan to be careful, but another part found his compassion very appealing. I offered him more corn bread. He smiled his thanks.

"I don't know," Meghan said.

He persisted. "There was something."

She took another drink of water. "This afternoon he called and wanted to take Erin out of school tomorrow. To have lunch with his mother. Erin had never met her. I told him no."

"You didn't want Erin to miss school," Ambrose said.

"She's in fifth grade," Meghan frowned. "It wouldn't have killed her to miss part of a day. I took her out for Walter's funeral on Monday."

"So she would have missed school for the second time in a week."

"Well, I guess that bothered me. But what really got me was how…off it sounded. Richard said his mother got in town Sunday. And he had Erin last weekend but brought her home on Saturday. He could have picked her up again on Sunday if he'd wanted. I don't know, maybe Grace was tired when she got in. But he also said his mother would be visiting for a week. Then she says she's leaving in two days. Either way, they could have spent the afternoon with her after school, so why take her out of school for lunch?"

I said, "His charming mother seems to decide what she wants, and she demands it immediately."

"I wish I knew what she wants. The way she acted with Erin tonight. It wasn't…"

"Grandmotherly," I said.

"No." Meghan looked at Ambrose. "So I don't have any proof of anything. I just felt scared."

He shook his head. "I'm not going to argue with a mother's fear. And you were well within your rights if you're the custodial parent."

"I'm so glad you came when you did. Does your presence always diffuse situations like that?" Meghan asked Ambrose.

"Rarely," he said with a wry expression, scooping the last of his chili into his spoon.

"They sure scooted out of here in a hurry," I said, glad he took Meghan's instincts seriously, and hoping he'd take my story about the truck seriously, too.

"Yeah, I noticed that." He finished off the corn bread.

"Want more?" I asked.

"No, thanks. That was great, though. Good chili's hard to come by."

I set a mug of coffee in front of him. "You take anything in it?"

"No, this is fine. Thanks."

Meghan stood up and gestured toward the living room. I limped behind them, carrying two more mugs of coffee. I sat on the sofa, and Ambrose sat beside me. Meghan took the armchair at one end of the coffee table.

"Now, what's this about someone attacking you, Sophie Mae?"

I hesitated. "Attacking?"

His eyes narrowed. "You weren't attacked?"

It wasn't the word I would have chosen, but I supposed it was accurate enough. So I told him. I'd been crossing Avenue A in the middle of the block. I'd checked for traffic first, but had lowered my head as I crossed, because of the rain. I'd heard the squeal of tires in time to see the pickup barreling toward me and had jumped out of the way, falling between the two parked cars.

Ambrose's face creased into a frown as I spoke, and I finished and waited for him to tell me it was all in my imagination, that I must not have looked where I was going. He pulled a notebook and pen out of his shirt pocket.

"You said she'd been attacked, Ms. Bly. But a near hit-and-run? You neglected to mention that."

"Sophie Mae didn't think you'd put much stock in what happened. Being almost run down sounds a bit…dramatic."

He looked at both of us. "But that's what happened, right?"

We nodded.

"Good God," he muttered. "Who else saw what happened?"

"No one," I said.

"No one? So close to downtown?"

"The street was empty. There may have been traffic a few blocks up, or someone could have been looking out a window. But the only person I saw was a young guy on a cigarette break. Works at the insurance office. He says he didn't see anything and made it pretty clear about not wanting to be involved. I got his name, though."

"Good. What is it?"

"Wait—I wrote it down when I got home." I got up and went into the hallway, returning with a sheet off the memo pad by the telephone. His lips thinned as he watched me limp back. I handed him the name.

"Have you seen a doctor about that ankle?"

I shook my head. "It's not my ankle. I hit my hip on the curb when I fell. I'm bruised, but nothing's broken."

Ambrose looked like he wanted to say more, but changed his mind.

"Tell me about this truck. Did you see the license plate number? What make was it?"

"I would have told you already if I'd seen the number," I said in a testy voice. Meghan coughed. I wiped the edge from my tone and continued. "And I couldn't tell the difference between a Chevy or a Ford or anything else, just by looking."

"Okay. That's fine. What color was it?"

"Blue."

"Bright? Dark?"

"Dark. And kind of dirty."

"Dirty dark blue," Ambrose said, writing it down. "Was it a truck you'd see on a new car lot?"

"Oh no. It was old. It seemed, um, wider than the newer trucks? Boxier. And there were rust spots. And the front grill was dented."

"But it wasn't a really old truck—like a classic."

"Huh uh. Maybe something from twenty years ago. Maybe older. Real square looking."

"Good. And the driver? What did you notice about the driver?"

"Nothing," I said, feeling defeated. "I didn't see the driver at all."

"Anybody in the cab besides the driver?"

"I don't…no, I don't think so. One figure outlined against the rear window." I closed my eyes, trying to remember. "The hands on the wheel were dark. Gloves? Or just my perspective. I don't know. The driver didn't have a face. Too dark. No features."

"Do you mean the driver was dark complected?"

"I don't think so."

"Why?"

I squeezed my eyelids together, trying to pry the reason out of my brain. "I didn't get the impression of *any* skin tone. I think it might have been fabric. Like a mask. Something with folds of fabric. Like a scarf or something." My eyes popped open. "It was a Ford."

"You remembered something."

"Yeah. That grill got damn close before I twisted out of the way. I saw the letters set into the chrome."

"Can you draw how they appeared?"

"I guess. I'm not a very good artist."

"That doesn't matter, I just want the general idea of placement. It can help us determine the year of the vehicle." He turned to a fresh page in his notebook and handed it to me. I sketched out the way the word "Ford" had looked on the grill of the truck and handed the notebook back.

"Excellent. Can you think of anything else?"

I shook my head. "I think that's the limit. You made me remember more than I thought I could."

Ambrose smiled. It was a nice smile.

"So, do you believe someone tried to run me down?"

The smile faded. "Why wouldn't I believe you? Have you lied to me about anything else?"

"No." I hadn't, not once. I might not have mentioned the boxes of paperwork, but that wasn't quite the same thing as lying, now was it?

"Tell me what you were doing downtown."

"I was in Piccadilly Circus, picking up some tea." But something in my voice or my eyes gave me away.

"And before that?" he asked, looking…amused?

Meghan said, "Tell him, Sophie Mae. He needs to know."

I sighed. "I was at Beans R Us. Talking to Walter's fiancée and that friend of theirs."

"What did you talk about?"

"I wanted to find out more about them, because I knew they both hung out with Walter. And I wanted to make sure Debby knew about the fire at Walter's—don't worry, I didn't mention arson—and I asked how to get a hold of them if I needed to. Jacob didn't want to tell me, but Debby said her last name is Silverman. Deborah Silverman. I got her phone number. I'll get it for you before you leave."

"Tell me why you've zeroed in on those two."

I shrugged. "They're the only ones I've found who might have wanted Walter dead. They knew he had the money from the lottery. I can't tell about Debby—she seems pretty upset that he died, but I can't be sure. But I think Jacob is in love with Debby, and he resented Walter. He also didn't like Walter giving all that money away to charities."

"He told you this?"

"When they came in while we were cleaning out Walter's place, he mentioned something about how Walter could have used that money in better ways."

"I heard him, too. He didn't sound happy," Meghan said.

Ambrose nodded, scribbling in his notebook.

Looking up, he said, "Did you say anything to either of them that would set them off somehow? Could one of them have left the coffee shop, gotten to the truck, and positioned it on your route home?"

"They said they hadn't heard about the fire. I gave them a copy of the paper so they could read about it."

"Yeah, I saw that. Nice picture."

I ignored him. "I can't think of a thing that would make them come after me. If they'd started the fire, I guess that could have been a sensitive point. And either of them would've had time to get the truck situated, since I was in the tearoom for at least ten minutes."

Ambrose shut his notebook. "I'll look into this, see if we can't pin down the owner of the truck. In the meantime you've got to stop poking into this on your own. I told you it could get dangerous—and today it did. I don't want something like that happening again. You might not be as quick on your feet next time."

Next time. That had an unpleasant ring to it.

"So can you tell us anything about your investigation?" Meghan said.

Ambrose looked pained.

"Of course he can't," I said. "We're suspects. At least I am."

"Is that true?" Meghan asked Ambrose. "You won't tell us what's going on even though we could be in danger because you think we killed Walter?"

He sighed. "It has nothing to do with you being suspects."

"So we are suspects," Meghan said.

"Not currently."

"Did you investigate us?" I asked.

"Enough to feel confident that neither of you had reason to be involved in the murder. Though I don't like how deeply involved you've become in the whole situation."

"I couldn't see any other choice," I said.

"You had a choice," Ambrose said. "You were just too…pig-headed to take it. And today you almost died because of it."

"Hey, that's not—"

"Tell him about the papers," Meghan interrupted.

"Papers?" he asked, giving me the evil eye.

"Oh, that's not important. I'm sure—"

"Tell him."

Meghan still had her back up from her encounter with Grace, and she wasn't too happy that someone had tried to kill me earlier. Fighting her now would be a lost cause.

"We took some papers from Walter's when we were cleaning out his house for his mother. We brought them over here. I thought I could get a handle on his financial situation from them. And I wanted to know why he committed suicide. Then later I thought there might be something that would help figure out who killed him."

He sighed. "Knowing full well you were withholding evidence from us."

"No! Well, not at first. Maybe later I sort of knew you'd want to see them. I planned to bring them to the station today."

His look said it all.

"I did! And you know, if I hadn't moved those three boxes of papers over here, they would have burned in the fire anyway."

"Three *boxes*? So why didn't you bring them to the PD today?"

"Well, for one, *someone tried to kill me this afternoon.*"

He looked a little sheepish until I went on in a much smaller voice. "And besides, they're gone now. When the thief took our jewelry yesterday, he took the boxes, too."

"Thief!" he said, his voice raising. "What goddamn thief?"

TWENTY-SIX

"Officer Danson hasn't had a chance to fill you in," Meghan said, a little too magnanimously in my opinion, and fleshed out the details of the burglary.

"Let me get this straight. You removed paperwork from a possible murder victim's house, which then burnt to the ground, but you didn't see fit to share it with the police. What were you thinking?"

"That you treated me like crap," I snapped. He looked bewildered. "Calling me down to your office, calling me a suspect. And besides," I finished lamely, "I knew you'd yell at me."

"Yell at you! *Yell* at you?" He took a deep breath. And another. With careful calm he said, "Is there anything else you've been doing on your own that I need to know about?"

"No."

He looked at Meghan. She smiled and shook her head. Darn those two, anyway. I'd had just about enough of their simpatico.

Ambrose drank some coffee, holding the mug in front of his face with both hands. I could almost hear him thinking. After several swallows, he put it down and said, "Did you find anything in the papers?"

"Walter took blood pressure medication. He went to the Evergreen State Fair this year. And he gave a ton of money away to children's charities."

He sighed. "Great."

We sat in silence for a few moments.

"Does anyone want more coffee?" I asked.

Ambrose ignored me. "Do you have someplace where you can go stay for a while?"

"Me? I can't leave. I have a business to run," I said.

He thought a moment. "You've pissed somebody off, and I don't know who. Or how. The department doesn't have enough manpower to assign someone to watch this house. I can ask the patrol cars to come by more often if you insist on staying, but that's all I can do."

"It'll have to be enough," I said.

"Are you staying, too?" Ambrose asked Meghan. She hesitated, then nodded.

"Well, it wouldn't hurt to move your daughter someplace else for a few days. If nothing else, it'll mess up any plans your ex-husband might have."

"We have friends she can stay with."

"Good. And I want you to call me immediately if anything happens. Immediately. These are my cell and home numbers if you can't reach me at work."

"Okay." I took the numbers. "Thanks. I'll get Deborah Silverman's phone number."

Meghan said good night to Ambrose and went upstairs, no doubt to talk to Erin about the scene with her father and grandmother. I gimped up behind her, fished the scrap of newspaper out of the slacks lying on my bedroom floor, and copied the number onto a fresh sheet of notebook paper. Then I made my geriatric way back down the stairs and handed it to him.

"See me out?" he asked, tucking it inside his notebook.

I followed him to the front door. He opened it and turned back to me. "I'll share whatever I can with you, just please stop asking questions. Will you do that?"

"I'll try."

He sighed. "You've already been hurt. Please, Sophie Mae. Be careful." Then he hesitated, opened his mouth, and then closed it again. He turned and walked outside without another word.

I found myself wanting to know what he had been going to say.

"Barr?"

He turned around, looking up at me from the front gate.

I wavered. "Never mind."

"You sure?" he asked.

"Yeah. It's nothing."

"Okay. I'll check in with you tomorrow."

I walked back inside, shutting the door firmly behind me.

I'd called him Barr without thinking. And he hadn't seemed to mind.

The kitchen was a mess. Lamenting the extra piece of corn bread I'd consumed out of cowardice, I carried dishes to the sink and put leftovers in the fridge. Once the dishwasher had started its wash cycle, I collapsed on the sofa to wait for Meghan.

Upstairs, she would be trying to explain to Erin how grown-ups could be assholes—though she'd use a term more suited for tender ears—and that Brodie was in no danger of being put to sleep. Then Meghan would have to turn around and tell her daughter to stay with her friend Zoe for a few days. How much would she say about why? How much would Erin figure out on her own? Considering her sometimes-disconcerting intelligence, probably more than Meghan wanted to divulge.

It would be just a few days, wouldn't it? Ambrose seemed smart and dedicated. He'd figure this out soon. I shook my head. Hope wouldn't make it so. Already I seemed to have discovered more than the police had. But with Ambrose playing his cards so tight to his chest, I couldn't be sure. Even though I knew it was childish, it didn't seem fair that I'd shared and he hadn't.

I got up from the sofa and began to check the windows. Most of them opened from the bottom, an old weighted-sash design. But in the kitchen, the basement, and the upstairs bathroom, Meghan had updated to modern double-paned windows with drop-in casings. These slid open to the side. All had sturdy locks, but adding doweling to prevent them from opening if the locks were broken would be fast and inexpensive. Not a lot we could do about someone breaking the glass, though.

I could…

…Oh God. My stomach flipped over as I realized that, just for a moment, I'd thought of asking Walter to secure the windows. I swallowed and continued checking the locks.

Okay, so I seemed to have gotten us into this pickle: possibly in danger (definitely, insisted a small voice), and having to live on the defensive as a result. I was thinking about how to make the house more secure. Erin couldn't live with Zoe's family—at least that's where I assumed Meghan would send her—forever. I couldn't just sit around while our lives closed in on us, afraid, jumping at every sound, counting on Ambrose. I'd started something, in ignorance of what I was getting into, and now I couldn't just call a time-out. Things had gone too far.

Problem was, even if I wanted to continue poking into Walter's death, I had no idea what—or who—to poke next.

Down in my workroom I checked the locks again, twisted the deadbolt to make sure it latched all the way. Feeling exposed, I turned off the lights and moved from window to window, standing back so I couldn't be seen. Light from the street filtered through toward the alley, pale and mottled by angled geometric shadows of house, fence, bushes, and…what was that one? The one moving back and forth? After a while, I traced it to a hanging bird feeder nudged by the wind.

Disgusted, I went back upstairs. For the first time since I'd lived with Meghan, I closed and locked the door that led from the kitchen to the basement steps. Not sure how much good it would do, given the wobbly, painted doorknob and delicate old-fashioned key. But it made me feel better to close off that part of the house, however ineffectively.

Brodie sat at the bottom of the stairs, looking up with a worried expression on his fox-like face. While I'd been in the basement Meghan had brought him down from Erin's bedroom, probably to take him outside, and neglected to carry him back up with her. His arthritis prevented him from bounding up the stairs the way he used to. I sat down and ran my fingers through his fur, smoothing the light strip that ruffled across his shoulders. Legend held that the fairies' saddles left this mark when they used corgis as steeds on their magical nocturnal wanderings.

"I don't want to disturb your girls," I whispered. "Or I'd carry you up myself."

Brodie sighed and slid his forepaws out a few inches. That was all it took for him to lie down. He laid his chin on his paws and looked up at me. Dogs must have a gene that tells them when to use that look to best advantage.

Standing up, I coaxed the little dog into the living room and lifted him up onto the sofa with me. Pulling the afghan from where it lay folded along the back, I rested my head on a throw pillow. Brodie snuggled up next to me, nestling the top of his head up under my arm. His warmth felt comfortable and solid. I closed my eyes, just for a moment.

I awoke with a start, and Brodie barked, a high, alarmed bark. Shushing him, I sat up, my heart pounding in my chest. Helping the dog to the floor, I strained to hear what had awoken me. I stood and moved quickly through the house, looking out the windows, checking the locks all over again. Brodie followed behind me, muttering but not barking again, his toenails clicking when we moved off the carpet. The only unusual thing was an unfamiliar white car parked across the street.

Other than that, nothing. Not a sound, not a movement.

In the kitchen the coffeemaker clock told me the time was two thirty-eight. And I became aware of how urgently I needed to go to the bathroom.

Great, Sophie Mae. Fall asleep on the couch, wake up because you've got to pee, and manage to scare both yourself and the dog in the process. No, living like this could not last long.

I used the downstairs bathroom, shut off all the lights, and hoisted Brodie. I walked with him to the front window and looked out at the white car again. Something shifted within the vehicle. Jerking back from the window, I hesitated, and then peeped around the curtain again. Was that a head, or just the headrest on top of the driver's seat? The steady rain softened the edges of everything, and I couldn't be sure. After staring at the motionless car for five minutes with Brodie clasped against my chest, I moved away, chiding myself for being an alarmist. With my bruised elbow throbbing from those twenty-five pounds of corgi comfort, I carried Brodie to the stairs guided by the orange glow of the streetlight outside.

The nightlight in Erin's room showed her burrowed under the covers. Meghan lay on top of the bedspread, curled around her daughter. I got a quilt from the closet, and she half awoke when I laid it over her. Mumbling her thanks, she went right back to sleep, obviously not as nervous as yours truly.

Meghan and Erin had each other. I took Brodie to bed with me.

TWENTY-SEVEN

At seven-thirty Wednesday morning I woke to find Brodie gone and the faint clatter of dishes drifting up the stairs. Reaching to throw off the covers, I gasped. Last night my hip and arm had hurt, but this morning I felt pummeled all over. As I slid one foot experimentally to the floor, dipping my toe into the day, so to speak, sharp pain ran up my side where I'd twisted away from the truck the day before.

With some effort I managed to sit up and take inventory. Besides the pulled muscle in my side, my elbow screamed when I rotated my arm. Not a something-is-ripped-or-broken sort of pain, but a loud protest of recent abuse. My hip sported a purple-black bruise extending from where low-rider jeans would sit to a third of the way down my thigh. No wonder I'd been limping the night before. These were the major causes of my discomfort, but my entire body seemed to want in on the act: every joint felt stiff; every bundle of muscle objected to flexing of any kind; behind my forehead the beginnings of a headache thudded in time to my pulse; and overnight my eyelids seemed to have turned to sandpaper.

Last night I had intended to apply arnica salve to my various painful parts, but between the stream of visitors and my falling asleep on the sofa, I'd forgotten. Now I regretted the oversight. Past experience with the little yellow flower's miraculous powers had made a believer out of me. Used topically (and only topically), it speeded the healing of bruises and muscle soreness to almost half the usual time. Ingested, it was toxic unless in a prepackaged homeopathic preparation.

I reached for my robe, then realized it still lay in an unwearable heap on the laundry room floor. Pulling on sweats was more work than I wanted, but I was cold so I didn't have much choice. After easing my softest and cushiest pair over my tender limbs, I splashed water on my face and doddered down to the kitchen, one step at a time. At least my fears from the night before seemed paltry in the daylight. I pasted a grin on my face and gimped in to breakfast.

Meghan stood in front of the sink, chewing on a piece of toast and staring out the window. She had rare blue circles under her eyes. Erin sat at the table, swinging her legs against the chair rung and reading. A bowl of cereal sat to one side of the book. Soggy flakes floated on the surface of the milk, and she hadn't touched her orange juice. I leaned over her shoulder to get a look at the book.

"Nancy Drew, huh? I used to read those."

Meghan snorted and rolled her eyes. I ignored her. Erin didn't look up. She said, "Huh," and kept right on reading. I poured some cereal and splashed milk on it. It tasted like sawdust. No wonder Erin hadn't eaten hers.

"What is this stuff?" I asked.

No one answered. I turned the box so I could see the front. Corn flakes. The way they tasted this morning I'd been sure Meghan was trying to slip some healthy super-fiber experiment by us.

The silence finally got to me. "Is anyone going to talk to me, or do I have to sit here and have a conversation with myself?" Not that I blamed them if they were mad at me.

"Well, Erin's not speaking to me right now, at least not if she can help it. I guess you've been included, as well."

"Mommmm!" Erin almost sounded like a teenager, the word was so angst-ridden.

"I'm sorry you have to stay at your friend's house for a while," I said.

"Oh, that's okay. I like it over there. We get to watch TV all we want, and Zoe has a Playstation, and her mom gives us donuts for snacks." She didn't look at her mom, but I could tell she was trying to push her mother's buttons.

"Oh. Well. That's good, then," I said.

Meghan gave me a wry look. "Go load your backpack, and I'll take you to school," she told Erin.

Sighing dramatically, Erin slid off the chair and walked toward the stairs, still reading her book.

"Why's she mad at you?" I asked.

"She's not, really. She's mad at her father and her grandmother, but they aren't around. I'm handy. Plus, I'm safe. She can be angry with me and know I'll still love her just the same."

"Lucky kid."

"Yeah. Unless I kill her."

I laughed.

"Will you be here when I get back?" Meghan asked.

I nodded.

"I've canceled all my appointments for today. Starting tomorrow I'm treating everyone in-home for a while—the atmosphere here is off, and I need my mindset to be right in order to give my clients the relaxation they pay me for. Tonight I've got an infant massage class over at the clinic."

"Okay. I'll be here when you get back from the school."

"I might be a while. I have to talk with them about Richard. And Grace. Besides the fact that I don't know what they're up to, maybe it'll put them on high alert regarding Erin's safety in general." Stress leaked through the seams of Meghan's usual aplomb.

"That's fine," I said. "But I think Ambrose's overreacting a bit. What happened to me yesterday was just someone taking advantage of an opportunity."

"Yeah, well, we don't know what kind of 'opportunity' they could decide to take advantage of next time."

"I'm ready," Erin said from the doorway.

"Let's get going, then." Meghan picked up Erin's duffel from the hallway. "I'll drop this at Zoe's on my way back so you'll have it when you go over there after school." She looked at me. "Sorry, that's going to make me even later."

"That's okay. Stop worrying."

She shot me a glance that said to shut up, she'd worry if she wanted to.

"Bye, Bug," I called. The door shut on Erin's farewell.

I dumped my cereal down the sink and heated a bowl of chili from the night before in the microwave. Adding cheese and onions, I took it to my workroom, holding the hot bowl with a dish towel and working my way down the stairs. My body seemed to be loosening up the more I moved around. Maybe I should go run around the block.

Maybe not.

While I slurped chili I checked my website. Two more orders since yesterday morning. I processed the buyers' credit cards, then typed up packing lists and printed them out, taped together two more shipping boxes, and gathered the merchandise to fill the new orders. Now twenty boxes marched down the counter in a neat row, waiting to be packed and weighed before I logged onto the UPS website to complete the labels and prepay shipping. Then to the UPS drop-off counter and they'd be on their way.

This process was simple but not fast. The last week had been anything but run of the mill, and I'd lost a lot of work time. Winding Road bookwork had piled up, my inbox overflowed with unanswered e-mail, the Christmas bazaars loomed, and I hadn't even begun to put together updated product pamphlets. The undone tasks, myriad and insistent, buzzed at the edge of my attention as I packed and invoiced and printed and labeled.

But Walter remained foremost in my mind. Why had someone been creeping around in Walter's house the night Officer Owens discovered me there? If they'd been looking for something, had they found it? If they had, why would they set the fire? For that matter, if they hadn't, why would they set the fire? Was the murderer the same person who burned down Walter's house, or could we be dealing with two nutcases?

That thought accelerated the pounding in my head, which in turn reminded me to find the arnica. I shut down the computer and went into my storeroom. One shelf is devoted to products I custom-make for Meghan to use in her massage therapy or that we use for ourselves.

I made the arnica salve by infusing olive oil with dried arnica flowers, either by heating it gently or by letting it sit in a jar in the dark for a month or so. Then I mixed the infused oil with melted beeswax to create a cream. Since shelf life at home wasn't much of an issue (and neither was liability), I didn't even bother with adding antibacterial preservatives like grapefruit seed extract or Vitamin E.

Of course, the one morning I needed a boatload of the stuff, the tiny tin was almost empty. Rooting through an assortment of jars and bottles, I located the Mason jar full of olive oil and arnica flowers. That would do. Skip the beeswax step and just smear on the infused oil. But when I opened the jar and sniffed, I decided a little lavender oil would mask the dusty cooking-oil smell of the contents, as well as add additional healing properties. I strained and mixed until I had a bottle of concentrated arnica oil from which the gentle scent of Lavandula angustifolia wafted.

On my way through the kitchen I put my bowl in the dishwasher and grabbed a Diet Coke out of the fridge. All my healthy eating was going to hell in a handbasket, but that was the least of my worries. I took a shower, hot then cold, and slathered on the arnica oil. I dressed in faded cotton hiking pants and a long-sleeved T-shirt, threw on a faded flannel shirt over the top like a jacket. After struggling with my braid for a brief time, my elbow finally won, and I gave up. The phone rang as I finished wrapping a hair band around my ponytail, and I picked up the receiver in the upstairs hallway.

"Hello?"

"Sophie Mae?"

"Yes?"

"Barr Ambrose here. I hope I didn't wake you up."

"Jeez, how long do you think I sleep in?"

"You looked pretty worn out last night."

"I feel better this morning. What's up?" I asked.

"Can you come down to the station?"

"Oh, God. Now what?"

"I need you to file a formal report regarding the truck incident yesterday, and then I want you to show me where it happened."

"Um, okay. Is this afternoon okay?"

"No sooner?"

"I'll try, I really will. It's just that my morning is pretty booked. Unless this is another 'come down here or I'll send a patrolman' thing."

"No. I just want to get moving on this."

So did I. "How long do you think it will take?"

"Hour or so."

"Tell you what. I'll come over right now, so I won't be holding you up." I'd make it back before Meghan came home. Probably.

"Really?" He sounded surprised. "Well, that'd be great. See you in a little bit."

As I cradled the phone, I mentally kissed my morning good bye. Between going over to the police station and following up with Meghan about what Ambrose had told us the previous evening, the orders I'd been hoping to ship would have to wait. Maybe I could do it all this afternoon.

TWENTY-EIGHT

ON THE WAY TO the police station I thought about why someone would try to kill me. I'd done a pretty good job of avoiding the question since yesterday. Now I took it out, dusted it off, and gnawed on it a while.

I didn't know squat about who killed Walter, had no hard evidence of any kind about anything. Instead, I possessed an abundance of useless speculation and what ifs. Was I getting close? I couldn't imagine how. Were they afraid I would get close? Well, in that case whoever had tried to run me down the previous afternoon had far more confidence in my investigative abilities than anyone else did, including me.

Someone thought I knew something I didn't.

My next thought threw a chill down my spine, despite the warmth from the truck heater. If they assumed I knew something, they also would assume Meghan knew. Ambrose was right. We were both in danger. And though Erin wouldn't be expected to know anything pertinent, if the person behind all this became desperate enough, they might not balk at using her as leverage.

Oh, for heaven's sake. This was getting ridiculous. We weren't living in some movie of the week. Get a grip on your imagination, Sophie Mae. It was even possible the driver of that truck simply hadn't seen me, that my near miss hadn't been anything personal. But the rationalization felt meager and unsubstantial to the part of me that knew better.

It wasn't until my tires screeched pulling into the police station parking lot that I realized how fast I'd been going. Urgency gripped me like a fist, propelling me through the building to Ambrose's desk. I must have looked like I knew what I was doing since no one stopped me, but that was a joke, now, wasn't it? Because I had no idea.

I pulled up short when I saw that Officer Danson, wearing navy slacks and a pressed oxford shirt, sat talking with Ambrose. Today the detective's string tie was a deep green disc of malachite, with a thin silver ring around it. It glowed against his ivory cotton shirt, worn with tan slacks and the requisite cowboy boots.

They both looked up, and Danson turned in her chair to send a disapproving scowl in my direction. I'd guess she came in before her regular shift to talk with Ambrose about our burglary, only for him to take her to task for not telling him sooner.

"Give me a minute, Sophie Mae?" Ambrose asked, and I nodded, backing out into the reception area.

He hadn't looked angry; he'd looked exhausted.

Green molded-plastic chairs sat in a row along the front window, but in deference to my hip, I chose to lean against the wall. A young woman with a cadet patch on her uniform instead of a badge walked by and raised her eyebrows in question. I answered with a smile I hoped exuded confidence. She walked on, her curiosity somehow assuaged.

After a few moments Danson came around the corner, directed a curt nod my way, and shouldered past me to the door. I walked to Ambrose's desk and sat down in the chair she'd vacated.

"I hope she's not in trouble."

"Why do you say that?" he asked.

"About the break-in, not telling you. I'm sure it was just a miscommunication."

"It was, and I'm partly to blame. But I don't have time to review every call in case it happens to impact one of my cases. Everyone's busy, of course."

"Isn't our burglary one of your cases?"

"Technically, but there's only one of me, so unless there's a problem we let patrol follow up on things like that. Don't worry, I'll be keeping an eye on it, now that I know. My sergeant may have had something to do with keeping it quiet, too. He's very political, and wants me working on this other thing."

"The toilet paper bandit?"

He looked surprised, then chagrined. "But I talked with him this morning and, given the fire and the attack on you, he's willing to pursue Hanover's death as suspicious."

"That's big of him." I tried to smile, but he saw something in my face.

"What's wrong? Did something happen?"

I shook my head. "Nothing new. But I've really screwed up, haven't I?"

Ambrose leaned back in his chair. "Well, maybe there was something in one or more of those boxes you took, and now someone sees you as a loose end."

"So now what do I do? Take out an ad in the *Eye* saying I didn't find a thing in the boxes, and would whoever took them please not try to kill me anymore?"

Ambrose smiled. "I doubt they'd believe you. You're not always truthful."

"I was kidding."

"So was I." But he wasn't, not entirely.

And he was right. I hated it, but he was right. If I'd turned the papers over to him immediately, I might not be in this trouble now. I'd been looking for something recognizably important, a will or insurance policy or threatening letter, but I could have easily missed something subtle, something even more important.

"Did your housemate make arrangements for her daughter to stay someplace else?" Ambrose asked.

I nodded. "She'll be at her friend's. And Meghan is talking to the school about Dick, so they'll be keeping a careful eye on her."

"Good. Now, I need you to write down what happened with the truck yesterday."

He got up and went to a filing cabinet, opened a drawer, and flipped through file tabs until he found the one he wanted. He drew out a form and placed it in front of me on the corner of his workstation. Then he took a pen out of his drawer and pushed it across to me.

"How much detail do you want?" I asked.

"Everything you can remember, everything you told me last night. When you're done we'll go down to Avenue A, and you can show me what happened."

I started printing my name and address. "Are you going to talk to the kid, Don whatshisname?"

"I already did, first thing this morning. He didn't see much. Debby and Jacob Silverman are next on my list."

I looked up. "Jacob's last name is Silverman, too?"

"He's Debby's brother."

My jaw dropped.

After a few moments, I managed to close my mouth. Grimaced. "Well, crap."

He grinned. "Kind of screws up your idea of Jacob as Walter's romantic rival, doesn't it?"

"Yeah. Sure does."

"Almost done there?"

I looked down at the form. "I've barely started."

"I have some things to do out front. Leave it on the desk when you're finished and come find me." He went around the corner.

It didn't take long once I stopped yapping. Placing it neatly in the center of his spotless desk area, I opened the top drawer.

And, of course, Ambrose returned as I was replacing his pen. I froze like a bunny caught in the headlights.

"Finished?" he asked, his face expressionless.

"I wasn't, I mean, I just wanted to put your pen away. I swear…"

"Well, let's go then."

I sneaked a look in his eyes as I passed, but he didn't look upset. He didn't look anything at all. I hate it when other people have great poker faces, especially because I have more of a hey-look-what-I'm-feeling-now face. And I was pretty sure it had guilt blazoned all over it right then.

And I'm not even Catholic.

TWENTY-NINE

OUT IN THE PARKING lot, Ambrose led me toward a silver-colored sedan that turned out to be a Chevy Impala. He opened the passenger door for me before going to the driver's side.

Inside, the car had a police radio, a holster on the dash holding a radar gun, and a switch for the lights I assumed were set into the grill. I was riding in an unmarked police cruiser, the bane of motorists everywhere.

I wondered what kind of car Barr Ambrose drove when he wasn't being a detective. A big SUV? I had trouble picturing it. A compact? Nah. A pickup, maybe, or a Jeep. Something functional and without a lot of frippery.

He paused while buckling his seat belt, sniffed a couple times, and said, "What's that scent?"

Oh, no. My nose had become inured to the lavender already, and I couldn't tell how much I reeked. "Sorry," I said, embarrassed. "It's the stuff I used on my bruises this morning."

"Wow," he said. "I thought it was perfume."

"You can open a window if you want."

He shrugged. "It's nice." And he cracked the window an inch.

As we pulled out of the parking lot I said, "Can I ask you something?"

"Like what," he said.

"Where are you from?"

"Came up here from Seattle last year."

"Before that."

"Grew up in Wyoming. My family owns a dude ranch there."

I nodded. I'd been close.

"I suppose the ties give me away," he said. "I hate to wear regular ties and the chief lets me get away with the bolos. My uncle used to collect them, left me a whole pile of them when he died. Figure I might as well get the use out of them." He stopped talking abruptly, as if he'd said too much.

We approached an intersection and a little red pickup, lowered to within an inch of the pavement, flew by on the cross street in front of us. I didn't need the radar gun to tell me it was going way too fast.

Ambrose frowned and said, "Idiot."

At the stop sign we turned toward downtown.

"And your accent struck my ear as familiar," I said.

"I don't have an accent!"

"Not really an accent. More like your diction."

"You from around there, too?"

"Around there. Northern Colorado."

The ensuing silence could have felt awkward, but didn't. Then Ambrose spoke again. "The state lab determined the lye we found

217

on your floor was a commercial brand that contains ingredients besides sodium hydroxide."

"Drain cleaner," I said.

He nodded.

"How long have you known?"

"Couple days."

"Would have been nice if you'd told me. You know, put my mind at rest."

He glanced over at me. "Sorry. You were so sure it wasn't yours I didn't think it'd be big news to you."

"Yeah. Well."

"Anyway, the drain cleaner wasn't mixed with water. Or at least, not only with water."

"One of those that comes as a liquid? Or gel?"

"It's sold in powder form. It was mixed with ethyl alcohol, sugar—looks like some kind of liquor."

"Peppermint," I breathed.

"What?"

"Peppermint schnapps. That's what we smelled in my work-room. And at Walter's that night…" I squeezed my eyes shut, re-membering. "That wasn't a glass that broke in Walter's kitchen. It was a bottle." How did I know that? "The label! There was paper mixed in with the glass."

"You get a good look at it?"

I shook my head. "No. Officer Owens hustled me out before I could. And then the next day, it was gone."

"What do you mean, 'it was gone'?"

"Someone had cleaned it up by the time Meghan and I went in to pack up Walter's things."

"You never told me that."

I held up my palms. "It just didn't seem important."

"So you didn't see what kind of bottle it was?"

I closed my eyes again. "Clear glass. The paper was black, maybe with a little red? But listen, um, Barr. Can I call you Barr?"

He smiled. "Sure."

"Walter was an alcoholic."

The smile slid off his face, to be replaced by puzzlement. "Well, the booze isn't a surprise, then. I don't know what his blood alcohol was—I'll have to check with the medical examiner's office. Maybe the guy did commit suicide."

"No, you don't understand. Walter was a recovering alcoholic, had been for years. He didn't drink alcohol—including peppermint schnapps—at all."

Ambrose pulled into an angled parking space on Avenue A and turned off the engine. I could hear his breathing.

"So. Where were you when that truck came at you?"

"Over there." I pointed.

We got out, and I led him to where I'd started to cross the street the day before. I described it all over again, demonstrating my position and how I fell.

"You said you heard a screech. From that direction?" He pointed up the hill. I nodded.

"Let's walk up that way," he said.

We stopped at the entrance to the alley that ran through the middle of the block. It wasn't paved. Ambrose stooped and looked at twin indentations in the gravel, ruts that by the spacing and width of them had been caused by tires, if I didn't miss my guess. His gaze moved to the pavement on the street as he stood up.

"They pulled out here, too fast and probably spraying gravel. Once they'd turned onto the street they punched it—see where they left those two short strips of rubber there in the middle of the street?"

"Are you sure? Wouldn't they be darker? And longer?"

"The rain reduced the friction. Made the pavement slicker. Probably slowed the vehicle down. If the street had been dry you might not have had a chance to get out of the way in time."

Though I'd already thought of that, I couldn't help arguing. "You really are a pessimist. If it hadn't been raining I wouldn't have had my hood up and my head down. I'd have seen the truck coming from the corner of my eye."

Ambrose narrowed his eyes. "Someone is having a whole lot of luck."

I bristled. "You mean me?"

He flicked a look at me and started back toward the car. "I mean whoever's behind all this. You, Sophie Mae, seem to have just enough luck to keep you alive."

THIRTY

MEGHAN SAT ON THE front step scooping the guts out of a pumpkin with a big metal spoon. Orange slime and shiny seeds made a pile on the newspaper she'd spread on the sidewalk in front of her. I stopped on the other side of the newspaper, already apologizing.

"I know I said I'd be here when you got back, but Ambrose called and wanted me to formalize my statement about yesterday, and then he wanted me to show him where it happened, and—"

A huge spoonful of pumpkin gunk landed on the paper in front of me, narrowly missing my foot.

I picked my way around the slime-ridden newspaper and sat down beside her. "I'm sorry."

The spoon made a hollow sound against the pumpkin flesh as Meghan removed the last of the fibrous pulp. She got up and went inside. I didn't know what to do; she'd never acted like this before.

She came back with a roll of paper towels and a bowl, sat down beside me again. Leaning forward, her fingers picked through the goo, extracting pumpkin seeds and dropping them into the bowl.

She turned to me. "Well, aren't you going to help?"

"Uh, let me go wash my hands."

I came back and dug into the orange muck, squirting the slippery seeds into the bowl. We'd soak them in brine and roast them in the oven.

"So, am I forgiven?"

"Don't you dare pull something like that again. Not while this is going on. I thought something had happened to you."

I felt mothered. I didn't like it.

But it wasn't her fault. "Okay," I said. "Point taken."

Then I filled her in on what Ambrose had told me about the lye. "I'm a little surprised that he told me. And last night he seemed…" I searched for a word. "…quite human." It fell short of what I meant, but I considered it a compliment.

Meghan looked at me sideways. "You're such a dope."

"What?"

"You. Are a dope. Otherwise you'd have picked up on the fact that Detective Ambrose likes you."

"Likes me? You mean, in the junior-high sense?"

"Yes. Detective Ambrose is attracted to you. Interested. Wants to get in your pants."

I stopped pawing through the pumpkin guts, stunned. "How can you tell?"

She shook her head, smiling. "How can you not? You've messed around in his investigation, been stubborn and combative, in short given him little but grief, and he's still solicitous and understanding and concerned about your safety. But, honey, that's nothing compared to the vibe between you two."

"Vibe? Really?"

She lifted her eyebrows a fraction. "You tell me."

I went back to sifting through pumpkin innards. Okay, the thought of Ambrose being interested pleased me. And maybe something about him drew my attention in an adolescent, stomach-fluttering way I'd tried to ignore. Because, I told myself, it didn't matter. Present circumstances didn't bode well for any kind of relationship between us.

On the other hand, loneliness had been a part of my life for so long it had become comfortable. Living with Meghan and Erin diffused the weight of it; we were a kind of family. But I missed the kind of intimacy I'd had with Mike. I missed the male perspective. I missed sex. I'd had a string of dates here and there, but nothing with teeth. And I got the idea any involvement with Barr Ambrose would have teeth.

Scary.

But maybe good scary.

I pushed the thought away. Never mind. Let Meghan play matchmaker. I didn't have to buy into her sentimental notions, vibe or no vibe. So there.

I swished my fingers through the accumulation of slick seeds in the bowl. "We need to find out more about Walter's money situation."

Meghan gave me a look, but let me get away with changing the subject. "I checked with the lottery commission. Three years ago Walter won $1.3 million dollars. He took it in one lump sum, though, which knocked it down considerably. Maybe Detective Ambrose can tell us if it's all gone, or if Walter had enough left to provide a motive for murder."

"I meant to ask him about that. He did say he's going to talk with Debby and Jacob this afternoon. Oh, and that reminds me. Debby and Jacob are brother and sister."

"Really? Yeah, I guess that makes sense. He seems protective of her."

"I'll say. To the point of being creepy. You think they could be, you know…?"

"Sophie Mae! That's gross."

Maybe so, but those two had something beyond the usual brother-sister stuff.

Meghan stood up. "Listen, I need to go get some props for Erin's Halloween costume. I hope this all blows over by then. It's her second favorite holiday." Christmas being number one, of course.

Costumes made me think of Tootie in the photo with the guy in the bunny suit. "Oh, no. I forgot to take the photos and stuff from Walter's over to Tootie."

She stared at me. "The fourth box, the one the thief missed. We never told Detective Ambrose about it!"

"It's just some old photos, a few other mementos."

"Sophie Mae, what if there's something there that's important?"

"Like what?"

"Like I don't know. Just call him, okay?"

"Sure. I'll do it now." I stood up to go inside, then stopped. "Meghan?"

Holding her pumpkin-slick hands out in front of her, she looked up. "What?"

"Do you think we should get a gun?"

Her face hardened. "Are you out of your mind?"

"Well…I just thought—"

"I will not have one in this house. You know how I feel about them. A gun's not going to solve our problems; it'd just give us a false sense of security."

I did know how she felt about guns. She hated them.

"Okay. It was only a thought."

Disgust on her face, she leaned forward to gather up the corners of the newspaper, bundling the pumpkin guts inside. I went upstairs to the spare room and dragged the box of photos from under the window and into the open space just inside the door. Opening the flaps again, I removed each item and set it on the floor, trying to consider each one as a clue. Everything seemed so innocuous.

The one thing that caught my eye was the photo of Walter with his parents, two brothers, and the woman I'd first assumed was his sister. But Tootie had mentioned only her sons: one dead from cancer, one dead in an accident, and now one dead from drinking drain cleaner. And Mrs. Gray had only talked about Walter's brothers. There was no sister. Now I looked closer at the picture. Two of the brothers stood with their arm around the girl, Walter's around her waist and the other man's encircling her shoulders. I turned the picture over and slid down the felt-backed piece of cardboard. No notations on the reverse of the picture to indicate who the subjects were or when it had been taken. Sliding the cardboard back in place, I turned the frame over again.

I was willing to bet the girl was Cherry, who'd married Walter and then abandoned him. Who wrecked his youth and stained his self-confidence for years.

The photographer had fit everyone completely into the frame of the black-and-white picture, head to toe, so the faces didn't hold a lot of fine detail. Still, I recognized Walter. The gray hair was dark, may have even been black then. The jowls that had developed later in life were missing, and brilliant laughter shone from his face. I'd never seen him look this happy when I knew him. I held the photo closer. Something about that young handsome face looked familiar, and not just because I knew the face when it was older and sadder. The angles and planes of the bones under his skin. I looked at the brother on the other side of Cherry, the one whose arm rested across her shoulders. That had to be Willy, the one she'd fooled around with while Walter studied at the University of Washington during the week. Not surprisingly, he had the same chin, the same brow I found so familiar in Walter's image. So did the third brother, though he looked thinner than the other two, almost gaunt.

I put the picture back into the box, along with the sparse collection of mementos we'd inadvertently rescued from Walter's little house. His face hovered at the edge of my thoughts, a constant image nibbling for attention. Something about the similarity he shared with his brothers.

Downstairs, I called Ambrose. He wasn't in, so I tried the number he'd given us for his cell phone. He answered on the second ring.

"Hello?"

"Hi. It's Sophie Mae."

"What happened?" Urgency rode through his voice.

"Nothing happened. I just forgot to tell you something, and thought I should. I mean, it's probably not important, in fact I can't imagine that it is, but Meghan said I should call, and—"

Ambrose let out a sigh.

"Are you busy? I can call back later…or you could call me back. I mean—"

"No, that's okay. I thought something was wrong. What did you want to tell me?"

"Oh. Well, there was another box we took from Walter's, and it wasn't stolen. I'd tucked it away from the other three, and I don't think the thief realized it was one of the boxes we'd packed up while we were over there."

"And you forgot to tell me about it?" He sounded incredulous.

"I did. I just flat-out forgot. So did Meghan. It doesn't have any paperwork in it. In fact, it doesn't contain anything other than pictures and a few other things that I thought his mother might want. That's why I packed it up in the first place, to take it over to Tootie. I thought I'd take it this afternoon."

On the other end of the phone Ambrose considered this. "I'll be back in my office after two, no, better make that two-thirty this afternoon. Can you bring it by?"

I sighed, thinking of everything I had to do. "Yeah. I'll drop by after two-thirty."

"All right. Bye."

And he hung up. I stood with the phone in my hand, wondering if he'd been so abrupt because he was mad at me again. It bothered me, how much I didn't want him to be mad at me.

"What did he say?" Meghan asked from the kitchen.

"He wants to see the stuff before I take it over to Tootie. Hey, come take another look at these pictures and tell me what you think." I went over and started laying the pictures out on the hardwood floor at the bottom of the stairs.

Meghan perched on a step beside me, her gaze flicking from picture to picture. She picked up the one of Walter's parents with the three boys and the girl I'd been looking at earlier. "Is that Cherry? The one Mrs. Gray told you about?"

I nodded. "I think so. Somebody there reminded me of someone I've seen recently, but I can't figure out who."

"Which picture?"

"Just look. I don't want to influence what you see."

"Well, Cherry looks familiar to me, but I'm not sure why. Is that who you mean?"

"No." I picked up the picture and squinted at it. The harder I looked the less clear the features became. "I probably want to find a clue so badly I'm making one up," I said.

Meghan gave me an understanding smile and began stacking the pictures. I remembered Walter's baby photo upstairs on my dresser.

"I'll be right back," I said and went up to retrieve it.

Meghan leaned over the open box, returning the last of the photos. I handed her Walter's baby picture to add.

Looking at my watch, I said, "If I hustle…" but trailed off at the sight of Meghan's face as she stood up. She'd gone pale. She stared at Walter's picture with a combination of fascination and dread.

"What's wrong?" I asked, moving to her side.

"Where did you get this?" Her voice shook.

"It's just a baby picture of Walter. It was on that shelving unit with the rest of them. Meghan, what's *wrong*?"

She looked up at me, biting her lower lip. "This isn't Walter. This is Richard."

THIRTY-ONE

"Richard?"

She nodded.

"Not Walter?"

She shook her head.

"What are you talking about?"

"Richard has a copy in an old photo album. His mother had it taken when he was a baby. He loves this picture."

Looking at the gorgeous baby, I could understand how it would support Richard's ego. "Why would Walter have a baby picture of Richard? Where would he get…?"

We stared at each other, minds racing. "No…that's crazy," I said.

But Meghan was already rummaging through the box, extracting the picture of Cherry.

"That's why she looks familiar," she said, holding the photograph close to her face.

"You think that's…?"

She nodded. "Richard's mother. Grace Thorson and Cherry Hanover are the same woman."

I leaned over, peering at the woman's face in the picture. "I don't know. It could be her. But it's so hard to tell. We need a more recent picture."

"Of Cherry? Or of Grace?"

"Either one. Both. You don't happen to have any pictures of Grace, do you?"

She shook her head. "I wonder if Tootie would have any of Cherry. Even if they were old, they might be clearer."

Walter's smiling face gazed back at me from the picture. It still looked familiar, and now I could see why. "Richard has Walter's cheekbones," I said.

Meghan said, "And the chin. The same as Walter, and the same as Willy, assuming this is Willy." She pointed to the man with his arm around Cherry's shoulders.

I sat down on the stairs. Meghan sat beside me, still holding the picture. I heard her swallow once. And then again.

"You okay?" I asked.

"No." She swallowed again. Inhaled deeply and blew out her breath through pursed lips.

"Well, this puts a different light on things," I said.

"Yeah." She did the breathing thing again.

"But we have to be absolutely sure."

"Yeah. Are you?"

Reluctantly, I shook my head. "Not absolutely."

"I guess we tell Detective Ambrose," she said. "Does he know about Cherry and Willy, that whole story?"

"Not from me. It was ancient history." A thought struck me, and I turned to face Meghan. "Mrs. Gray! She could tell us if Grace is Cherry. She knew her way back when."

"But she's never seen Grace."

"Detective Ambrose can pick up Grace and then have Mrs. Gray come in and make an identification. But we'd better not be wrong. Remember how Richard and his mother reacted last time they saw Ambrose?"

"Oh, God. You're right. And Grace is a particularly nasty hornets' nest to stir up," Meghan said. Then she narrowed her eyes. "On the other hand…having Ambrose pick Grace up and take her to the station might get her to back off. I'd have to put up with some crap from Richard for a while, but it'd be worth it if Grace left Erin alone as a result. I know the woman's her grandmother, but no way will I let her be alone with my daughter."

"Do you think she killed Walter?"

Meghan closed her eyes, grimacing at the thought even though it had been hovering in the back of both our minds. "I don't know. But don't you think it'd be a heck of a coincidence if she wasn't involved somehow?"

I agreed. "So, we need to tell Ambrose the story about Cherry and Walter and Willy, and about our suspicions about the picture. If he wants to haul Grace into the police station, fine. If not, we can figure out something so Mrs. Gray can get a look at Grace in the flesh. And we should show her this picture, make sure it's really Cherry."

"Tootie could tell us that, I bet," Meghan said.

"You're right. Let's see what Barr has to say about this, first."

"Okay." She looked at her watch.

"Is Richard involved?" I asked.

"Richard? Involved in murder? Can you see that?" She laughed, a slightly hysterical sound edging toward tears.

"I suppose not. Petty stuff, but not murder. On the other hand, it's easy to believe Grace capable of five murders before breakfast, just to whet her appetite."

I called Barr Ambrose's cell phone again.

"Sophie Mae?"

I'll never get used to caller ID. "Meghan and I discovered something that may help solve Walter's murder."

"I'm in the middle of something right now. If it's not an emergency, meet me at the PD at two and fill me in."

I looked at my watch. It was just past noon. "Okay," I said. "See you then."

Meghan was unhappy with the delay, but I hurried down to my workroom, determined to plow through a big chunk of my to-do list before I had to leave. I sped through four hours of work in under two, plowing through bookwork and answering email, and then running out to move my truck around to the alley. Loading orders onto the two-wheel hand truck and then into the camper-shell-covered bed of the Toyota made my abused muscles ache at first, but after a while my body shed some of its stiffness. Still, my elbow throbbed when I'd finished shuttling the boxes, and my jeans, though my comfiest pair, creased painfully against the massive bruise on my hip when I slid behind the wheel.

And the puzzle of how the long-gone Cherry fit into Walter's death fermented in the back of my mind. The first question was, of course, did Grace's sudden presence in Cadyville have anything at all to do with Walter's death? At this point there was no way to know, but as Meghan pointed out, it was an unbelievable coincidence if the two events weren't connected. I was willing to assume they were. Given that, why would Grace have wanted to kill Walter? Not that I didn't think she had it in her; the woman was a viper. If Walter had stood between her and something she wanted, she'd eliminate him with no compunction.

So how would Grace Thorson/Cherry Hanover have managed to get Walter to drink the lye? Had she been trying to make it look like a suicide? And why would she have done it in my workroom?

A horn honked on the edge of my awareness, then louder. I'd slowed to a crawl. Accelerating, I returned to thinking.

Was Meghan right about Richard not being involved? Did he even know Walter was his father? For that matter, was Walter his father, or was Willy? I hoped he didn't have anything to do with Walter's death, for Erin's sake, but if the motive were the lottery money, Dick would have his fingers in the pot somehow. His relationship to money was like some kind of congenital defect.

I pulled into the parking lot of an L-shaped strip mall and shut off the engine. Walter had doted on Erin. Had he known she was his granddaughter? And if he did, would he have left her his lottery winnings? I swore under my breath. If only we'd found a will, we'd know. But Grace might have thought so, and that would explain both Meghan's intuition about protecting Erin from her grandmother and Grace's odd, ungrandmotherly behavior.

The more I thought about it, the less I trusted Dick to be any kind of safety barrier between his piranha of a mother and his daughter. I hoped we wouldn't have to ask them to the house in order to identify Grace, but it might come down to that if Ambrose didn't think what we had discovered merited official action.

As excited as I was about finding a significant clue, a real wowser that might be able to solve the mystery of Walter's death, I had, in the course of the last week, at least learned to tread a bit more carefully and not assume too much. Jacob and Debby had turned out to be brother and sister, not the erstwhile lovers I'd posited. For all we knew, Cherry, or Grace, could have a sister or a doppelganger.

I unloaded the boxes at the UPS drop-off counter and sped home. Before I left again I had time to call Kyla at home. She'd just come in the door and sounded breathless on the phone. I told her I was caught up for the moment and asked her if I could commission a painting. Though she insisted she only dabbled, the girl had talent, and had done murals for two of our friends. I wanted a big acrylic painting to hang over or behind the Winding Road booth. She agreed with alacrity, full of ideas for what to paint. I said as long as it had the logo and conveyed the kinds of products we made she had free reign.

"Don't worry, Sophie Mae. I know just what we need."

Her adolescent surety amused me. But I knew she'd do a good job.

"By the way, Kyla. Did you happen to mention where we keep the spare house key to anyone?"

"The house key? Oh, you mean the one under the rock? No." The last word came out sounding defensive. I couldn't blame her.

"Okay, just wanted to check. I'll let you know when we figure out a new place to keep it. Until then I'll make sure someone is always here to let you in." Meghan had told me she'd briefly explained why the key wasn't under the rock by the side of the house anymore.

"Okay. Um, Cyan was wondering if maybe she could help with the bazaars."

"Yes, and double yes. They'll be long, and you'll need someone to spell you. We can talk later about specifics."

Technically the booths don't have to be manned all the time at most holiday bazaars. But I'd sell twice as much if someone were there to chat with the customers, answer questions, and keep the display in top shape all the time.

The phone rang seconds after I finished talking with Kyla: Meghan calling from the clinic where she was setting up for her infants massage class that evening.

"I'm running late for the meeting with the detective," she said.

"I'll wait for you."

"No, go on over. I'll meet you there."

"Will you be long?" I asked, reaching for my wallet.

"No—I'll be finished here in ten minutes or so."

"See you at the station."

THIRTY-TWO

I HAULED WALTER'S MEMENTOS out to my truck and buzzed over to the police department. Inside, I maneuvered the awkward box back to Ambrose's pristine desk. "There it is, for what it's worth."

He opened the cardboard flaps and peered inside. Took out the chicken bank and shook it, removed the rubber stopper and peered inside. Pried open the locket and showed it to me: nothing. Flipped through the book on baseball collectibles, the Bible, the field guide.

"I already looked to see if something was hidden in those," I said, lifting out the photos and stacking them on his desk.

He grinned. "I bet you did." He put the box on the floor and spread the pictures out on the desk. "So this is all you thought his mother might want."

I nodded. "Kind of sad, isn't it?"

"It is. Kind of…pathetic."

"No. Please don't say that. Walter wasn't pathetic. He did the best he could with what he had."

Ambrose looked up from the images on the desk. "Sorry." Like I had with the picture of Walter and Cherry and his brothers, he slid the backs out of the other photos, then removed the photos themselves, looking at all the surfaces. "Sit down. I found out something you should know." His voice was low.

I sat. Looked around. The other desks were empty, except for a cadet doing paperwork across the room. Didn't any of the other officers ever need to fill out paperwork?

"What did you find out?" I asked. Had he found the truck that almost ran me down?

"First off, I flat-out shouldn't be telling you, but knowing may increase your safety, so I'm telling you anyway. Deborah Silverman has a history of mental instability. She's been in and out of treatment, and her last stint in an institution ended about two years ago."

"My God. She's sort of out there, but I wouldn't call her loony. What kind of mental instability?"

"She's manic-depressive. With at least two violent episodes. She has a criminal record for assault."

I wrinkled my forehead. "I didn't know manic-depressives were dangerous. Except to themselves."

Ambrose said, "I don't know if her mental illness had anything to do with the assault charge, to be truthful. But she has a mental condition that requires medication, a record for assault, and a fiancé who died violently. I don't care for the combination."

Neither did I.

"Okay, thanks. I'll keep it to myself."

"Go ahead and tell Meghan," he said.

"Okay. You said you had Walter's bank records. Did he have any of that lottery money left?"

"Not much. A little over thirty thousand."

"Sheesh. He really went through it, didn't he? But thirty thousand dollars would be a lot to some people," I said. "Like me, for instance."

"Me, too." He started putting the photos back in their frames.

"Meghan and I think we know who killed Walter."

He glanced up at me. "Oh yeah? Who?"

I pointed at the photo he held. "The girl in that picture. Her name's Cherry. She married Walter and they had a son."

Ambrose leaned against his desk. "You're serious."

"Yes. Very." I gave him a brief version of the story Mrs. Gray had told me.

"That's sad, but I don't see how you got from there to deciding this Cherry killed Hanover."

"There's more." I pointed at Richard's baby picture, grimacing at the thought that I'd had it sitting on my dresser for two days. "Meghan says this picture isn't Walter. It's Richard."

"Richard?"

"Her ex-husband. From the other night?"

"Oh, him. Right. So, why would Hanover have a baby picture of Meghan's ex-husband?"

"Because Cherry and Richard's mother, Grace Thorson, are the same person."

Ambrose raised one eyebrow, then reached for the picture of Cherry and the Hanover boys. He squinted. Whistled. "Could be. Hard to tell from this. Might explain why Walter had a baby picture of your housemate's ex, but so might some other things."

Like what? Richard handed out his baby picture to all the neighbors? Right.

"Can you find out anything about Cherry? See what happened to her after she left Cadyville?"

"I'll see what I can do," Ambrose said. "And when you take this stuff over to Mrs. Hanover, ask if it's Cherry in the picture with her boys."

"It's her," Meghan said from behind us.

"Ms. Bly. Come sit down." He pulled over another chair for her. He perched his lanky frame on the edge of his desk.

"You sound sure," he said. And she did, more than she had with me.

"I think you should talk to Grace Thorson, see what she has to say about it."

"How long did you say she was going to be visiting your ex-husband? We might want to wait until we learn a little more about this Cherry person, confirm Grace Thorson's identity as Hanover's ex-wife."

"Last night she said she was leaving in two days. And if she leaves, I imagine it will be hard—and expensive—to talk with her once she's back in California."

"I see," he said, watching her. "Any other reason you might want me to talk with your mother-in-law?"

Meghan met his gaze.

"Well, it's okay if you don't want to go talk with her," I said. "We can do it. In fact, we'll run by there on our way home. I'll drop this stuff by Tootie's tomorrow. C'mon, Meghan." I stood up.

Ambrose laughed. "Okay, you win. Give me the address, and I'll go by tonight and talk with his mother. Leave those two pictures with me."

"I thought you worked the day shift."

239

He sighed. "I do. And then some."

"Can't you do it now?" I said. Meghan didn't try to shush me.

Ambrose saw our expressions and sighed again. "I guess I could."

"Good. Let's go," I said.

"Huh uh. You're not going. Or the deal's off."

"What deal? The one where you're doing your job?" I said.

"You're not coming with me."

I pasted on my sweetest smile.

For some reason, he grumbled all the way out the door.

THIRTY-THREE

Since Ambrose had flat-out refused to let us come with him, Meghan and I followed in her old Volvo. We didn't even try to be sneaky about it. All that earned us was a glare in the rearview mirror when we pulled up behind him at a stop sign. But we parked down the block when he pulled to the curb in front of Dick's and Ambrose didn't get out and bluster at us to go away, so I decided to interpret that as tacit approval.

He narrowed his eyes at us when Meghan shut off the car engine, but when we made no move to open the car doors, he strode up the short sidewalk and poked one long finger at Richard's doorbell.

Dick lived on the corner of Root and Tenth, in a slate-blue box divided into eight apartments: four on the first floor, four on the second. Exterior stairs on each corner of the building led to the upper units, while the lower ones had nine-by-nine-foot pads of concrete to approximate patios in front of their doors. The concrete pads met the concrete sidewalk without the bother of anything green and growing in between. His neighbor had made the most of the patio idea, outlining the cement square with pots of flowering kale and winter pansies and placing a small bistro set next to a humongous gas grill.

Dick's outdoor décor consisted of a hibachi and a doormat.

Ambrose waited. We waited. He pushed the bell again and then knocked on the door. No one answered. Even though Richard had quit the job he'd been complaining about, the one where he was so abused and underpaid he had to borrow money from Meghan to take his kid to a movie, it didn't mean he'd be hanging around the apartment, especially with his mother in town. Maybe he'd taken her, or more accurately she'd taken him, to some tourist hot spot for the afternoon. I tried to imagine Grace mincing around Seattle's Pike Place Market in those godawful high heels, or Dick nodding sagely as a docent explained Caravaggio's use of light at the Seattle Art Museum. Ambrose approached and caught my grin as I rolled down the window.

"What?" he said when he saw my expression.

"Nothing. I take it they're not home."

"No. And I'm not leaving my card because I don't want to spook them."

"Yeah. It would suck to lose our only decent suspect," I said.

He gave me a look.

"I'd like to find a phone, check in on Erin," Meghan said. Neither of us carried cell phones, since we both worked out of the house and were pretty easy to track down.

Ambrose reached into his jacket pocket. "Here, use mine."

"Thanks," she said, punching in numbers and turning away from us as I began to speak.

"So how do we know when they get back?"

"I'll run by again tonight. They're probably just gone for the afternoon."

"I could stay and watch for them," I said.

"Oh, for God's sake. Will you please stop trying to play detective?"

"Hey, if it weren't for me and Meghan, you'd never know about Grace's connection to Walter."

"If there's a connection. That hasn't been established."

"Even so. You'd never know to check if it weren't for us. And having his ex-wife show up out of the blue, right when he dies, has to mean something."

"If she's his ex-wife."

"Yeah, yeah."

"Okay, you're right, it would mean something. But the connection to Meghan and her daughter I find a little hard to take, given the first connection, which isn't a bona fide connection, yet."

"You're starting to sound like me."

"Great. Just what I need. What I mean is, don't you find it odd that Walter just happened to be living right behind his granddaughter and daughter-in-law?"

"Too much coincidence?"

"Exactly."

"What if it wasn't."

"Wasn't what?"

"Coincidence. What if he knew Erin was his granddaughter?"

"I wonder how long he's lived there."

"Mrs. Gray said he moved from one of her other properties to that one right after Meghan and the Dick moved in. Erin would have been a baby, then. Walter said he liked the little cottage better than the other place he rented, and asked to move in there. Could be he knew who lived in the yellow house across the alley, don't you think?"

"Maybe," he conceded.

Meghan handed Ambrose his phone. "Erin and Zoe stayed after school to help their teacher decorate the classroom for Halloween," she said. "They should be home soon. I'm thinking I might drop by and see if they want to go grab some ice cream."

I looked at my watch. "Kind of close to dinnertime for that, isn't it?" And the temperature had dropped in the last hour. I wrapped my arms around myself and shivered at the thought of eating anything that cold.

"We'll keep them small." The ice cream was just an excuse. Not knowing Dick and Grace's whereabouts had pushed her "Mom" button, and Meghan needed to see that Erin was okay.

I turned to Ambrose. "Can you give me a ride back to my truck?"

"Sure," he said, and I followed him to his departmental car while Meghan climbed back in her Volvo and drove away.

Once we were on our way back to the station, I broached the subject of showing the picture of Cherry to Mrs. Gray.

"She's the one who told me about Cherry and Walter in the first place. I can go over as soon as I get home and see if she recognizes Grace."

Ambrose gave me a sideways look. "Really."

But when I followed him into the station and reached for the picture still in the box on his desk, he shook his head. "I don't think so."

"But—"

"It's not a bad idea to show the pictures to Walter's landlady. So that's just what I'm going to do."

"Pictures? As in more than one?"

"Before we left I asked one of the cadets to track down a copy of Grace Thorson's California driver's license. With her picture on it."

"Excellent! But you should let me go with you, and not just because I'm trying to be a pain in the ass."

He raised one eyebrow.

"No, wait. Listen. Mrs. Gray knows me. She doesn't know you. She's the one who told me the story about Walter and Cherry and Willy, and I think she'd respond to questions about it better if I were there."

"She'll talk to me."

"I'm sure she would. But she wouldn't tell you as much, or the same things."

"The chick factor," he said.

"Something like that."

He sighed and turned toward the door. "Well, come on."

THIRTY-FOUR

Ambrose retrieved an enlarged printout of Grace Thorson's driver's license photo. She looked awful; the harsh lighting revealed every meretricious skin-pull, gob of makeup, and strand of brassy red hair. I swore I'd never complain about my driver's license photo again.

Ambrose followed my little truck down Mrs. Gray's street and pulled to the curb behind me in front of her house. She answered the door wearing her usual gray sweatsuit and a black baseball cap that had "Girl Power" embroidered in royal purple across the front. I introduced Ambrose and asked if we could come in and ask her some questions about Walter. She agreed and offered tea. Ambrose accepted for both of us.

"We have some pictures we'd like you to look at," I said as I slid onto a red kitchen chair. Ambrose pursed his lips, and I shut up, mentally drumming my fingers as he chatted a bit about Walter in general. Mrs. Gray assembled cups and waited for the water to boil, and he asked questions about how long Walter had lived in the cottage and how long she'd known him, most of which elicited information I'd already told him. But Mrs. Gray seemed more at ease when the tea had brewed, and she sat down at the table with us, smiling at Ambrose in an almost flirtatious way. It felt more like a few old friends gossiping than an interrogation. I had to give the man credit.

"So what's this about pictures?" she asked.

"We have—"

Ambrose cut me off. "I'd like you to take a look at a couple of photos, just to see if you recognize anyone."

He moved the teapot to one side and opened his briefcase. First he laid the still-framed picture of Cherry and the Hanover boys on the table. Mrs. Gray drew it toward her, then shook her head. She got up and went to the kitchen counter to retrieve her reading glasses and perched them on the end of her nose. The half-moon frames matched the purple embroidery on her hat.

"That's better. Let's see what we can see, then." She cocked her head to one side, perusing the faces. Pointing, she said, "That's Walter, there. And that's Willy, and there on the end, Wayne."

I realized I hadn't known the name of Walter's other brother. "Is he the one who died of cancer?"

"Yes, and Willy died when a crane down at the mill dropped a huge log on him."

Eeew.

She pointed at the picture again. "And that's probably that girl I told you about, Sophie Mae."

"Cherry?" I said.

Ambrose looked at the ceiling and then at me. I ignored him.

Mrs. Gray nodded. "That's right."

"Are you sure?" Ambrose asked.

"Well, it would be, wouldn't it? They look to be about the right age, sometime around the end of high school or the beginning of Walter's time in college. Who else would it be?"

"But do you actually *recognize* the face," he persisted.

"Oh. Well, it's hard to tell. If she weren't with the boys I might not think of her first thing, but why would I? I haven't seen her in over forty years. But I do think that's her in the picture."

"Do you happen to remember what Cherry's last name was?"

"Hanover," she said.

"Before she got married. Her maiden name."

"Oh. Um, Dodds, I believe. Yes, her father was Ethan Dodds. And her mother was Nellie Marston before she got married. I went to school with her. But I don't think I ever knew what Cherry's first name really was. Everyone always called her 'Cherry.'"

"It wasn't her real name?" I asked.

"No, it was a nickname, from when she was just a baby. Because of her hair. If this were a color photograph I'd be able to tell you for certain if that's her. She had the most gorgeous red hair, bright but not carroty. Deeper than that."

"Is there anything else you can remember about her?" Ambrose asked.

"Not really." Her eyes took on a speculative gleam. "You don't think she had something to do with what happened to Walter, do you?"

"We're just trying to find out as much as we can about him," Ambrose said.

"Oh. Well, I haven't been much help."

"Now don't you worry about that. You've been able to tell us more about Walter than we've learned from anyone else," Ambrose said. Mrs. Gray looked pleased. He put the first picture back in his briefcase and pulled out the printout from Grace Thorson's driver's license. They had removed the license information and blown up the picture a little, but not so much as to lose any significant resolution. "Now, take a look at this one, and tell me if you've seen her before."

Again Mrs. Gray drew the picture toward her and cocked her head to one side. "I think so," she said. "That poor dear needs to do something about her hair, doesn't she?"

"When you say, 'I think so,' do you mean you've seen her lately?" Ambrose asked.

"Oh. That could be it. But there's something else. Good heavens! Let me see that other picture again."

Ambrose removed it from the briefcase again, his face neutral. I took a sip of tea, shielding my face so Mrs. Gray wouldn't see my excitement.

Her gaze swung like a pendulum between the two images, now side by side in front of her. She looked up at Ambrose, then back down. "This older woman could be Cherry all grown up and weathered badly."

I put my hand over my mouth and waited for the urge to laugh to pass. I could just imagine how Grace would like hearing she'd "weathered badly."

"And her hair is close to the same shade of red. It's a dye-job, I know, but Cherry was so very proud of that fiery head of hair. I can see her trying to keep it after time robbed her of it."

The phone rang, and Mrs. Gray rose to answer it.

"What do you think?" I asked Ambrose.

"I don't know. I wish she could be more definite about Grace Bly being Cherry Hanover, or Dodds, or whatever, but at least she's being honest. And now that we know that 'Cherry' was a nickname we might have more luck tracking her down. Her name's probably always been Grace."

"Tootie would know."

"She didn't seem all that, uh, there, when I spoke with her."

"She's there. Let me take the pictures to her. Along with the others I'll be taking over there anyway."

Ambrose shrugged. "I'm going to give these pics to the state crime lab guys, let them do their thing with computers. Even if the subject has aged, they should be able to tell if they're the same woman."

"How long will that take?"

"Don't know. A few days, probably more like a week. But I'll do my best to light a fire under them."

"Yes, she's right here, dear," Mrs. Gray said as she entered the room. She held the cordless phone receiver out to me.

I took it and said, "Hello?"

Meghan wasted no time with preliminaries. "Erin didn't come home from school with Zoe."

"You're over there now?"

"Yes. Zoe came home by herself. She doesn't know where Erin is. She went off by herself and didn't tell anyone where she was going." Her words tumbled over one another, fear raising the pitch of her voice. My stomach muscles clenched.

"Okay, Meghan, slow down. Zoe said Erin went off on her own? Not with anyone else?"

Ambrose's head jerked up, but I ignored him, trying to concentrate.

"They stayed late to help Mrs. Kreagle decorate the classroom for Halloween. They helped for half an hour, but when they started to walk home, Erin told Zoe she'd meet her at Zoe's house, that she had something to do."

I tried to sooth her. "Well, she'll probably be there soon, then." Ambrose held out his hand for the phone.

"Listen, Detective Ambrose wants to talk to you."

"He's with you? Put him on." I handed the phone to him.

"Ms. Bly? What happened?" He was silent as Meghan told him.

"Is the mother there?...Good. I'm coming over. What's the address?...Okay, got it. I'll be right there." He pushed the disconnect button and handed the phone back to Mrs. Gray, who had been watching with a worried expression.

"Thank you," he told her. "You've been very helpful. If I think of anything else I'll give you a call. That all right?"

"Of course, Detective," she said, then, "Is Meghan's little girl okay?"

"I'm sure she is. Kids'll wander off sometimes, by themselves. We'll track her down." He was already walking toward the door. But the look on his face, which I could see and Mrs. Gray couldn't, told me he was worried. I ran after him.

"Let me get my coat, and I'll ride with you."

He started to shake his head, then said in an irritated tone, "Hurry up."

I ran, I mean really ran, around the side of Mrs. Gray's house, skirted the stinking pile of soggy charcoal that had once been Walter Hanover's house and through our backyard, loping awkwardly as I approached the back door, trying to extract my keys from the front pocket of my jeans. The bruise in the fold of my hip screamed as I dragged them out. I fitted the key into the lock and turned, pushing the door too hard so that it banged open. Dashed up the stairs, through the kitchen and to the front hall where I grabbed the first thing that came to hand: a fleece vest. Good enough. I ran back downstairs and out the still open door, remembering at the last minute to close and relock it.

As I turned, Erin walked around the side of the house. Her backpack hung over one shoulder and tiny raindrops had collected in her curls. I stared for a moment, panting and hot, the fleece vest lying on the ground where it had landed after slipping through my fingers.

"What?" she said.

Five steps later, I had her wrapped in a tight hug. Only as relief flooded through me did I realize how scared I'd been, how certain that Richard and his mother had taken her.

"Mmmph," she said, wiggling in my clasp.

"What?"

"Lemme go. I can't breathe."

"Oh. Sorry." I loosened my hold and backed off a half step, one arm still around her shoulders.

"What was *that* all about?" she asked.

"Where have you been? We were all worried sick about you. Do you know how worried your mother was? Is. I have to go call her. C'mon—I'm not letting you out of my sight. You know, I'm sorry you have to stay at Zoe's for a while. I said I was sorry this morning. But you do have to. You can't come home yet, even though you miss us. We miss you, too, but it's just for a little longer. You have to go back."

"Jeez, Sophie Mae. I only came home to pick up a book I needed for school."

"Oh."

"But the key's gone, so I couldn't get in. So I was waiting for someone to come home. I thought I heard the back door bang open and came around to see if you'd parked in the alley.

"Oh. Well, you should have told someone where you were."

"Sorry." She didn't sound all that sorry to me.

"Or better yet, called your mom to have her bring the book to you." By now we were upstairs. I reached for the phone in the hallway.

Erin said, "What's the big deal? How come you don't want me here?"

"I…it's not that we don't want you here, Bug."

"Did I do something wrong?"

"No!"

"Is this about Grandma Bly? I mean, *Grace*," she said, remembering her grandmother's admonition to call her by her first name.

"What did your mom tell you?"

"She said to trust her and go to Zoe's. So she didn't tell me anything, and if I'm going to get yelled at—" She put her fists on her hips and glared at me. "—then I think I have the right to know why."

"Oh, God, Erin. I need to talk to your mom. Then—"

"Sophie Mae? Where the hell are you?" Ambrose bellowed from downstairs.

253

"Up here," I yelled. "What's Zoe's number?" I asked Erin. She told me, and I punched it in as Ambrose's footsteps approached.

"How long can it take to get a coat, woman?" He stopped dead in his tracks when he saw Erin.

"Woman?" I said, amused. The phone was picked up at Zoe's house. I asked for Meghan, and in two seconds she came on the line.

"Erin's here," I said.

"Where? Is she okay?"

"Home. She's fine. She just stopped by to pick up a book for school, then couldn't get in because we don't have the extra key outside now."

"I'll come get her."

"I can bring her over," I said, and to Erin, "Go get your book." She turned and went up the stairs to her room.

"No," Meghan said. "I want to talk to her, and it would be better if it wasn't in front of her friend."

"Yeah. About that. Don't be too mad at her. She didn't know she'd be worrying you. She doesn't know why you sent her to Zoe's."

Meghan sighed. "She'd barely talk to me on the way over here, and besides, I hadn't thought of a good answer anyway. I didn't want to scare her."

"I know, I know. But she wants to know what's going on. We have to tell her something. You can blame it all on me," I said.

"It's not your fault." When I didn't respond she said, "Anyway, I'll be right home."

After we hung up I turned to Ambrose and gestured him into the kitchen. "You heard what happened?

254

He nodded. "Everything okay now?"

"Yes. And no. We still have to figure something out to tell Erin so she'll understand why she can't be here, put her on her guard a little without terrifying the poor kid."

"Try the truth."

"What, that her mom's afraid her grandmother is going to kidnap her?" The words, finally said, seemed almost silly. Except I'd seen the look on Meghan's face when Grace was in our kitchen, and that hadn't been silly at all.

"Well, that's one reason. The other is that someone came after you, and I suggested it would be easier to learn who did it without everyone being worried about whether Erin would be safe or not."

"We can't tell her that," I said. "She wouldn't understand."

"Right," Erin said from the doorway. "I'm not stupid, you know. What did you do, Sophie Mae?"

I glanced at Ambrose, then rubbed my hands over my face. "I don't know, Bug." Ambrose rolled his eyes. I added, "At least not specifically."

"Is it because of what happened to Walter? Did you find out why he died?"

Ambrose threw up his hands. "What is it with the women in this house?"

Erin smiled at him.

The front door opened, and Meghan came in. She went straight to Erin and enveloped her in her second bear hug of the day. But this time Erin didn't struggle, just waited until her mom let her go.

"I'm so glad you're okay. But we need to talk," Meghan said.

"We sure do. I know someone's after Sophie Mae, but maybe you could tell me more about Grandma kidnapping me, 'K?"

Meghan turned disbelieving eyes on me, and I went back to rubbing my face with my hands. Ambrose chose then to clear his throat and say he was going to go let Mrs. Gray know everything was all right.

Traitor.

"C'mon, Mom. You can tell me in the car. They eat early, and I don't want to be late for dinner." She tugged her mother toward the door, the surliness from earlier in the day completely gone.

I hoped Meghan would regain the ability to speak on the drive over.

THIRTY-FIVE

I COULDN'T WRANGLE THE picture of Cherry and the Hanover boys from Barr Ambrose, but he did allow me to make a copy of it at the police station. It was a pretty good copy, and, after much wheedling and begging on my part, he also let me have a copy of the driver's license picture.

"Use it wisely," he said, and his face held reluctance when he handed it over. I knew he would have insisted on going, but he had two other cases he'd neglected all afternoon, and his shift was already over. I wondered if the department paid overtime, or if Barr had to eat all the extra hours he worked.

Still, with high hopes I buzzed over to Caladia Acres, armed with the photocopies and the pictures and mementos Ambrose had declared unrelated to the murder investigation. Perhaps the sight of them would shake Tootie out of her funk.

Ann, the nurse who seemed to be always on duty, flagged me down as I carried in the carton.

"Here to see Tootie?"

I nodded. "How is she?"

She grimaced, and it was enough to convey Walter's mother wasn't any better than when Meghan and I had seen her on Sunday. "Did Meghan come with you?" she asked.

"Not this time," I said.

"Well, can you tell her she's got the gig?"

"What gig?"

"She called and wanted to set up a time to offer massages to the residents here."

"Oh. I didn't know."

"And next week we'll ask the board to approve the classes she proposed for the nurses and attendants, to train how to give hand and foot massages to those residents who request them."

"I'll tell her."

It was dark by the time I'd pulled into the parking lot, and Tootie hadn't turned on a light in her room. I didn't want to wake her.

"Tootie?" I called softly from the doorway.

A rustle, then a soft voice out of the darkness. "Yes?"

"It's Sophie Mae." I put the box on the floor and walked in, using the light from the corridor to find the lamp I remembered from before, fumbling for the switch for a moment before turning it on.

She had plummeted downhill, far more than I'd gathered from Ann. She looked out at me from dull sunken eyes, her unbraided hair spilled across the pillow in a snarled mass. At only a few minutes after six in the evening, I didn't think she'd gone to bed early. She'd never bothered to get up. Someone had turned the thermostat too high. The stuffy room smelled of dust…and I realized with a start that I could smell Tootie herself.

"Good God," I said, and marched out to the reception desk.

"What's going on? She hasn't even had a bath lately."

Ann nodded. "I know. We've tried. She fights us. It's the only time she shows any animation at all now. At some point the doctor will prescribe tranquilizers just so we can clean her up."

I stared at her. "Drug her? To give her a bath? That's barbaric."

Ann looked apologetic. "So is the alternative."

Shaking my head, I went back to Tootie's room. Pausing in the doorway, I studied her. Her eyes were open, but she was staring at the ceiling.

"You have to stop this," I said.

Silence, then finally a little sigh.

"You have to stop this pity party of yours."

She blinked.

I took a deep breath, crossed my fingers, and followed my instinct. "Walter's death had nothing to do with whatever feud you two had going on, and nothing to do with anything you ever said to him. In fact, he must have taken some of what you said to heart, because after spending so long mentally crippled by losing his wife and son, he put that aside and got on with living. He kicked the booze. He fell in love with a woman named Deborah Silverman and asked her to marry him. He helped hundreds of kids—maybe more—with money he won from the lottery and donated. Even dead he's helping people. He was a good man. And you know what else? He was pretty darn strong after all. You had a lot to do with that. He was his mother's son. He didn't commit suicide, Tootie. Someone killed him. The police are investigating it as a suspicious death as we speak."

She turned her head, and her eyes met mine. At least I had her attention now, though her face remained expressionless.

"I have something to show you. Will you at least sit up in bed long enough for that?"

Nothing. Then a light shift under the covers. A deep breath, and she moved again. I went over and helped her sit up, then plumped her pillows, and assisted as she settled back into a more upright position.

She glared at me as I went and got the box. Good. Better anger than nothing. I unloaded the framed photos, one by one, setting them on the coverlet.

"These are from Walter's house, what I managed to get out before it burned down. This one is of you, isn't it?"

She glanced at the picture I held, of Tootie in her youth, standing in a shirtwaist dress in front of a house, and looked away.

Putting down that photo, I picked up another one. "What about this one?" I'd selected the one of Walter as a little boy, giggling open-mouthed as a beagle puppy lapped at his chin. Hallmark would have snapped it up in a second.

Her eyes flickered to me, and her hand crept out from under the covers. She took the picture from me, considering it for several moments. Then she drew it to her chest.

"I'll keep this," she said.

"Tootie," I said, exasperated. "You can keep all of them."

She shook her head. "I don't want all of them. I only want this one."

"Well, what about his stuff?" I took out the Bible and the chicken bank. She shook her head.

"There are other pictures," I said.

"I only want this one."

I regarded her for a few moments, and her eyes sparked in rebellion. She'd shown the most animation when the Caladia Acres staff had tried to make her do something she didn't want to do. There was life in the old girl yet. Just had to find the right buttons to push.

"I'd like you to look at one more thing. Well, two, actually."

She turned her face to the wall. It was like dealing with a stubborn six-year-old.

I stood up, started putting the pictures back in the carton. "No? Okay. Probably just as well. You wouldn't remember who the people were anyway. It was a long time ago. And Mrs. Gray has told us most of what we need to know. You know Mrs. Gray—Walter's landlady? Oh, she said you'd know her as Mavis Smart. Anyway, she's told the police enough, I suppose, though it's too bad we can't find out for sure who's in these pictures, since it would probably help find Walter's killer. But I wouldn't want to bother you, Tootie…"

My words had spilled out as I got ready to leave, and I hadn't tried to be tactful. Tact wasn't working with Tootie, and it couldn't hurt to try and startle her out of her funk. But still, I was unprepared for her reaction.

She hissed.

I whirled in surprise. Tootie Hanover's eyes blazed at me. I controlled the urge to smile.

"So am I to take it you do want to help?" I asked, feeling smug.

"Walter rented from Mavis Smart? Is that who I talked to on the phone that day you went through his things?"

"Um, yeah. Why?"

She barely breathed the words: "That whore."

"Mrs. Gray?" I said, dumbfounded.

Tootie started to look at the wall again, then turned back to me. "You think just because someone is old and gray they're sweet and stupid."

"I do not. You, for example, are neither sweet nor stupid."

We glared at each other for a while. Then she held out her hand. "What do you want me to look at?"

"These," I said and pulled out the photocopies Ambrose had given me.

She took the first one and held it at arm's length. "Hand me those," she said, pointing to her dresser. I saw a pair of black-rimmed reading glasses and retrieved them for her. She perched them on her nose and peered at the group of people on the page.

"This is my family, just before all the boys left home. And this is my husband—" she glanced at me over her glasses, "—who had been spending more time than he should have with Miss Mavis Smart for almost two years by then. And the girl is that good-for-nothing Cherry Dodds."

"You're sure that's Cherry Dodds?"

"Of course I'm sure. I remember the day her sister took this picture. What can this have to do with Walter's death?"

My heart beat a little faster. "And this woman? Do you recognize her?"

Tootie studied the photocopy of Grace Thorson's license. Her eyes narrowed and found mine. "She's back?"

"Who?" I asked, just to make sure.

"Cherry."

"Do you remember her real name?"

She pursed her lips. "Grace. Grace Dodds."

"Well," I said, taking the page back from Tootie. "I guess the answer is yes, then. She's back."

THIRTY-SIX

THE SMELL OF PEANUT butter cookies hit me like a sledgehammer when I opened the front door. Meghan was pulling a pan of them out of the oven, while Erin sat at the table and flattened another batch onto a cookie sheet with a fork dipped in sugar.

"What are you doing here?" I asked.

Meghan straightened. "We decided Erin would be safer with us. And she promised to be very, very careful." She gave her daughter a look, to which Erin responded with an earnest nod.

"Well, I'm glad," I said.

"Why?" Erin asked.

"Because I like having you around."

She grinned. "You just want a cookie, huh?"

"You bet. Gimme."

She grabbed one off the pile on the plate beside her and handed it to me. Fiifteen seconds later she had to give me another one.

"Don't spoil your dinner," Meghan said, but her voice was mild. I looked at Erin, but she wasn't eating anything.

Oh.

"I won't," I said around the second cookie. "What're we having?"

"Pizza. It's on the way."

"Thank God. I don't feel up to cooking tonight. I've just been over talking to Tootie."

"What'd she have to say?"

Since Meghan didn't give me any sign that she didn't want Erin to hear, I told her how Tootie was doing, and about our conversation. When I'd left, Tootie had still been lying in bed, but at least she seemed to inhabit her own body again. She hadn't had any other pictures of Cherry, though. I'd also driven by Richard's apartment on my way home, but the windows were dark, and I didn't see his car or the white Camry he'd been driving with his mother the day of Walter's memorial service.

"She didn't want Walter's things?" Meghan asked.

"Only that one picture."

She cocked her head at her daughter. "What's wrong, Bug?"

Erin looked thoughtful. "Nothing's wrong. I was just thinking…since Grandma Grace was married to Walter, that makes Walter my grandpa, right?"

Meghan glanced at me and seemed to make a decision. "Yes. And I bet he knew it, too, because he kind of acted like a grandpa, didn't he?"

I piped up. "Do you want any of his stuff? The photos are kind of cool. And there are a couple books, and a funny bank shaped like a chicken."

Erin made a face. "Nah." Saw her mother's look. "I mean, no thank you."

Ah, unsentimental youth.

But she wasn't finished. "So his mom would be my grandma, too?"

"Your great-grandma," Meghan said. "She was the lady with the white hair you met at the funeral. Do you like the idea of having a great-grandma?"

Erin considered. "I only met her once. I'd want to know her better before I decide whether I like the idea or not."

Meghan and I couldn't help smiling. "That makes sense," Meghan said. Given how Erin's last "new grandma" encounter had turned out, I had to agree.

"I'm going to call Debby and see if she wants any of Walter's things," I said

Meghan nodded. "Good idea."

After we ate pizza and Erin had gone up to do her homework, I asked Meghan, "Do you really think Walter knew she was his granddaughter?"

"You know, thinking back on how he was with her, I really do."

"You're from Seattle."

"Yeah."

"And Richard's from California."

She nodded.

"Then how the heck did you two end up in Cadyville, where Richard was born? Unless he's known about Walter all along?"

Meghan stared off into space for a few moments. Then she looked at me and shook her head. "I could be wrong, but I don't think he knew. At least, not that Walter was his father. He would have acted differently around him. Richard might have known he'd been born here though. I don't know. It was his idea to move here. I didn't want to, thought living in a small town would be too boring. But he talked me into it."

"Did he want to move to any small town, or just to Cadyville?"

"Just Cadyville. See, he went to the University of Washington, at least he did for a year before he quit to sell office machinery, because his mother told him that was the one school she didn't want him to attend."

"He rebelled."

"Uh huh. And he told me she used to talk about Cadyville—she hated it—so one day we came up here, and it turned out to be this cool little town. He decided then and there this was where he wanted to live."

"The best way for his mother to keep him away from Cadyville would have been to tell him how great it was."

Meghan laughed. "Right. She might as well have bought him a plane ticket and a map for all her insistence that he stay away."

"When you were married, did he ever go visit his mother in California? Or suggest that you all go?"

"Never. I only met her one time, when we drove down the coast before we were married."

"She treats him like crap," I said. "Or she did the other night."

"I noticed that. And he takes it. No wonder he wanted to live someplace she wouldn't want to visit."

Debby wasn't home when I called, but she had an answering machine, and I left a message about Walter's things. I went downstairs, put molds for the lotion bars in the dishwasher to sterilize, and gathered the ingredients for the next day. I had just finished rubbing arnica oil into my bruises again and putting on my pajamas, when she called me back.

"Yes, I want anything you have of Walter's. When can I come over?"

"I'm making an early night of it," I said. "Can you come over in the morning?"

"Um, not until about eleven. Is that okay?"

"Sure. Come around to the back door. I'll see you then."

Meghan had taken off for her infant massage class, so Erin and I flopped on the sofa together to read. Erin seemed restless, which at first I put down to too much excitement. But she didn't settle down, and she had a peculiar look on her face. Finally, I put my book down.

"What's up?"

"I feel kind of funny," she said.

"Sick funny?" I put my hand on her forehead. Felt a little hot.

"I don't know."

I went into the bathroom and hunted up a thermometer. She had a temperature of one hundred point two. Not too bad, but she was coming down with something. I gave her some Tylenol and bundled her into bed. She was asleep by the time I went to bed at nine.

I was still reading Margery Allingham when I heard the front door open downstairs. Brodie didn't bark, so I knew it was Meghan, and minutes later she stood in my doorway saying good night.

"Erin's got a fever," I said, and filled her in.

"Poor kid," she said. "The stress of the past week has probably weakened her immune system. I'll keep her home tomorrow. Can you watch her after two?"

"Sure. How'd the class go?"

"It went well. Eight couples showed up. Three heard about me through word of mouth."

"The best advertising. Oh, hey, I forgot to tell you. Ann over at Caladia Acres asked me to tell you that you 'got the massage gig.' And something about the board needing to approve the classes you wanted to offer the staff?"

Meghan looked pleased. "Oh, good. I was hoping they'd let me work on the residents."

"So, you're going to be around tomorrow morning?"

"Uh huh. I have two clients in the early afternoon, but I'm open in the morning. Why?"

"Debby Silverman's coming over around eleven." And I related what Ambrose had told me about Debby's manic-depression and past violence.

Meghan looked unhappy. "That poor woman. No wonder her brother's so anxious about her. But I'm surprised Ambrose told you her diagnosis. He must really be worried about you."

"I think he was more worried about her criminal record. But frankly, I'm more concerned about Grace."

"So am I."

———

I was out by ten. And awake again at midnight. After listening to the quiet and staring at the ceiling in the dark for almost an hour, I got up and padded downstairs. I thought I'd seen some melatonin in the kitchen cupboard, and if I had to, I'd suffer through a cup of valerian tea, even though the stuff tasted like sour dirt. I needed to sleep.

No melatonin. Tea it was, then. As I waited for the kettle to boil, I wandered the perimeter of the house in the dark, checking the window locks like I had the night before. Pushing aside the living room curtain, I stopped cold. The white car from the night before sat across the street again. It hadn't been there all day, but there it was, back again tonight.

It's someone new in the neighborhood, I told myself. They work all day, so their car is only here at night. But as I watched, I could clearly see the silhouette of a head and shoulders on the driver's side.

In the kitchen I turned off the burner under the kettle, then went back upstairs and put on my jeans and sweatshirt. I felt my way down the basement stairs and let myself out the back door. I went down the alley until I came to the sidewalk, and then around the corner and quickly across the street, hoping whoever lurked in the white car didn't look in the rearview mirror right then. I sidled up the street behind the car, hugging hedges and dodging behind bushes like some crazed character from *Get Smart*.

As I neared the car it occurred to me I might need a weapon. Swearing under my breath, I scanned the shadows. A glint caught my attention. Edging toward it, I saw someone had left a trowel out next to a half-full basket of spring bulbs. Better than nothing. Snagging it, I crept on.

Upon reaching the car, I approached from the blind spot and then crab-walked along the curb until I crouched directly beside the passenger door. Whatever happened, I wanted to make sure I got a good enough look at whoever was inside to recognize them. Slowly, I rose and looked in the window.

And locked eyes with Barr Ambrose. I let out a yelp, and Ambrose let out a yell. I stood up and turned, leaning against the car and holding my palm to my chest. If it had been Richard I probably would have folded into an unconscious heap. What a trooper.

The window slid down. "What do you think you're doing?" Ambrose asked. Feeling sheepish, I opened the door and slid into the passenger seat.

"Well?" he said.

"I was trying to find out who was watching the house."

"You came out here not knowing?"

"Well…yeah."

"Would've been better to call the PD, have someone check it out, don't you think?"

I was glad he couldn't see my face turn red. "Just what *are* you doing here?"

"Like you said: I'm watching the house."

"You were here last night, too?"

He nodded.

I thought about it. The short-handed police department. Ambrose had mentioned they couldn't spare anyone to keep an eye on us. So he'd taken it on himself. No wonder he looked so tired.

"Is this your car?"

"Yeah."

"I thought you'd drive a Jeep or something."

"Sorry." He sounded irritated.

"It's nice. You doing this," I said.

"It's my job."

"Not exactly," I said.

This time he shrugged. "Maybe not."

"You should go home. We'll be okay."

"I will. In a bit. What's that?"

"Garden trowel."

"What were you going to do, plant me?"

I smiled. "You should see me with a pair of pruners. I'd scare you silly."

"Sophie Mae, you already scare me silly. Among other things."

Like what, I wanted to ask but didn't. We watched a car turn into a driveway. A woman got out and went inside her house.

"Do you want to come inside, at least? Where it's warm?"

Oh, God, did that sound like an invitation? And then I realized I rather hoped it did.

"That's okay," he said.

I shrugged off a twinge of disappointment. "Go home, Barr. Really. We'll be fine."

"Well, now that I know you have your garden trowel, I'm sure you will. I'll take off. Go to bed."

"You promise?"

"Uh huh."

I got out, shut the door, leaned in the window. "Thanks for taking such good care of us."

He grinned at me. "Not a problem, ma'am."

Inside, I made my nasty-tasting tea, climbed back into my pajamas, and then into bed. An hour later, still unable to sleep, I slipped back downstairs. Pulling back the curtain, I saw Barr Ambrose still sitting in his car, watching.

THIRTY-SEVEN

I SWEAR: EVERY TIME I think I've finally caught up, it turns out I'm low on something. These days, lotion bars are all the rage. A solid emollient molded into a pretty shape, a lotion bar looks a lot like a bar of soap, but when you rub it between your hands the cream melts into lotion. I make mine out of spicy beeswax, olive oil, and non-deodorized cocoa butter, with some grapefruit seed extract thrown in as an antibacterial agent. I like the non-deodorized cocoa butter because it smells so delicious.

The lotion bars started as one of those items I made for personal use because in spring and summer Meghan and I do a lot of gardening, and our hands suffer for it. In the fall, we preserve fruits and pickles and jams, which means constant hand washing. The cocoa butter works better than anything else to heal the damage from all that scrubbing.

I was weighing chunks of dark, spicy beeswax on a kitchen scale when I heard the rapping of knuckles against the windowpane.

Wiping my hands on an old flour-sack dishtowel, I went to open the door.

"Come on in," I said.

Debby entered, and Jacob followed, shuffling his feet and looking around.

"Looks like a big kitchen in here," he said.

I propped the door open. "Well, in a way I guess you could say I'm a cook. Or at least part cook. It's just that my recipes aren't for things people eat."

"Maybe not," Debby said, "but it smells yummy in here."

I inhaled the chocolate scent, smiling. "That's the cocoa butter melting right now." I picked up the beeswax and carried it to the stove. "Give me a sec, and I'll get that stuff for you to look through."

Once I'd stirred the beeswax into the olive oil and cocoa butter already in the large saucepan and lowered the heat, I retrieved the box of Walter's mementos from the storeroom where I'd stashed it earlier in anticipation of their visit. I put it on the center island and stood back.

"I'm sorry there isn't any more than that. But with the fire and the police taking a couple of the pictures, that's all that's left. Oh, and his mother took one picture, too. The one of Walter as a little boy, with the beagle?"

Debby nodded, either remembering the picture or acknowledging Tootie's right to take it. "I've never met her."

The first time I'd met Debby she didn't have anything good to say about Walter's mother, but now her words held no heat, only a soft sadness. And until I told her, Tootie hadn't even known her son was engaged.

"Why don't you go visit her?" I asked.

Debby shrugged.

"How long had you and Walter been, uh, an item?" An item? Good Lord, Sophie Mae.

But Debby just said, "A little over a year," and went back to pulling items from the box and spreading them across the butcherblock counter.

Over a year, and he'd never taken her to meet his mother, even after he'd asked Debby to marry him. His mother, who lived only a mile away.

Debby sniffled and wiped the back of her hand across her face. I glanced at Jacob in time to see something indefinable cross his features as he watched his sister sort through her dead lover's things.

"Her name's Tootie," I said. Debby raised her head. "Walter's mother. Tootie. Short for Petunia. I think she'd like to meet you."

She looked down. "Oh, I don't know." Then back up at me. "You think so?"

I nodded. Maybe Walter had been right not to subject his fiancée to his mother's judgment earlier, but somehow I didn't think Tootie felt the same way now. Regret had altered her outlook more effectively than anything else might have.

So was it better for bitterness to be replaced by sadness? I'd get an argument from some, but I think so. Sadness is real, grief is real, and ideally a stage you move through to get to the other side where life goes on, while bitterness is a protective façade, static and hard. My father turned brittle with bitterness after Bobby Lee killed himself, and I struggled against doing the same thing when my husband died. Debby seemed to be doing okay, inviting the sorrow from losing Walter to sit with her a while. Maybe a lifetime of battling depressive episodes gave her a special understanding of the process. Or maybe she was on really good drugs. But Tootie had forgiven Walter only to turn around and judge herself. If only she could release some of her self-recrimination.

As for what was going on with Jacob, I had no idea.

Debby pulled out the ceramic chicken bank, turning it in her hands.

"That looks old. You might be able to get somethin' for it," Jacob said.

Debby glared. He hung his head and stubbed his toe into the concrete floor like a little kid.

Fingering the worn paint on the bank, she looked back at me. "You think you could go with me? To, you know…"

"Like, to introduce you? Yeah, I could do that."

"Okay. I'll um…I'll let you know."

"What's back there?" Jacob asked, gesturing with his chin toward the storeroom.

"I keep my product inventory in there, as well as some of the raw ingredients I use."

"That where you keep your lye?" It was a shock to find him looking directly into my eyes as he said it, and I realized it was the first time he hadn't shunted his gaze off elsewhere when I looked at him.

I didn't look away. "No. That's not where I keep it."

"Stop it, Jacob," Debby said. "It's not her fault, what happened."

Jacob shrugged and shuffled toward the storeroom, pausing in the doorway and then continuing in, head craned up to see the contents of the high shelves.

"Sorry 'bout that," Debby muttered.

"He knows, right?"

"Knows what?"

"That Walter didn't…commit suicide." It was still hard for me to say.

She was silent. Then, "Well, that policeman sure talked like someone killed him. Jacob's not taking it too well. Doesn't want to believe it. 'Course, the guy made it sound like Jacob or me had done it, and *that* made him mad."

"The policeman—was it Detective Ambrose?"

"That's the one. Promised he'd let me know when they caught the bastard who did that to Walter, but I haven't heard anything. Probably just gave up." She sounded resigned, like she didn't expect Ambrose to spend more than the minimum required time on Walter's case. It had only been a day since he'd spoken with her, and only a week since I'd found Walter.

"He didn't give up," I said. "In fact he's got a good idea who did it. Now he just has to catch them. Trust me, Ambrose knows what he's doing."

Jacob peered around the storeroom door, saw Debby's face. "What's wrong?" he asked, scurrying like a monkey to her side.

Debby ignored him, her gaze boring into me. "Who killed Walter? Do you know?" When I hesitated, she said, "Tell me."

"I'm sorry, but—"

"*Tell me.*"

The look Jacob sent my way could have started a brushfire, and I took an involuntary step backward. "What the hell kind of nonsense are you fillin' her head with now?"

Debby grabbed his arm. "Stop it. I'm sick of being treated like an invalid. I want to know the truth."

He snorted. "Truth? This woman just wants a little excitement in her life. Don't got nothin' to do with the truth."

Well, naturally that rubbed me the wrong way. "Hey. If you could just—" *pull your head out of your ass...* "—listen for a moment. I'm not making it up. The police are very close to arresting the murderer."

Jacob's nostrils flared.

Debby said, "Really?"

"Yes!"

"Prove it. If you know so much, tell me who killed my Walter."

"I bet I know who they're looking for," Jacob said.

Debby whirled. "Who?"

Jacob paused, then said, "Walter's first wife. She's been in town. Guess the police heard that, too." He squinted at me. "Am I right?"

I didn't answer, but my face must have given it away, because he nodded and turned to Debby. "I figured as much."

"His first wife! But why...how do you know she's here?"

"I, uh, saw her. With Walter. She was lookin' for money, I guess. And he said she's a real piece of work—meaner 'n a snake."

An accurate assessment.

"Why didn't he tell me?" Her momentary grit had vanished, and only the little girl voice remained.

"He just wanted her gone, Debs. He didn't want you bothered with any of it." Jacob's expression now held nothing but concern for his sister, and I could have been on Mars for all he noticed me. I found his focus on his sister a little unnerving.

"Debby," I said. "Are you okay?"

She turned bewildered eyes on me. "What's her name?"

"Debby!" Erin's voice from the bottom of the stairs saved me from answering. "What are you doing here?"

Debby blinked, then turned to Erin. "Honey, how are you?" She held out her arms, and Erin glided into the hug as if from long practice.

"Um," I said. "You two know each other?"

Erin nodded happily, ignoring my questioning look. Little imp.

Debby said, "Walter introduced us. Turns out Erin's quite the little Mariners expert."

"Not like Walter was," Erin said. "He knew everything about baseball, and not just the Mariners, either. He had all kinds of stories."

"Really?"

"He did," Debby replied, more at ease in this conversation and with Erin than any of the times I'd seen her with her brother. Now he shuffled backwards, physically extracting himself from potential conflict. He went back into my storeroom. Had he been jealous of Walter? Was he still?

Debby continued. "Walter loved two things: baseball and nature. He was going to be a scientist once, did you know that?" I made a noncommittal sound, and she continued. "But I bet he knew more about baseball than any commentator."

"I don't think Tootie knew that about him."

"Well, maybe I'll tell her."

Erin skipped into the storeroom. I heard her say, "Hi! I'm Erin. Doesn't it smell great in here? This one over here's my favorite."

The sound of footsteps on the stairs preceded Meghan into the room.

"Have you seen my offspring?" she asked.

I gestured with my elbow. "She's in there."

"Okay. Don't tell her I asked."

"Stalking your kid again?"

Debby looked puzzled.

"Funny," Meghan said, leaning against the end of the counter. "But she is getting pretty sick of me dogging her heels."

"At least she's feeling better," I said.

Meghan nodded. "Seems to be."

"Uh, Sophie Mae?" Debby said, and my eyes followed her gaze.

Grace Thorson stood in the doorway, a scrawny silhouette against the bright daylight.

"Where's my granddaughter? Where's my sweet little girl?"

THIRTY-EIGHT

SHE MINCED INSIDE ON her spike heels and peered around the room. Richard followed behind. Meghan and I gaped.

"Where's little Erin? She's not in school today. I want to see my granddaughter!" Then her gaze fell on Debby. "Who are you?"

I jumped in. "I'm sorry, Mrs. Thorson. Erin isn't here right now." From the corner of my eye I saw Jacob moving toward the storeroom doorway. Grace couldn't see inside the storeroom from where she stood. With my hand at my side, I waved him back without moving my head. Erin's small hand snaked out and grabbed his sleeve, pulling him back out of my sight.

"Well, where is she? When will she be back?" Her face twisted, and she turned on Meghan. "You can't stop me from seeing her forever."

"I'm sorry, but it'll have to be another time," Meghan said, her composure returned. She shot a meaningful look at Richard. It was either lost on him or else he didn't care if his mother made a scene. "I'll call you, and we can set something up."

"Nice try, honey. But I want to see her now. I know she's not in school. Where is she?"

"She's not here." Meghan spoke as if to a slow child.

"I *know* that. You *said* that. So call and have her come home." Her eyes took on a calculating gleam. "Or Richard and I could just go pick her up. Have that lunch you were too high and mighty to take her out of school for."

Richard said, "She with your new boyfriend?"

"What?" Meghan looked confused.

"Ha!" Grace said.

Richard stuck his chin out. "What, you think I couldn't tell how chummy you were the other night? And then you drag him over to my apartment. What did you think you were doing?"

"Wait a minute. You mean the detective who came over when you were here the other night?"

Richard snorted. "You're right, Mother. Won't even admit what she's exposing my daughter to."

"Exposing…? You've got to be kidding."

They glared at each other in a moment of electric silence. Grace hummed under her breath and looked on with an indulgent gaze that made my skin creep.

Meghan said, "He's not my boyfriend. He's a police detective."

"So you said. What was he doing here? Huh? And why was he with you when you came over?"

"Why didn't you answer the door?" I asked.

He sent me an acidic look. "I wasn't home. Or else, believe me, I would've been happy to give the guy a piece of my mind."

"Sure you can spare it?" I mumbled, and beside me, Debby smiled.

Richard's chin jutted forward again. "What did you say?"

"I asked how you knew Meghan had been there if you weren't home."

"My neighbor told me." He turned on Meghan. "And if he's not your boyfriend, why would you bring this detective guy around, anyway? Trying to get me in trouble?"

Why, I wondered, would she bring Ambrose around if he *were* her boyfriend? I mean, it'd probably be worth a lot in the romance department to never expose a man you were interested in to Dick.

Her eyes met mine. She didn't want to tell Richard that Ambrose wanted to question his mother about the murder.

"We had a break-in," I said.

Richard's eyes narrowed, then he gave an elaborate shrug and examined the ceiling. "So?"

"So Detective Ambrose wanted to question everyone who might know where the spare key was."

His gaze reverted to me. "You bitch. You told him I did it."

"Richard…" Meghan began.

"Did you?" I asked.

He gave me his best glare. I bet he practiced it in the mirror, it was so good.

"Well, did you?" Meghan asked.

"That's a stupid question," he said.

But he didn't deny it.

"Come on, Mother," he said.

Grace swung her head back and forth. "No. I want to leave something for Erin first. In her room."

"Mother, there's nothing…let's just go, 'K? We'll take her out another time."

"You're such a pathetic sap, Dickie-Bird. Your wife, excuse me, *ex-wife* pushes you around like you're nothing. Of course, it's a miracle you found anyone who'd want to marry you in the first place. I suppose it'd be too much to expect that you stand up to her like a man." Grace drifted around the room as she spoke, not looking at anyone, trailing her fingers along surfaces as if marking them with her scent.

A waxy pallor overtook Richard's usual healthy tan, and his Adam's apple jogged convulsively up and down his neck. He looked at the floor as she went into her diatribe, shouldering her vitriol like a helpless child, and my perception twisted for a moment, allowing me to see this obnoxious man as an emotionally abused boy. I thought of how that beautiful child might have turned out had he been raised by a loving father, by Walter Hanover, and how Walter's life might have been so different from the train wreck it turned into if only he'd been able to raise his son. Anger flooded my veins as I watched Grace's blithe destruction of a man I didn't even like, her casual delivery of insults as if from long practice.

"But I guess there isn't a lot I should expect from you, is there, Dickie-Bird? After all, you are your father's son. Too bad. Too bad you weren't Daddy Bly's. Maybe you'd have picked up his knack for making money. I hoped maybe he'd rub off on you, but no such luck. You just have to do the best you can with those useless dreamer genes you got from your father."

"Is that why it was so easy to kill him, Grace?" The words spewed out before I even thought of stopping them. The look on her face granted me a disturbing feeling of satisfaction. Debby stared at me, then swiveled to Grace, to Richard, and back to me again. Richard's eyes flicked up at me, then back to the floor. I didn't dare look at Meghan.

The shock on Grace's face faded, to be replaced by lip-curling scorn. "Well, aren't you clever."

Revulsion curled my own lip back. "Did you kill Walter, Grace? He was just a dreamer, so why not? What was it? He make you mad? Did you want something from him? What miserable reason did you give yourself to justify it?"

Richard seemed to shake himself. "Don't be stupid, Sophie Mae. My mother had no reason to kill Walter."

He still didn't get it. But Debby had connected the dots. A distilled moan escaped her lips.

"Shut up, Dickie. I don't need you to speak for me." Grace turned to face me, and the force of her animosity backed me up against the stove. "You are a stupid little bitch. I didn't kill that old drunk. Find some other sap to pin it on."

I shook my head. "I can't believe you show up here out of the blue and it has nothing to do with Walter's death."

A primitive, guttural cry beside me cut off her retort. Debby stood with her hands clenched white around the ceramic chicken bank, her pale face suffused with blood, and the tendons of her neck standing out under her skin. The sound built and seemed to take on a life of its own, a reverberating ululation of naked anguish that made my jaw ache.

Jacob erupted from the storeroom, scuttled to his sister, and wrapped both arms around her as if he could smother her cries with his body. Debby twisted from him and launched the chicken bank at Grace. It flew over her head and exploded on the cement floor at the far end of the room. Meghan, standing against the wall by the stairway, flinched away from the porcelain shrapnel.

Grace's eyes bulged, and her mouth dropped open. She recovered quickly and began fumbling in her capacious handbag, scattering the contents on the floor around her feet. Her search netted a nasty-looking pewter-toned gun. When she pointed it toward Debby, Jacob, and me, clustered together in front of the stove, it looked even nastier.

"Mother, what are you doing with my gun?"

Fury overcame Meghan's features, and she turned on Richard. "*Your* gun? You have a gun? Around your *daughter*? Have you *completely lost your mind*?"

"She doesn't know where I keep it," Richard said.

"But your mother does?"

Richard, confused, looked back at Grace. "How did—"

"Oh, will you two shut up!" Grace rolled her eyes and brought her other hand up to help grip the gun.

Jacob ignored the gun, focusing on calming his sister. The horrible noise she'd been making broke and faded. I groped for how to get the abruptly perilous situation under some kind of control. Grace seemed to be watching the Silvermans, and I reached behind me to the burner control on the range and gave it a twist. Soon I felt the increased heat against my lower back.

Meghan had been slowly backing toward the staircase, but Grace saw her from the corner of her eye.

"Stop her!" she yelled at Richard, who moved with sickening alacrity to cut Meghan off.

"Mother didn't do anything wrong," he said. "She didn't hurt anyone. So she'll just put the gun away, and we'll leave. Okay?"

It was Grace who said, "No."

For the first time Richard looked worried. "Mother. We need to go. They'll find who really killed Walter. I know it wasn't you. You barely knew him."

"You really think a police detective was at your apartment about a stupid key? Don't be so dense. They wanted me." Grace laughed. First it was just a strange, inappropriate chortle, but it grew to a staccato giggle. Then the laughter stopped like she'd run into a wall, and she pointed the gun at Richard and Meghan. Well, really at Meghan, since Richard had moved behind her and stood with his hands on her shoulders. Grace's finger twitched on the trigger. My breath caught in the back of my throat.

"Maybe you should tell your son how well you knew Walter," I said, trying to get her attention.

It worked. The barrel of the gun moved toward me. "Shut your mouth," she hissed.

THIRTY-NINE

WOULD SHE SHOOT ME? I honestly didn't know. But I did know we needed Richard as an ally.

"Richard," I said. "Your mother was married to Walter Hanover. She married him, cheated on him, and took his child and deserted him. You were that child. You were born Richard Hanover. And your mother never told you, even when you lived right next door to him."

The stunned look on Dick's face would have been comical under other circumstances.

He turned to Grace. "Mother?"

Her eyes flashed, and her chin lifted. She waved her hand, red nails flashing like talons.

"Irrelevant. A long time ago, and unfortunate. But irrelevant."

"Jesus Christ!" Richard yelled, making me jump.

Her voice took on a whining undertone. "How was I to know he'd moved in next to you? I didn't think he knew anything about either of us, about where either of us lived. How could I tell you?

I didn't even know if he still lived in Cadyville until he contacted me. You have to understand, Richard, I did it for your own good. Think about it. Think about that old man. You knew him. Can you imagine being his son? A nothing, a nobody? Daddy Bly gave you so much more than Walter Hanover ever could have, and I gave you Daddy Bly. I did it all for you, to save you from squalor and poverty and obscurity." Here she pursed her lips. "Not that you did much with the opportunity, Richard."

After several seconds Richard blinked and looked away. "I'm sorry, Mother."

Meghan's eyes closed for a moment, her dismay mirroring my own. It didn't matter whether it was fear, guilt, habit, or a moral compass permanently knocked askew by his caustic upbringing that caused him to capitulate so easily; any hope of him going against his mother to help us had retreated into the distance.

Mama's boy. Useless, pathetic little mama's boy. I wondered what he'd do if I said it out loud, if I could goad him into rebelling.

And I discovered I didn't want to know. As much as I despised the man, I couldn't bring myself to taunt him the same way I'd seen his aging mother do. And reasoning wouldn't work, that was obvious. Swinging him to our side was a lost cause.

Grace directed a triumphant smile my way, and I returned it with a sarcastic grimace. The heavy scent of beeswax infused the air as the chunks rapidly melted into the cocoa butter behind me. The heat from the burner felt uncomfortable against my back, and with a casual flip I drew my braid forward over my shoulder, afraid my hair might suddenly combust.

"Now then," Grace said, considering Debby and Jacob. She pointed the gun casually at Jacob. "You, I know. Walter's friend.

The one who stayed quiet and sat in the corner like a good little boy. But who are you, honey?"

"Nobody to you," Jacob said.

"I was Walter's fiancée," Debby said, the words like sandpaper in her throat.

"Oh! So you're the one he was so worried about. The poor little wacko. Wouldn't want to upset the fragile bird—might send it back to its cage, with the bars and the needles and all sorts of other unpleasantness, I should imagine. But you don't look so delicate to me. And let me tell you, honey, Walter's no great loss."

It was like jabbing a wounded animal. Debby charged. Grace pointed that stupid gun at her. Wiry little Jacob grabbed his sister and spun her around. She fought him, adrenalin against adrenalin. I thought of running, then, with Grace distracted, but the Silverman's struggle blocked my path to the back door, and Richard stood with Meghan in front of the stairway.

I stayed where I was.

The gun went off.

The bullet would have hit Debby except Jacob knocked her feet out from under her so she fell out of the way.

"I did it," Jacob shouted. "I killed Walter."

All movement ceased. Whiter than humanly possible, Debby stared up at her brother, confusion and disbelief on her face.

Grace laughed.

"But he wasn't supposed to die. Honest, Debs, it wasn't supposed to be Walter who drank the schnapps. He'd been sober for years—I never thought he'd drink it. It was an accident. I meant it for her." He pointed at Grace.

He held out a hand to Debby. Slumped on the floor, she didn't take it. She pulled her knees to her chest in a fetal position and covered her face.

I could barely make out her mumbled words. "You were his sponsor. You were his friend. Oh, Jacob, what were you thinking?"

At least Grace had stopped laughing. "You little worm. You tried to kill me?"

Jacob watched Debby, as if trying to make her look at him through sheer force of will. Finally, he closed his eyes and nodded. "You wanted to meet Walter in a bar, both times he came to see you in Seattle, an' he was afraid between your spite and his worries he might be tempted to have a drink. So he asked me to come along."

Grace shook her head in wonder. "Pathetic."

On the floor, Debby made a noise somewhere between a growl and a whimper.

Jacob sighed. "And both times you and Walter got together, you drank Rumple Mitz. Tossed the stuff back like it was water. I knew you'da never noticed a little addition until it was too late."

Grace glared at him, and I wondered for a brief moment whether he was trying to get her to kill him. But she had rested her forearms on the island counter to take the strain off them and seemed more interested in Jacob's tale than in shooting him.

"I bought a bottle of it—wasn't easy—I hadn't bought a bottle of booze for almost twelve years—and some drain cleaner from the Safeway. Got the idea from Walter himself, joking about drinkin' drain cleaner and talkin' about how Sophie Mae here made her soap. I 'member my grandmamma used to make soap with lye from the grocery store, too. You 'member that, Debs?"

Debby didn't respond. After a few moments, Jacob continued. "I mixed it up with some water, and I mixed it strong. Then I worked off the seal of the Rumple Mintz, poured out half, and replaced it with the lye. Then I reattached the seal with a dab of superglue."

Crude, but effective.

"I gave the bottle to Walter to give to you," he said, looking back at Grace. "A kind of send-off gift, get on your good side a little. I figured you'd drink it after you got home, and since you said you hadn't told anyone you were up in Seattle, no one would think of looking up here if you died."

Grace looked angry, sure, but also oddly speculative. "Clever," she finally said.

But Richard looked confused again. "I don't understand. I thought you flew in on Sunday. But you were here before Walter died?"

"Yes, Dickie-Bird. I was here before he died, and I didn't tell you."

"Why?"

"Because I didn't want you to cock it up."

"But…"

"Oh, shut up, Richard!"

"Why?" Meghan asked Jacob. And while I could understand someone wanting to pour lye down Grace's throat on general principle, I wanted to know what Jacob had had in mind, too.

"She wouldn't give Walter a divorce. He'd tracked her down in California and asked her to sign the papers, but she kept putting him off. She'd ask for money, and he'd give it to her, but then she'd want some more. Two times he gave her money to fly up here so's she could sign them. The first time she changed her mind. And he knew she'd do the same thing this time, too.

"How was he gonna marry my sister if he couldn't get a divorce from that one?" He pointed at Grace, who regarded him with a spellbinding stare. "She told him to go ahead and get married anyway. She'd done it. Twice. But Walter didn't want to do that. He said he was goin' to take her to court, get the divorce anyway, even if it made a stink." He pointed at her again. "And you threatened to bring Debs into it. I couldn't let you do that. She didn't even know he was still married to you."

"Well, you've certainly brought her into it now, haven't you?" Grace said.

Jacob looked at Debby, who sat rocking, her knees up to her chin, both arms wrapped around her legs. His eyes filled with tears.

"I was only tryin' to make it better for her. Make it so's she'd get somethin' she wanted for once. She deserved to be happy," he whispered.

Grace sniffed. "You all heard him, right? So you know I didn't kill Walter."

Unenthusiastic nods all around.

"So how did he die?" I asked. "He didn't drink. Why would he have decided to jump off the wagon that particular morning?"

Jacob shook his head, at a complete loss for words. Meghan frowned. Debby was off in her own little world. Richard looked confused again.

But Grace watched me, her dark eyes glittering with…satisfaction?

"You were there," I said.

293

She didn't respond, but the corners of her lips turned up an infinitesimal degree.

"You made him drink the schnapps."

"I didn't even know about the schnapps," she said.

"What did you say to him?"

She shrugged, a tiny movement of her shoulders to indicate how trivial my question was. "He threatened me. He said he'd have me arrested for bigamy."

"Bet you didn't like that."

"Not much," she admitted. "I said a few things to discourage him."

"Like what?"

She waved me off.

But I'd seen how she laid into Richard on a whim, heard about how she'd treated Walter when they were young, and he'd only recently recovered. I could imagine how she'd react to a direct threat.

Grace had been there at Walter's house that morning—she'd told me as surely as if she'd spoken the words—and he told her he wouldn't put up with her manipulations any more. She'd pulled out the big guns. Debby. Erin. Richard. Direct attacks on Walter himself.

After she'd left, he'd remembered the Rumple Minze Jacob had given him. Poured himself a glass. Didn't drink it. Took it outside. Debated. Tried to distract himself by looking at his job for the morning, the raised bed he'd be building in our backyard. Couldn't quite put the glass down. Thought about calling Jacob, his AA sponsor. Didn't make the call.

Finally gave in.

And when the burning started, he ran to the closest faucet. In my workroom. And there he'd died.

Even if it hadn't happened exactly like that, I was close. We'd never know for sure, because no one had been there when Walter died. But two things I knew without doubt: Walter's weakness for alcohol betrayed him, and Grace had been the one to drive him over the edge.

I looked at Meghan and found an echo of my own profound sadness.

"Jacob," I said, still looking at Meghan. "Were you in Walter's house the night after he died?"

In my peripheral vision I saw Debby's head come up to watch her brother. I turned to Jacob. He radiated misery as he nodded. "Yeah. Earlier I heard the sirens and saw the ambulance and everything. So I knew somethin' was going on, but not for sure what. So that night I went to Walter's to see if he could tell me, but he wasn't home. So I let myself in with that key he left out for us, and I saw the Rumple Mintz bottle on the counter, open and with part of it gone. I still didn't know what happened, but I knew it was time to get rid of it. I'd just finished pourin' it down the sink when you came in. I waited in the kitchen, scared you'd find me and hopin' you'd just leave. But you didn't leave. And while I'm standin' there, I lose my grip on the bottle, and it broke on the floor. So I left."

"And came back later to clean up."

"I didn't want that bottle around!" His vehemence took me off guard.

I held up my hands. "Okay. What about the fire?" I didn't know what Grace was planning next, but I knew it couldn't be good. And as Richard stood listening to Jacob, I'd seen Meghan very slowly moving back toward the stairs. If I could distract Grace—and Richard—for long enough, she'd have a good jump at getting upstairs and locking the door before Richard could catch her or Grace could shoot her.

Jacob nodded, wretched. "Yeah, that was me, too. I got to worryin' about that stuff they can do on TV, you know, the crime-scene people? I thought they might be able to figure something out about how I'd done that to the peppermint schnapps, and I'd get in trouble."

Debby started sobbing. "Oh, Jacob."

"It wasn't 'cause I'm afraid of goin' to jail for what I done, Debs. I knew I deserved that. But then who'd take care of you?"

"You know you'll have to go to jail, don't you, Jacob?" I kept my voice gentle, but if he still posed a threat, I wanted to know now, while Grace still had her gun on him.

Rebellion crossed his face, then slid off. "Yeah. I know." And he started to cry. "I'm sorry, Debs."

"But that wasn't you driving the truck that almost ran me down, was it?"

Jacob wiped his eyes—and nose—on his sleeve. "Huh?"

"Downtown, Tuesday afternoon after I talked to you at Beans R Us. Someone tried to kill me."

He shook his head, a bewildered expression on his face.

I looked at Grace. She wore that tiny smile. More of a smirk, actually. I longed to smack it off.

"What did I ever do to you, Grace?"

"You're snotty, and you're nosy. And I'm sure you were keeping Erin from me, along with her mother. But hurting you wouldn't have done me any good."

"But you drove that truck, didn't you?"

She gave a little nod of acquiescence. "I thought you were Meghan. I saw you come out of your house, and I went and got the truck—Richard has a neighbor who leaves the key in his vehicle, can you believe that in this day and age?—and then came and looked for you on the street. I saw you walking home from downtown."

Meghan and I exchanged glances. "You thought I was Meghan? We look nothing alike."

"Your hood was up. You came out of her house. I'd only met her once, and Richard neglected to tell me his ex-wife had a room-mate." She directed a sharp look at her son.

"I get it. You wanted to kill Meghan so Richard would get custody of Erin."

"Not kill. Just…hurt a little. Enough so he'd have Erin for a while." Grace smiled at Meghan, not a nice smile at all. "Richard, you're not paying attention to your wife. She's trying to get away."

Absently, Richard moved Meghan further into the room. "You tried to hurt her?" he asked in a hushed voice, as if amazed his mother could do such a thing.

"Oh, for heaven's sake, nothing happened," she snapped.

"Nothing my aching, bruised ass," I said.

She ignored me. "What's in there?" She pointed to the storeroom.

"Just some inventory," I said.

"Is there a lock on the door?"

"Why?"

She sighed and pointed the gun at me. "Because I'm going to lock you all in there. I need a little quiet time upstairs before I leave." She looked at Meghan. "You can save yourself some heart-ache if you'll just tell me where it is."

"Where what is?"

"You know."

Meghan shook her head, baffled.

"I want what Walter gave Erin."

Meghan drew her eyebrows together. "I have no idea what you're talking about."

"Oh, come on, honey. You're her mother. Mothers always know. He gave her something—cash or jewelry or something worth a decent chunk of money. Money he owed me. You know, he never paid a cent of child support. And, as his wife, I should have received half his lottery winnings."

Meghan could have been looking at a gross but fascinating insect. "You stole Walter's son and disappeared. Now you're mad because he didn't give you child support? And you think you're eligible for community property even though you've committed bigamy not once, but twice? You're kidding, right?"

Grace's nostrils flared in anger, not a flattering look for her.

Meghan continued. "Walter gave Erin time and attention, but nothing of monetary value. You must know that after you searched the house, when you and Richard broke in on the day of the service."

"She hid it, that's all. Either you're lying, or she didn't tell you, because Walter assured me he'd arranged it so our granddaughter would be able to afford college. And that's not cheap. So I'll have to wait and ask her." She gestured to Richard, not quite pointing the gun at him, but not being very careful with it, either. "Help me get them all in that room. If it doesn't have a lock, we'll have to jam it shut."

Meghan sent me a panicked look as Richard pushed her toward the door to the storeroom.

"Get up and get moving," Grace walked over and prodded Debby with her toe. Jacob bent and began talking to his sister in low tones. "Hurry up," Grace said. "I don't have all day."

Erin shot out of the storeroom, dodging Grace and running for the door to the backyard.

"Hey!" Grace yelled. And she pointed the gun at Erin's back.

Meghan screamed and Richard shouted, and I reached behind me without thinking, grabbed the handle of the saucepan and flung the searing contents at Grace. The molten blend of oil, butter, and wax looped through the air and struck her on the shoulder. It splashed up her bare neck and splattered onto the side of her face. She howled. The gun dropped from her hand.

I lunged for it, but Jacob reached over and picked it up first.

"Drop it!" came the command from the doorway.

Suddenly the room was full of people, and at least half of them wore uniforms. Jacob put the gun on the island counter and again bent to his sister. Debby had stopped crying and stared straight ahead of her with no expression on her face at all. Sergeant Zahn scooped up the gun, put it in a bag, and took it out to his car. Barr Ambrose shouldered his way into the room and over to where I stood rooted to the spot.

On the floor, Grace moaned and wept. She was a wicked, destructive, self-serving bitch, but I couldn't quite believe I'd hurt her so badly. I'd never intentionally hurt anyone. Richard moved toward his mother, but Meghan stepped in front of him. Behind her, the paramedics hustled in and began tending to the burned woman. They were the same ones who had told me Walter couldn't be saved.

"Sophie Mae?" Ambrose said in a low voice.

I looked at him standing there next to me, all detective-looking with his belt and gun, and saw a tenderness in his eyes that nearly shattered my tenuous control. I felt my lower lip quiver, and promptly fastened it between my teeth.

"She deserved anything she got," he said, putting his hand on my shoulder and squeezing. I wanted to close my eyes and fold against him, feel his arms encircle me. I wanted to let go and not have to deal with any of what was coming. I wanted to rest. I wanted to be taken care of, for a change.

And I could tell he'd be amenable. His hand on my shoulder held warmth and reassurance. And warning. Sergeant Zahn had reentered the basement and watched us from across the room. This was not the time. Not the place.

The sound of a slap cracked above the voices of emergency personnel. The paramedics continued to murmur to one another, but everyone else fell silent, their attention captured by Richard and Meghan. His cheek blazed red, and her hands were clenched into fists by her side. The next blow wouldn't be open-handed.

"What the…?" Richard said, staring at his ex-wife.

"You stupid *shit*. How could you endanger your daughter like that?"

"I told you, Erin didn't even know I had a gun."

"Not the gun, you moron, though that's bad enough. Your mother. She was trying to get at Erin, and you knew it! How could you?"

At least he looked sheepish. "Mother wouldn't have hurt her. She only wanted whatever Walter had given Erin."

"He didn't give her anything!" Meghan shrieked, finally free to lose control. She tried some deep breaths. Didn't work, except to bring her voice down a few decibels. "And if he had, it was for Erin, not, not…oh, you stupid…oh, god!" Frustration at his deliberate obtuseness choked off her words.

"I didn't know," he said. No one said anything. Erin sidled over to me, and I put my arm around her bony shoulders.

He turned to Erin. "I didn't know," he said again.

She turned her face into my side. Sergeant Zahn walked over to Richard. "You need to come with me, sir."

"Erin?" Richard said.

"Come on." Sergeant Zahn took his arm and led him outside. I ran my fingers through Erin's curls.

Meghan came to us then, and Erin transferred her grasp to her mother. Ambrose's hand left my shoulder, and he began reading Jacob his rights. The paramedics wheeled Grace out to the ambulance, which waited in the alley.

And the questions began.

FORTY

Erin, listening to everything from the storeroom, had started up my computer and instant-messaged her friend Zoe. Zoe's mom had called the police. Erin had had the foresight to shut the speakers off before she started, so the usual resounding greeting from the operating system wouldn't give her away. Smart kid.

When the police got there, they saw through the window that Grace had a gun. They had just decided to shoot her through the window when Erin made her move, and I disabled Grace with the medieval weapon of burning oil.

They searched Richard's apartment and found some of our jewelry and the three boxes of Walter's paperwork. They didn't find Meghan's engagement ring or my grandmother's gold broach.

Or Mike's wedding band.

My wedding set was there, but not Mike's band. Richard denied selling anything, as did Grace. One of them was lying. Probably Richard.

Barr Ambrose put in more overtime hours perusing Walter's paperwork, but didn't find anything of consequence. Walter didn't have an insurance policy. He didn't have a will. His last thirty thousand dollars will be tied up in probate forever and a day, given the tangled family tree and a few relatives that might be spending time in jail.

Grace was charged with bigamy, but it turned out Mr. Thorson had lost his fortune so she wasn't losing out on anything there. The money she'd gotten from Mr. Bly, Richard's supposed step-father, was either gone or well concealed someplace offshore. The California authorities were looking into it, but Ambrose told me Grace didn't look too worried.

Jacob was charged with second-degree murder, but there is some question as to whether the county prosecutor has a good case. He admitted to spiking the Rumple Mintz, but since Walter didn't usually drink, Jacob's lawyer may try to claim Walter committed suicide after all. Grace Thorson, Hanover, whatever—her role is too difficult to define or prove. Ambrose said it probably wouldn't enter into things at all.

Richard took all the blame for our burglary, saying his mother had nothing to do with it. Again, it didn't matter that she'd practically admitted her involvement to us; we couldn't prove anything, and Richard refused to implicate her.

And he had the unmitigated gall to call Meghan and ask for legal help. She can still practice law in Washington State, but she was never a criminal lawyer. She had the sense to tell him to go talk to somebody else, but I think she felt kind of bad about it.

Sheesh.

Debby went into the hospital for a few days, but while there she decided to try making it on her own, without her brother's help. She has a good therapist, she says, and a lot of experience with her own demons. We all wish her well.

She decided to wait a while before meeting Tootie for the first time. So Meghan, Erin, and I went to see Erin's new great-grandma a couple days after the craziness in my workroom. Ambrose had already told her the whole story, and I'd called to warn her that we were coming.

When we arrived, Ann gave us a cheerful wave I found encouraging. In her room, the bed was made, and Tootie, dressed in deep-red rayon slacks and matching silk tunic, stood gripping the silver-headed cane.

Erin, sober and polite, explained to Tootie exactly who she was. Her grandmother listened with attentive seriousness, and they agreed to spend some time catching up on family history. Then Erin asked if we could go out into the garden we could see from Tootie's window. The sun shone bright and warm out there, and for a moment I thought of the perfect fall weather on the day of Walter's death.

Tootie agreed and even acquiesced to using a wheelchair. Meghan pushed and I trailed behind, while Erin, loosening up after her initial apprehension about having a new grandmother, walked backwards in front of the chair, chattering away. I could tell that Tootie adored her already.

They were discussing what Erin should call her. In their increasingly lightening tones, it sounded like "Nana Tootie" was the favored candidate.

FORTY-ONE

THE DOORBELL RANG, AND I got up from where I'd been attempting to write copy for a flyer about Winding Road Bath Products for our upcoming booths. Barr Ambrose stood on the front porch, grinning at me like a fool. And, God help me, I grinned right back.

I stepped back so he could enter the house. He gave me a quick up and down perusal, no doubt because of the white bodysuit I wore. The sandwich boards depicting the chocolate wafers of an Oreo cookie leaned against the wall, but I wasn't going to put them on until the trick-or-treaters started arriving. It was too hard to sit down in the thing, so for now I was just cream filling.

But he didn't comment, just walked past me and went into the kitchen. Sat at the kitchen table like he belonged there. I found it didn't bother me a bit.

"Coffee?"

"Got any tea?"

"What kind of a cowboy drinks tea?"

"The kind that doesn't like coffee much."

"You know, they might drum you out of the ranks of the rough-and-ready club for talk like that."

"Might." He paused, and his expression became serious. "How are you?"

"Not bad. Actually, better than that. Oolong?" He shook his head, pointed at the Earl Grey on the counter.

I rolled my eyes. "I'm so glad that whole mess with Grace and Dick is over. And knowing how and why Walter died. At least as much as we can know. I mean, I hate that he died by accident, well, sort of by accident, you know what I mean, but just knowing, you know, not having to wonder and worry—it's great. So. I'm doing great."

He laughed.

"What?"

"You sorta bubble."

"*Bubble*?"

"Barr!" Erin came barreling into the room, gave the startled man a big hug, and bounced into a chair. "Hi! What're you doing here?"

"Well, I—" he began.

But Meghan walked in then, dressed as an umpire. "Hi, Barr. Don't mind us. Erin and I are eating early so we can get going on the trick-or-treating as soon as it's good and dark. Got a lot of houses to hit."

She might be strict about some things, including Erin's consumption of candy, but Meghan loved Halloween. Plus, her response to the resolution of the mystery surrounding Walter's death bordered on giddy. Tonight she was ready to rock and roll on the treat aspect of the evening. I, on the other hand, got to stay home and parcel out goodies for the ghosts and goblins—actually I suspected they would be more along the lines of Harry Potter—who came tramping to our door. I'd planned to pop corn and indulge in Laurie R. King's newest mystery between rings of the doorbell.

Then Barr had called, and I ended up inviting him over. Or he invited himself. Actually, I'm not sure how it happened, but here he was. Ms. King, move over.

I watched Meghan as she heated soup on the stove for her and Erin's early dinner. I'd been worried about her reaction to Dick's slime-ball behavior. He hadn't stood up against his vile mother when it came to his own daughter, and given that, Meghan was ready to believe the worst about him.

Meghan was kicking around the idea of trying to adjust their custody agreement, even more uneasy than before about his ability to take care of Erin, even for a couple of days at a time. But since asking for her help, Dick wasn't calling, wasn't making a peep. He hadn't shown up to get Erin last weekend, either. Meghan had heard from a mutual friend that he'd said something about how much Cadyville sucked and how he wanted to move back to California. I think she was hoping he'd do so as soon as he was allowed to leave the state.

As for Erin herself, she seemed to be on an even keel. Somehow the kid was able to accept things, not fight against them, and not expect them to be different. The rest of us, the grownups at least, tended to rail against the inevitable with remarkable regularity. She coasted along in the present like a little Zen monk with a wicked sense of humor. Her dad was a creep? Yeah, well…what about it?

Then I remembered her sitting on the sofa, acting like she was reading *The Wolves of Willoughby Chase* but feeling lower than slug snot because Dick had brought her home early. Maybe her aplomb wasn't quite so seamless. Maybe Meghan and I should be keeping a close eye on the little one for cracks and broken places.

"So, what's your costume going to be?" Ambrose asked Erin.

Her mouth full of the cheese and crackers her mom had put in front of her, Erin pointed to her chest. She was wearing a knockoff Seattle Mariners jersey with a big 51 on the front.

"You're going as a baseball player?"

She chewed and nodded emphatically, pointing at her chest again.

"You're going as Ichiro."

Her head bobbed in the affirmative.

Ambrose sat back. "Cool."

Erin swallowed. "I'm gonna slick my hair down, and I've got these cool shades just like his. And I've got a bat and a ball and a glove and stuff."

"Sounds like a lot to carry," Ambrose said. "Good thing your mom'll be along."

Meghan grinned. "I may have to charge a percentage for hauling around all that candy."

"Oh right, Mom. Like you won't eat half of it, anyway."

Meghan waggled her eyebrows at her daughter, and they both giggled.

"Do you play baseball?" Ambrose asked.

"No. I suck at sports," Erin said. "But I like to watch."

"Erin," Meghan said.

"Sorry. I'm *really bad* at sports."

"No, you're not."

"Whatever. I'm gonna go get my stuff and show it to Barr."

"But your soup's ready," Meghan said—to the sound of Erin pounding up the stairs to her room.

Moments later, she came back into the room with a Mariners cap on and lugging a ball, bat, and glove. Meghan set a bowl of soup on the table and pointed at the chair.

"Eat."

Erin wrinkled her nose and set her props in the corner.

I got up and dug salami, olives, and pickled asparagus out of the fridge to round out the snack, and Erin ate her soup while we chatted. When she'd finished, she rinsed her bowl and put it in the dishwasher. Meghan got up, and they both went upstairs.

When they returned, Erin's hair was gooed down to her skull and tucked into the back of her collar. Meghan had drawn thin sideburns and a narrow moustache on her heart-shaped face with eyebrow pencil and smudged a hint of a beard across her chin. Erin put on her shades and struck a pose, then bent to put on her tennis shoes.

"That'd be easier if you could see what you were doing," I said.

She ignored me, squinting, but after a few more moments gave up and removed the sunglasses.

Meghan looked up. "Ready?"

"Uh huh," Erin said, gathering her baseball paraphernalia.

Barr cocked his head. "What's on the ball?"

Erin held it up, turning it in order to see better. "Just a bunch of names."

"Let me see," he said.

She brought him the ball. As I leaned closer, he rotated it so we could see all the signatures.

"Where did you get this?" he asked, reverence in his voice.

"Walter gave it to me. He made me promise not to play with it, but since I don't actually like to play baseball, that was okay. And this isn't playing with it, is it?" She seemed worried.

Meghan had been watching Barr's face. "What is it?"

He took a deep breath. "I think it's a 1927 World Series ball. Yankees—see, here's Ruth, and Meusel, and Gehrig. Lazzeri, Huggins, Pennock." He looked up. "If it's real, it's worth at least twenty grand."

Meghan's eyes widened.

"He gave me other ones, too," Erin said. "I just thought they were plain old baseballs."

Barr stood up. "Where are they?"

Erin leading the way, we all trooped up to her room. She knelt and dug into the junk on the floor of her closet, pulling out four more baseballs. All had signatures.

Barr identified one as a Yankee World Series ball from 1928, and another from 1932. The other two he wanted to have someone look at. In fact, he said, we should have the balls appraised by a professional and then put them in a safety deposit box.

Erin agreed, but still wanted to take one trick-or-treating.

Meghan considered her for a long moment. "Okay. But take that one—" she pointed to the one Barr said was worth the least, only five or six thousand dollars—"and only this once. These are going to pay for your college."

Just as Walter had intended. And Grace had probably looked right at them while rifling through Erin's room.

Barr looked appalled as Erin skipped down the stairs with her collector's item. He turned to me. "She's letting her…?"

I took his arm and led him back downstairs. "It'll be fine."

"Be careful," he called out before the front door closed.

In the kitchen, he helped me put away our makeshift dinner. I was starting coffee when the doorbell rang for the first time. I slipped on my sandwich boards and went to hand out miniature Snickers bars to a little dinosaur and a tiny tiger, barely able to walk. I gave one to Mom, too, figuring she could use the energy tonight.

Back in the kitchen, Barr had finished the coffee. I put some of Meghan's peanut butter cookies on a plate.

"Wanna cookie?"

And as Barr Ambrose stood looking me up and down, I realized what I'd said.

He blinked. Slow.

Like a cat about to lick the cream filling out of an Oreo.

Oh.

Oh, my.

I decided right then and there Halloween was my new favorite holiday.

LYE IN WAIT RECIPES

OATMEAL MILK BATH SALTS

1 cup powdered goat's milk

1 cup colloidal oatmeal

1½ cup Epsom salts

Scant ¼ cup dendretic salt

½ teaspoon liquid glycerin

½ teaspoon essential oil (lavender, orange, balsam peru, sandalwood, fir needle, or rosewood)

In bowl large enough to provide plenty of stirring room, combine Epsom salts and dendretic salt. Stir together with a metal whisk. Dribble glycerin and essential oil over salts. Stir well with whisk. Add oatmeal and goat's milk and stir with whisk. This makes enough for at least three baths.

Dendretic salt helps avoid clumping and distributes the fragrance more thoroughly in the mix. The liquid glycerin does the same thing. Colloidal oatmeal suspends in the bathwater, and most powdered goat's milk is full fat, which makes it very softening. For immediate use you can also make this without the dendretic salt and glycerin, and substitute nonfat dry milk and baby oatmeal cereal for the goat's milk and colloidal oatmeal. The result will be a little different, and you will have to rinse a little oatmeal fiber out of the bottom of the tub when you're done, but it's a wonderful, soothing soak!

EASY LIP BALM

1 oz. beeswax

½ cup olive oil

¼ to ½ teaspoon essential oil—peppermint, spearmint, or
lemon

Melt wax and oil together over very low heat. Stir in essential oil
and pour into small tins, lip balm tubes, or any other suitable, lid-
ded containers. Allow to cool.

This recipe will fill about twenty-five .15 oz. lip balm tubes.

STOP 'EM IN THEIR TRACKS LOTION BARS

3 oz. beeswax

3 oz. coconut oil

3 oz. cocoa butter

Heat wax, oil and butter together over very low heat. Pour into six 2 oz. molds. Allow to harden and remove from molds. Given the 1:1:1 ratio of ingredients, it's very easy to increase or decrease this recipe.

Using non-deodorized cocoa butter gives the lotion bars a yummy chocolate scent, but if you can't find it you can add ¼ to ½ teaspoon of an essential oil or oil blend of your choice.

In addition to soothing "garden hands", try rubbing a lotion bar on rough feet and putting on cotton socks before going to bed.

SUPPLIER WEB SITES FOR INGREDIENTS, PACKAGING, AND LOTS MORE RECIPES!

www.fromnaturewithlove.com

www.camdengrey.com

www.glorybee.com

www.snowdriftfarm.com

If you enjoyed *Lye in Wait*, read on for an excerpt from the next
Cricket McRae Mystery

Heaven Preserve Us

ONE

"You don't have to fix any of the callers' problems; you just pass them on to someone else who can."

I nodded. "Got it."

"Okay, babe. I'll leave you to it. I'm going out back to have a smoke."

Smiling through gritted teeth, I tried to ignore the acrid stench of cigarettes that permeated his clothes. Philip Heaven could spend the whole evening toasting his lungs in the alley if it meant I wouldn't have to listen to him call me "babe" one more time in that gravelly, know-it-all voice. I'd handle every incoming call to the Heaven House Helpline if I had to. I mean, how hard could it be?

"Take your time," I said, aligning my list of referral numbers with the edge of the blotter and lacing my fingers together on top of the cheap laminate desktop. I glanced hopefully at the multi-line phone.

"Thanks, babe." He pointed his finger at me and made a gun-cocking sound with his tongue.

Yuck. Thank God, the phone rang. I reached to answer it.

———

After I referred a nice-but-scared-sounding lady to the next AA meeting in the basement of the Cadyville Catholic Church, the phone was silent for several minutes. The whooshing of tires across wet pavement on the street outside filtered into the spacious old building where I sat, a comfortable, lulling sound. I'd worked my way to forty-two across on the *Seattle Times* Tuesday crossword only to puzzle over a six-letter word for an exclamation of annoyance when the phone rang again. This time I gave a runaway boy an 800 number he could use to find a safe place to stay down in Seattle. I felt pretty satisfied with the whole volunteer gig after that one and picked up the next call feeling helpful as all get out.

"I have the knife against my wrist. It shines in the light. And it's cold. I bet this thing is so sharp I won't even feel it slice through my skin."

Uh oh.

I struggled to remember what I was supposed to say, but Philip's meager training hadn't prepared me for anything like this. Where was he? He couldn't still be working on that cigarette, could he? I mean, I hadn't really meant that about him hanging out in the alley all night. It was my first night manning the Helpline at Heaven House, and Philip Heaven was supposed to be mentoring me. Sheesh.

So I said the only thing I could think of: "Wait!"

"Why should I wait? I've been waiting my whole life to die."

Oh, brother. A philosopher. And a melodramatic one at that. "So have I," I said.

"What?"

I looked at the caller ID, so I could jot it down on the call sheet. It read *Private Call*. Great.

"I've been waiting my whole life to die, too," I said.

"You have?"

Yeah. Right along with all us other mortals.

Hush, Sophie Mae. He may be a moron, but he sounds pretty serious.

"But I'm not going to die today. And I'm not going to tomorrow, either, at least not if I get a vote in the matter," I said.

Silence.

"And neither should you. What's your name?"

"It's…just call me Allen."

"Okay, Allen, listen, I'm going to—"

"What's yours?"

"What's my what?"

"Your name."

"Allen, I need you to write down a number. This is someone who knows how to help you."

"I don't want another number. I want to talk to you. Tell me your name."

"Sorry, it's against—"

"I told you mine."

No, you didn't, I thought, but stopped myself before I said it out loud. Just call me Allen? That's not how you tell someone your name, for Pete's sake.

"Call me Jane."

"No! I want your real name. Tell me."

An icky feeling crawled up my spine. I put some steel in my voice. "Allen, take down this number: 555-2962. There's someone there who's trained in how to help you deal with your suicidal thoughts."

"What the hell? You're trying to foist me off on someone else? All I want to know is who I'm dealing with."

My resolve wavered. It was against the rules of Heaven House to give out our names to the people who called the Helpline. For that matter, I shouldn't still be talking to this guy. Volunteers were armed with a long list of experts who dealt with all sorts of different problems, from teenaged runaways to unplanned pregnancy, depression to spousal abuse, alcoholism to…suicide. If Philip had been honest enough to list Heaven House as a Help *Referral* Line in the phone book, maybe this guy wouldn't be so angry about having to call someone else.

Still. There was something about him that gave me the creeps.

"No, Allen. I'm not going to tell you my real name. That's against the rules here. I'm here to help you find someone to talk to. Are you going to let me do that?"

"You stupid bitch! All I want to know is who—"

A finger came down on the disconnect button. I went from staring stupidly at the phone to staring stupidly up at Philip. His cousin, Jude Carmichael, stood slightly behind him. I hadn't heard either of them come in.

"Should you have done that?" I finally managed.

"I could hear him yelling. He's a crank," Philip said.

I licked my lips, ambivalent about the intense relief I felt at the timely rescue. "But what if he really needed help?"

Jude, his coat collar still turned up around his ears, shuffled his feet and looked at the floor. In the brief time I'd known him, I'd noticed that he did that a lot. When he spoke, I leaned closer so I could hear his soft voice.

"Then he should have taken it. You don't have to put up with abuse, Sophie Mae. Philip should have told you. Sometimes people call in just to call in. They're lonely." He shuffled his feet again. I had the feeling he knew about lonely. "Or they're weirdos. Like this guy. His next call will probably be heavy breathing and obscene language. He's just bored."

"Well, he better not call back here, then."

Philip bent toward me. "Tell you what, babe. It's your first night. Your shift's almost over. Go ahead home."

"You sure?"

"Yeah. It's fine. My boy here can start his overnight shift early."

"That okay with you?" I asked Jude, since Philip hadn't bothered.

Jude shrugged and tried a smile. "Sure. I forward the calls to my cell and keep it on my nightstand. It hardly ever rings." He pulled a phone out of his pocket and started pushing buttons.

"I hope that guy didn't scare you off," Philip said.

"No, I'll be back," I said. "Friday, right?"

"That'll be great. We'll need your help. Friday night'll be hoppin'!" He made it sound like great fun, taking all those desperate phone calls from people in horrible situations.

Woo hoo!

———

Just after nine I pulled to the curb in front of the house I shared with Meghan Bly and her eleven-year-old daughter, Erin. I jumped out of my little Toyota pickup and ran up the sidewalk. Rain spattered down for the twentieth day in a row, and the temperature hovered around forty-two degrees—typical weather in the Pacific Northwest in February. The damp air smelled of rotting leaves and wood smoke.

In the foyer I shook like a dog, scattering the stray drops I hadn't managed to avoid in my mad dash from the street. I waved at Meghan as I passed the doorway to the kitchen on my way to the stairs, breathing in the scent of freshly baked bread.

"Back in a sec," I called over my shoulder and climbed to the second floor.

I poked my head into Erin's room. "How's it going?"

Meghan's daughter sat in bed, wedged in on one side by a stuffed platypus and on the other by a big purple hippo. Brodie, Erin's aging Pembroke Welsh corgi lay on his back, legs splayed open as he slept by her feet. His right eye cracked open so he could peer at me upside down, then squeezed shut again. A textbook lay open on Erin's lap, and she looked up from scribbling on loose-leaf notepaper when I spoke. Her elfin features held pure disgust.

"I hate math. I hate algebra, I hate geometry, and I plan on hating trigonometry and calculus as well." She squinted blue-gray eyes at me and shook her head of dark curls for emphasis.

"Trig? When do you start that?" Could be next week for all I knew. She was in an advanced class and last year had blown by everything I'd retained from my English major's admittedly pitiful math education. But trig? In the fifth grade?

"And proofs. I hate proofs, too."

I had no idea what proofs were. I went in and looked at what she was working on. Drawn on the wide-ruled paper was a y-axis.

And an x-axis. Lines connected some of the points in the grid. I still had no idea what proofs were.

"Looks like a graph," I said. "What are you supposed to be proving?"

The look she gave me was full of pity.

"Okay. Well, I'm going to change my clothes and go talk to your mom. So, er, g'night."

She sighed. "Good night, Sophie Mae."

I smiled to myself as I went down the hallway to my room and changed into my flannel pjs. Erin was a drama queen. It would only get worse as she morphed from tween to teen, but at heart she was such a great kid I knew she'd make it through okay.

I just hoped Meghan and I made it through okay, too.

Cricket McRae is a full-time writer, living in the Pacific Northwest. This first book in her new Home Crafting Mystery series features soap making, a craft in which Cricket is experienced. Her other crafting skills include food preservation and spinning, which will be featured in future books in the series.

www.MidnightInkBooks.com

From the gritty streets of New York City to sacred tombs in the Middle East, it's always midnight somewhere. Join us online at any hour for fresh new voices in mystery fiction, book club questions, author information, mystery resources, and more.

Midnight Ink promises a wild ride filled with cunning villains, conflicted heroes, hilarious hazards, mind-bending puzzles, and enough twists and turns to keep readers on the edge of their seats.

MIDNIGHT INK ORDERING INFORMATION

Order by Phone:

• Call toll-free within the U.S. and Canada at
   1-888-NITEINK (1-888-648-3465)

• We accept VISA, MasterCard, and American Express

Order by Mail:

Send the full price of your order (MN residents add 6.5% sales tax) in U.S. funds, plus postage & handling to:

Midnight Ink
2143 Wooddale Drive, Dept. 978-0-7387-1116-4
Woodbury, MN 55125-2989

Postage & Handling:

Standard (U.S., Mexico, & Canada). If your order is:
   $24.99 and under, add $3.00
   $25.00 and over, FREE STANDARD SHIPPING

AK, HI, PR: $15.00 for one book plus $1.00 for each additional book.

International Orders (airmail only):
   $16.00 for one book plus $3.00 for each additional book

Orders are processed within 2 business days. Please allow for normal shipping time. Postage and handling rates subject to change.